Praise for
Dead Letters from Paradise

"From one of our best—a blend of literary mystery and history in a pitch-perfect evocation of a pivotal year of growth in our nation. Featuring a solitary woman and the new, sassy, ten-year-old neighbor who opens the world to her, this tender, humane story illuminates the nature of discovery and courage."

—Katherine V. Forrest, author of *Curious Wine*
and the Kate Delafield Mystery Series

"If you're looking for hardcore bullets, booze, bodies, blonds, and blood—this isn't the book for you. But if you're after a beautifully crafted story, one that blends elements of mystery, history, and romance, I guarantee this clever, intelligent and surprisingly gentle novel will not disappoint."

—Ellen Hart, Mystery Writers of America Grand Master

"Within the construct of a fascinating mystery, Ann McMan asks important questions and unflinchingly implores us to explore our own ideas about who we are, where we come from, and the assumptions we make. Rich language, characters to root for, and a precocious ten-year-old from whom we could all learn a great deal. Brava!"

—Lynn Ames, author of *Secrets Well Kept*

"*Dead Letters from Paradise* is a brilliantly wrought, multi-layered work made sweet and tender by an emerging community of loving and lovable characters. The richness of Ann McMan's achievement has seldom been equaled in contemporary lesbian literature."

—Lee Lynch, trailblazing author of *The Swashbuckler*

T0037821

DEAD
LETTERS
FROM
PARADISE

ANN McMAN

Bywater
BOOKS

2022

Bywater Books

Copyright © 2022 Ann McMan

Print ISBN: 978-1-61294-235-3

Bywater Books First Edition: June 2022

Printed in the United States of America on acid-free paper.

Cover design by TreeHouse Studio

Bywater Books
PO Box 3671
Ann Arbor MI 48106-3671

www.bywaterbooks.com

Excerpts on page 277 quoted from:
Patricia Highsmith (writing as Claire Morgan),
The Price of Salt, New York, Coward-McCann, 1952

1761 map of the *hortus medicus* medicinal garden
at Bethabara made by surveyor and naturalist Christian Reuter,
courtesy of Historic Bethabara Park

For Ms. Alma Penn, who has the head of a realist, but the heart of a woman who still believes in the innate goodness of people.

Books by Ann McMan

Novels

Hoosier Daddy
Festival Nurse
Backcast
Beowulf for Cretins: A Love Story
The Big Tow
Dead Letters from Paradise

The Jericho Series

Jericho
Aftermath
Goldenrod
Covenant

Evan Reed Mysteries

Dust
Galileo

Story Collections

Sidecar
Three Plus One

Author's Note

This novel departs from the U.S. Postal Service's standard and historical procedures for the handling and processing of mail that cannot be delivered through normal mail processing channels. I have taken liberties with the actual location of regional Dead Letter Offices, which were consolidated by the USPS in 1957, and, for the purposes of this story, I've chosen to set one of those regional offices in the city of Winston-Salem, N.C. Also for the purposes of this story, I have moved the *hortus medicus* garden, located in the historic Moravian settlement of Bethabara, to the larger Moravian settlement in Old Salem. This book is a work of fiction and is not intended to serve as an accurate historical record of daily life or events in the city of Winston-Salem in 1960. However, it *is* an accurate reflection of the lives and times of the characters you're about to meet.

DEAD
LETTERS
FROM
PARADISE

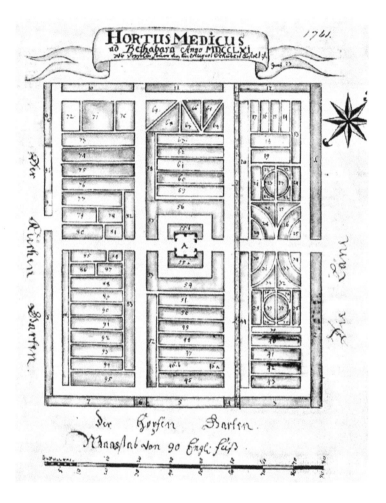

Der Kirchen Garten.

HORTUS MEDICUS
ad *Bethabara Anno* MDCCLXI

1761.

Der Hopfen Garten.

Maasstab von 90 Engl. fuss.

"The past is never dead. It's not even past."

–William Faulkner, *Requiem for a Nun*

Archangelica
(Angelica)

"Better is a dinner of herbs where love is . . ."
–Proverbs 15:17

I was knee-deep in bitter herbs when the first batch of letters came my way. It was a Saturday in mid-April of 1960, and I'd just spent two hours weeding rows of tiny new Angelica plants—the first to emerge after the cold nights had retreated and the days began to grow warmer.

Evelyn Haas, the master gardener of our *hortus medicus* in Old Salem, thrust a flat cardboard box at me, and brusquely suggested that its contents were something I "needed to tend to." It was clear that the shallow tray had originally been used to transport seedlings. Its sides and bottom were still damp and spotted with tiny clots of rich, black potting soil. It now contained a half dozen or so letters, all written on the same pale stationery, and all addressed by the same hand. They each were stamped and postmarked, and appeared to have been delivered to a Miss Mary Ann Evans, c/o The Gardens at Old Salem.

I had no idea why Evelyn was handing them off to me, but I suspected it had something to do with my job.

I processed dead letters for the Winston-Salem Post Office.

It's important to understand that most people, including Evelyn, have broad misconceptions about "dead letters." It's not hard to figure out why. The term itself is a misnomer. That's because Dead Letters aren't actually *dead*, as if they were once alive and now aren't. They're just *stuck*—caught in a transient space that's like a bureaucratic way station. Letters that become classified as "dead" fall into a state of limbo. It's an unhappy fate. One that can divide deepest expressions of love, longing, hope, despair, joy or grief from their intended recipients. Each letter represents an intentional demonstration of good faith and an implied trust in a sacred delivery system—and it is my job to realize the intent of the sender, and to connect the letters with their rightful beneficiaries.

But in this case, the letters Evelyn expected me to "tend to" had already *been* delivered—if not to the correct person, then at least to the intended destination.

"What are these?" I asked.

Evelyn shrugged her narrow shoulders. "Dead letters, I suppose."

"But they were *meant* to be delivered here." I held one of the letters up. "To the gardens."

"Maybe so. But there's never been anyone here by that name."

I quickly flipped through the stack. All six of the letters were addressed to Mary Ann Evans.

"No one named Mary Ann Evans has ever worked here?" I asked her.

"No."

"Could she have been a volunteer?"

2

"Not during my tenure—and I've been the master gardener here for nearly twelve years."

It wasn't usual for us to receive letters *back* into the postal system once they'd been delivered, but this did appear to be an odd circumstance.

"I suppose I can take these in and try to figure out what to do with them." I turned one over. No return address. "Did you try refusing delivery?"

"Of course not." Evelyn's response was curt and delivered with the same dispatch she used to snap dead blooms off late-season plants. It was clear she was losing patience with our conversation and wanted to be done with the matter. She had already pulled off her gloves and was busy clearing bits of soil from beneath her fingernails. "No mail is ever delivered here. Anything intended for the garden gets sorted in the administrative office for Old Salem and dropped into a box for me. I only pick it up every couple of months, because there's rarely anything of consequence. Seed catalogs, mostly. Or sometimes I get requests for tips on growing certain kinds of herbs. Those?" She gestured at the flat box of letters. "Nothing like that has ever been sent here before. At least, not that I know of."

"I'm not sure what to do with them, either."

"Isn't that your job?"

Evelyn's directness made me feel guilty—like I'd been trying to shirk responsibility for taking the letters off her hands. "Well, technically," I said. "But letters aren't normally returned to us *after* being delivered."

"Judging by the dates on the postmarks, these have been arriving about once every ten days. So, the sender must be unfamiliar with your policies. Either way, I don't have time to bother with these." She turned on her heel and started back toward our small potting shed. "Do whatever you want with them."

I watched her walk away.

Just super.

I examined the stack of letters. The handwriting was even and precise with notably few flourishes. The style wasn't exactly lacking in character, but it did manage to convey a hint of impatient proficiency. I collected them all from the box and placed them in the cleanest compartment of the big leather satchel that today contained my own gloves and gardening tools. The commodious bag had belonged to my father when he'd been a mail carrier. It was large enough to accommodate all my various paraphernalia, and something about carrying it just made me feel better and more connected to him.

I'd take the letters to work with me on Monday, and sort things out from there.

But it was nearly eleven o'clock, and I had to hurry home to take a quick bath and change clothes before meeting my neighbor, Fay Marian, for lunch.

Fay Marian owned a large house that years ago had been converted into five apartment units. It was located on Main Street, directly behind my more modest home at the end of South Church Street in Old Salem. Fay Marian lived in one of the smaller apartments and managed the rest of the property herself. We'd been backdoor neighbors for nearly two years, but had only struck up a speaking relationship recently. Fay Marian had approached me early one evening about a week ago, when I was sitting on my small front porch, and had stopped to ask if I would be interested in helping her reclaim the large garden space that used to dominate the lot between our two homes. I was surprised by her request and said as much.

"I know you volunteer in the old herb garden up on Salt Street," she said. "I've heard that you know your way around the plants pretty well and wondered if you'd be interested in helping me bring this space back to life." She waved at the lot behind her house, a scrappy bit of ground that was mostly overgrown with weeds and a few determined clumps of Lenten roses. "My daddy never much cared about how things looked—or worked, for that matter. I've been so focused on fixing up the interior of this place, I haven't had much time to turn my attention to the outside. If you could help me out—even if it's just by making some suggestions about plants and things—I'd be extremely grateful."

She looked so earnest and sincere, it was hard for me to say no. And, truthfully, I'd been wishing for years that someone would do something to clean up that space. It was an eyesore.

"Well, I suppose I could help you out a little bit." I wasn't sure what else to say.

It was a cool evening, and I felt guilty letting the woman continue to stand on the sidewalk in front of my porch in the early night air. "Would you like something hot to drink?" I offered.

To my surprise, and chagrin, she accepted my offer immediately.

"I'd love that. Thanks." She climbed the steps to join me. "What are you having? It smells great."

"This?" I held up my old chipped mug. "It's just Postum. But I could make you some hot tea or coffee."

"Postum is great. My daddy loved the stuff, so we always had it at home. It was the first thing I remember drinking that made me feel grown up. I didn't figure out it wasn't actually coffee until I got old enough to read the label. Whoever figured out that a powder made from ground-up grain could taste so exotic to a child was a genius. I drink it straight up, too—just like he did." She smiled. I noticed that she had beautifully straight teeth. "Come to think of it, he drank just about everything else straight up, too."

I got to my feet rather nervously. I wasn't used to having company—especially in the evening, after supper. I'd seen Fay Marian Vogler often enough, though, puttering about behind her house. My kitchen windows looked directly out over the overgrown area between our two homes. From a distance, it had been hard to make out anything particular about her features. So, when I stood up beside her, I was surprised to discover how much shorter than me she was. She was sturdily built, too. Not stocky or mannish, exactly, but decidedly not feminine, either. And she was wearing trousers with the cuffs rolled up at her ankles, and a heavy wool shirt. She had a head full of frizzy-looking hair that appeared to have been hastily pulled back, away from her face. Untamed strands of it had escaped and were shooting out in all directions. I guessed her to be about forty-five years old—the same age as me.

"I'm Fay Marian, by the way." If she'd noticed me taking in her appearance, she didn't show it. I was grateful for that. She extended her hand, and I shook it belatedly. "I inherited the house after my daddy passed away."

"I was sorry to learn of his passing. My name is Esther. Esther Jane Cloud." I knew I was rambling—mostly to cover my unease. I wasn't used to talking this much to a stranger. "But please call me EJ."

"You work at the post office, right?"

I was surprised by how much Fay Marian seemed to know about me. But, in truth, Old Salem was a small community and there were few privately owned homes left. Most of the former residences were landmarks that now belonged to the college or the Wachovia Administration that operated the old Moravian village as a historic site.

"Yes." I explained. "We've always been a post office family, so it was natural that I'd end up working there, too. Please," I gestured toward one of the chairs on my porch, "make yourself comfortable. I'll be right back."

I excused myself to scurry inside and heat more water to make Fay Marian's beverage.

What a strange experience. I fumbled getting another mug down from the cupboard and nearly dropped it. *Why was I so nervous?* True . . . I hadn't had company since—well. I couldn't remember the last time. *But who called on their neighbors this late in the evening?*

I glanced at the clock above the wall oven in my small kitchen. It was barely six forty-five.

Still . . . It *was* evening, and it seemed like an odd time to make a social call on someone you'd never met before.

The kettle whistled, and I poured the water over a heaping tablespoon of dark granules and stirred the beverage until it was nicely blended and frothy. When I carried the mug back out to the porch, Fay Marian was comfortably settled on a wicker chair, flipping through the book I'd been reading.

I felt a surge of mortification.

I handed her the steaming mug. She took it gratefully.

"Thanks. This should take the chill off." She sipped it and smiled at me. "This tastes exactly the way I remembered it: exotically grainy." She held up the book. "So, you like mysteries?"

I tried to hide my embarrassment. I'd been reading the latest Erle Stanley Gardner novel, *The Case of the Shapely Shadow.* It wasn't something I was eager to admit to, but I actually loved the mildly racy novels. I'd look for them whenever I had occasion to visit the Walgreen's on Fourth Street.

"I read them from time to time—mostly because they're simple stories and are easy to digest in small bits of time."

Fay Marian set the book back down on the table beside my chair. "Do you watch the show on TV?"

"Not often. I don't much care for the actors."

"Me either. Raymond Burr is always too brooding for me. I never imagined Perry Mason that way. I always saw him as a bit more dashing. Not to mention the TV depiction of Della Street. In the books, she's sultrier and more alluring."

Her observation made me feel antsy. It felt vaguely inappropriate.

"So, you've read some of the novels, too?" I asked her, to cover my unease.

"A few. I have to sneak to read them—or any dime-store novels. My neighbor, Inez Bell, likes to chastise me for having what she calls 'plebeian' taste in books." Fay Marian sipped her hot beverage. "I just tell her to go pound salt." She smiled at me. "Inez teaches English literature at the college."

"Salem College?"

Fay Marian nodded. "She rents one of my apartments. In fact, she was the one who suggested I approach you about helping with the restoration of our garden. You need to meet her. I think you two will discover many things in common."

I had no idea what to make of that suggestion. And how in the world did this woman, Inez, know anything about me? Occasionally volunteers from the college would help out in the community gardens, but I didn't recall ever meeting anyone named Inez.

But Fay Marian wasn't ready to let go of her idea.

"Tell you what," she said. "How about you come over for lunch next weekend? You can meet Inez, and the three of us can make a plan for how to begin tackling that tangled mess back there."

"Um . . ." I had no ready excuse to refuse her invitation. "I suppose I could do that."

"Great. Saturday? Around noon? We'll make something simple." She laughed. "In fact, just about *anything* I cook is simple. But if it's between slices of bread, I do okay."

"May I bring anything?" It seemed appropriate to offer.

"Just yourself. Or maybe any gardening resources or seed catalogs that might be helpful."

"All right." I struggled with what else to say. In the space of fifteen minutes, I'd somehow ended up with a new acquaintance, a commitment to work in yet another garden, and a spontaneous social engagement.

So many firsts were unsettling for me. More than anything, I wanted to retreat to the safety of my living room and be left alone to read my book in peace.

But thanks to this brash woman named Fay Marian, that was about to become a thing of the past—starting with lunch on Saturday.

I arrived at Fay Marian's large, yellow frame house promptly at noon. Even though she'd instructed me not to bring anything, I felt it unseemly to show up empty-handed. So I made time to stop by Winkler's Bakery and picked up some orange scones.

When I arrived, Fay Marian exclaimed over the box of scones

before leading me to her kitchen, where another woman was busy setting a small table.

"Esther, meet Inez Bell," she declared. "Inez, this is EJ Cloud, our green-thumbed savior."

Inez crossed the small space to warmly shake my hand. "What a pleasure to meet you. Your work in the community garden is legendary."

I was nonplussed by the compliment. "Thank you, but I hardly think that's true."

"Oh, it's true all right." Fay Marian began to unload the box of scones. "Evelyn Haas raves about you."

"Evelyn?" I was incredulous. *Raving* didn't sound like something the dour woman would ever do—about *anyone*. Not unless someone mentioned John F. Kennedy.

Evelyn was an unapologetic Democrat.

"That seems . . . unlike her." I didn't quite know how else to respond.

"Don't be so modest." Inez's tone was light and teasing. She exchanged glances with Fay Marian. "I see you weren't exaggerating . . . for once."

Fay Marian winked at me. "I told Inez you had a voice like Julie London."

"Oh." I was addled by her comparison to the sultry-voiced singer. "I've . . . never heard that before."

"*Ignore* her." Inez chose to take pity on me. "As I was saying, EJ—Evelyn and I are in the same book club. I've learned to appreciate that when she's enthusiastic about something, it must be genuine. Believe me, it happens infrequently enough."

I smiled at her.

Inez was an attractive woman. Petite and well put together—a complete contrast to Fay Marian, whose rumpled appearance

10

was at odds with the more buttoned-up professor.

"She's certainly a taskmaster when it comes to maintaining the garden," I said.

"What first led you to volunteer there?" Inez indicated that I should take a seat at the table.

"Oh, we've always worked in Moravian gardens. I mean," I clarified, "the women in my family always have. My mother and grandmother were both devoted to maintaining a *hortus medicus*. The herbs were practically sacred to them. Growing up, I can't remember a time when I didn't accompany my mother to work in one of the gardens on weekends."

"That's fascinating." Inez took a seat opposite me and commenced pouring three glasses of lemonade. "I've never understood the mystique surrounding the continued cultivation of medicinal herbs, and why they still matter so much to the Moravians—especially when they're no longer compounded into cures."

In truth, I'd never questioned the activity myself—I simply accepted it as something we did. As something all the women in my family were expected to do. That same process of acceptance applied to most things I learned from my parents.

"I suppose," I said, "I enjoy this simple link to a shared past. I grew up in a Moravian family. Well, at least my mother's family were Moravians. I never asked or questioned their ties to the herb garden—or to any of their other faith traditions. They all just seemed *normal* to me. As I grew up, I developed a deeper understanding that Old Salem was a special place where the earliest German-speaking protestants who had fled persecution in Europe settled to worship and live communally. The medicinal herb gardens became an essential part of their ability to survive, and later to thrive, as a center of commerce."

"And yet," Inez noted thoughtfully, "we have to acknowledge that there is a problem implicit in the preservation of *some* old-world traditions that fail to change with the times."

I wasn't sure what Inez was referencing, but Fay Marian succinctly dispatched any mystery about her remark.

"She's talking about segregation . . . *again*." Fay Marian clarified. "As we all know, the Moravians didn't have the best track record on civil rights."

"Still don't," Inez added.

I felt strangely indicted by her observation. Was I expected to agree with her assessment, or to rise up and defend the perceived inaction of the church?

Fay Marian joined us at the table and deposited a platter of tiny, cut-up sandwiches. "She thinks you're a kindred spirit, EJ." She winked at Inez. "See? I told you that you two would get along."

Inez swatted her with a napkin. "Behave."

"Oh, you're all show and no go." Fay Marian handed me a plate. "Don't be shy, EJ. Help yourself."

I was relieved when our conversation shifted away from race relations to details about the steps involved in clearing and planting Fay Marian's garden space. It took an effort for me not to feel conspicuous when Fay Marian extracted a dog-eared notebook from beneath a stack of catalogs and began taking copious notes. When we finished eating lunch, we walked outside together to look over the space.

It was an even bigger mess than I imagined. Not only was the area choked with weeds and sinewy vines of English ivy, but there appeared to be an impressive amount of cast-off junk, too. I could make out old buckets and broken clay flowerpots, a set of white sidewall tires, and the remains of a rusted bicycle frame.

I squinted at something projecting from a dirt pile. Sun was glinting off the unmistakable chrome contours of a car bumper. I pointed at it.

"Is that . . . ?"

"Oh, yeah." Fay Marian sighed. "Daddy had a thing for junked cars . . . ancient Simcas, mostly. None of them ever ran, as far as I can tell—not even in the 30's and 40's when they were new. It's like a French burial ground out here. Every time I think I have them all cleared out, I find another damn artifact."

"Don't curse, Fay Marian. EJ will think you're a heathen."

"Give it up, Inez." Fay Marian laughed. "Better she should know the truth up front, don't you think?"

"I fear that some of this is beyond my purview." In fact, I was talking as much about the easy camaraderie between the two women as I was the horrendous condition of the garden. I was out of my depth on both counts.

A horn sounded, and Fay Marian whirled around to take in the station wagon that had just pulled into her driveway.

"Well, damn." She looked at her watch. "They got here early." She waved at the driver. "Excuse me, you two. New tenants moving in today. I'll try not to be too long." She jogged off to greet her new lodgers.

Inez and I watched her go.

"That's a sad story," Inez shared with me. "Single man and his ten-year-old daughter. From Reidsville, I gather. He just took a job at RJR." She shook her head. "Pity he had to take his little girl out of school in the middle of the year. His name's Johnnie Hart."

"You said he's single?" I asked. "What happened to his wife?"

Inez lowered her voice. "We have no idea. We just know she isn't in the picture. Fay Marian said he's a distant cousin of her mother's. Otherwise, I don't think she'd have rented to a single man."

That made sense to me. New people were always moving into Winston-Salem to work at the tobacco company. My daddy used to say you couldn't throw a rock without hitting somebody who worked for R.J. Reynolds. I carried his assessment a bit further: you couldn't walk ten feet in this town without stepping on one of Mr. Reynolds's cigarette butts.

It was an epidemic of bad manners.

I watched our new neighbor talking with Fay Marian.

"He looks like a young man to have lost his wife," I observed. The door on the passenger side of his car flew open, and a wiry young girl with scabbed-over knees and a pixie haircut tumbled out. She greeted Fay Marian with an energetic wave before making a blurry beeline for the house.

"That must be Harriet, his daughter," Inez explained. "Fay Marian said she's rather a pistol."

"Pistol" didn't begin to describe all the things Harriet Hart was destined to become to me. But even without the benefit of that understanding, on this strange and uncharacteristic afternoon, I had already acquired a nagging suspicion that my life was about to change in ways I never could have predicted.

It was nearly 2 p.m. when I finally returned home. Saturdays were normally my housecleaning days, and it had taken most of the afternoon to organize garden tasks—beginning with the removal of any submerged car parts—and pull together a rudimentary materials list for Fay Marian.

I was already running far behind on my chores, and I knew that the time it would take to finish up would intrude on the rest of my evening. I wanted to complete them because I didn't like

14

doing housework on Sundays—and not just because my mother had always frowned on the commission of any chores on the Sabbath. For me, it was more about balance: I wanted to have one day a week that was free from obligation.

Housework was definitely an obligation.

Growing up, my mother had been an unrelenting taskmaster about adherence to unwritten rules. There were so many it became impossible for me to keep track of them all. She expected me to assimilate her proclivities through some kind of filial osmosis. I learned quickly that the key to maintaining felicity in our home environment hinged on following her lead and not asking too many questions. It took many years before I realized that Daddy did the same thing, although he had the latitude to ignore most of her behavioral directives. I was not as fortunate. Sometimes, Daddy would try to intercede with Mother on my behalf.

"Minerva, why don't you leave that poor girl alone and let her make her own decisions?"

Mother's litany of reasons why I lacked the competence to navigate my own life choices was so exhaustive that Daddy would soon give up the fight. He'd smile at me apologetically before offering her a defeated shrug and heading outside to take up some emergent lawn task.

Under normal circumstances, I'd have gotten right to work—even if it meant I'd have no time to finish reading *The Case of the Shapely Shadow*. But *that* Saturday, I admitted an exception. *NBC Theater* was broadcasting an afternoon performance of *Don Giovanni*, and I was determined to watch it. I'd been a fan of this opera—and most others—ever since I attended a live performance of *Lakmé* in Philadelphia during a sophomore year college trip. That performance had featured the celebrated American soprano, Lily Pons, who was part of the Metropolitan

Opera's spring tour. I had never experienced such an emotional performance. And the way the sheer beauty of the music and the grand emotion of the story swirled together was a kind of awakening for me—particularly the sonorous opening duet between the heroine, Lakmé, and her maid, Mallika.

I'd previously read that several television stations across the South were refusing to air the broadcast because it starred the Negro soprano Leontyne Price. But I was relieved to discover that our affiliate in Winston-Salem was showing it. Last year, I'd purchased a record by the lyric soprano and had been instantly charmed by the virtuosic purity and sheer power of her voice. To me, the ethereal beauty of the sound she created transcended time and all barriers—including color.

The opera was being performed in English, which I found unfortunate. English lacked the fluidity and poetic resonance of the original Italian. But even with that disadvantage, I was captivated by all the signature performances—Price's, in particular. She was singing the role of Donna Anna, a woman of great contradiction. As many times as I'd listened to the opera, I remained unclear about whether Donna Anna had been cruelly used by the rake Don Giovanni—or whether she'd been a willing participant in his seduction and had later become enraged by his rejection of her attentions. I thought Price's enigmatic performance straddled that ambiguity perfectly.

By the time the opera ended, it was too late for me to make any progress on housework. So I made myself a cup of Postum and carried it out to the front porch to enjoy what was left of the evening. The night air was a tad chilly, but not prohibitive to sitting outside, so I donned my father's old gray sweater. It had been a ubiquitous part of his post office uniform. My mother never liked it when I'd taken to wearing it after his death. She thought the oversized garment with its worn elbow patches made me look too blowsy and masculine. I did my best to imitate Daddy's feigned obliviousness and ignored her remonstrances. I hadn't often been successful.

I smiled. *But wearing the sweater did remind me of how Fay Marian looked in the mannish clothes she seemed to favor.*

I didn't care. I *liked* wearing it. And even though it had been laundered many times, I still imagined the thing smelled like Daddy: a tumbled confluence of fresh air, tobacco, and the bittersweet aroma of the horehound candies he always carried in its oversized pockets.

It was a quiet evening. By now, most of my neighbors would be inside, watching *American Bandstand* or *Bonanza*. I didn't tend to watch much television on the weekends—except for special occasions like today's opera broadcast. In fact, I couldn't recall watching anything since the Winter Olympics in Squaw Valley had concluded. People were still talking about how the U.S. Hockey team had finally beaten the Soviets, and how that event signified the start of some new world order.

I had my doubts. I didn't see how winning an ice hockey game could signify much of anything other than . . . well . . . winning an ice hockey game. But we seemed to be living in a time when people attached metaphorical significance to just about everything. But then, I'd always lived in what effectively was a two-hundred-year-old monument to the past. Old Salem was frozen in time like a quaint little snow globe. I loved it here. And yet . . .

Maybe I did need to get out more?

One of the best things about living on a dead-end street was the absence of through traffic. Evenings were generally uneventful, and uninterrupted by passing cars or people out walking with children or pets. I looked forward to these quiescent evenings when the air grew warmer and made sitting outdoors possible. After spending eight hours a day working in a basement with no windows, it was a luxurious release. It was regrettable that our local postmaster equated the "dead" aspect of undeliverable letters with a morgue—and, according to him, morgues were *always* located in basements.

On impulse, I retrieved the odd stack of supposed "dead" letters from my leather bag and took them outside with me. I had resolved not to deal with them until Monday morning at work. But I couldn't resist looking them each over more carefully for any clues I might've missed that morning.

Once I was situated, I picked up the letters and sorted them in order by the dates on the postmarks. All the letters had been mailed from the same post office in Paradise, Virginia. I had a vague recollection that Paradise was a small town located somewhere on the outskirts of Roanoke, but I wasn't certain. I'd have to look it up on Monday.

A mild, intermittent breeze was billowing in from the east. I could smell the fresh-cut grass from the grounds around the old St. Philip's Church which sat on a rise across the street from my house. That meant Nelson had been there today, mowing and tidying up. He must've come while I'd been at Fay Marian's. I was sorry to have missed him. Nelson Porter and his family lived across the creek in the Negro neighborhood called Happy Hill, and every weekend during the spring and summer, he volunteered his time to maintain the land around the original African Moravian Church. We'd struck up a friendship many years ago, and sometimes he would help me set bulbs in the front beds. While we worked, he reminisced about how he had always helped my daddy with that same task in the past. In fact,

Nelson had been the one who'd discovered Daddy's body, lying in a bed of liriope beneath a big tulip poplar tree. He'd collapsed on a late-spring day while working in the yard. I remembered how tentatively Nelson had approached our front door to knock and tell us that Mr. Walter had fallen into the shrubs out front. I never forgot his kindness or how gently he talked with Mother while we waited on the ambulance to arrive.

It had been too late, of course. Daddy had always suffered with the permanent lung damage he sustained after being gassed by the Germans near the Somme River during the Great War. When he returned home, Mother tried, unsuccessfully, to get him to give up his job as a mail carrier, and to seek a different assignment inside the post office. But predictably, Daddy refused. So he dutifully carried his bag along the same old city streets, rain or shine, for the next twelve years. All the while, his heart grew weaker and weaker, until it finally gave out—three days before my eighteenth birthday.

Yes. I was sorry to have missed Nelson today.

The breeze picked up again. It carried another scent—this one sweet and vaguely spicy—almost like Earl Grey tea. *Strange.* Nothing was blooming yet. It was still too early in the season. It took me a few moments of reflection to realize that the scent was coming from the letters. I lifted one to my nose. There it was: that same heady scent of bergamot, jasmine and vanilla. I checked each letter in turn. They all carried the same whisper of fragrance.

Curious. Whoever wrote these took the time to perfume the stationery. That clearly had to indicate that these were not business letters, or anything related to commerce . . . or to any kind of bad news. They had to be personal. Which made the fact that they'd all been addressed to an unknown person not now connected with the gardens even stranger.

Why on earth had these been sent here? And why were there so *many* of them?

I had already checked the telephone directory for any Mary Ann Evanses listed. There were none. It had become clear that we'd have to open at least one of the letters to look for any clues about the intent of the sender. But only after I'd researched the feasibility of even accepting the letters back into our system.

In truth, I shouldn't even have been looking at them on my front porch at home. That action was a gross violation of protocol—something I'd never done before.

I hastily restacked the letters and set them down on the table beside my chair.

I resolved not to think any more about them until Monday morning. But the rest of the time I tarried outside, I occasionally caught traces of the spicy sweet fragrance floating on the falling night air.

After early church, I sat down to read the paper. I always liked reading the magazine first, before moving on to the local news and front section. National news was still consumed by continuing coverage of the horrible Northwest Orient Airlines crash in Indiana. It had been a catastrophic event. The plane had blown apart in midair and all sixty-three people on board had died. No cause had yet been identified, but suspicions and wild speculations abounded—primarily because another midair explosion had just occurred on a National Airlines flight over Bolivia in Brunswick County, a small town near the North Carolina coast. It was suspected that a passenger carrying a makeshift bomb in his luggage had caused that crash, resulting in the deaths of all thirty-four people aboard.

I had already read enough of the cascading news reports suggesting a possible connection between the two plane crashes. The horrific event in Indiana had been enough of a tragedy without amplifying sensational rumors about bombs or midair collisions.

Another article reported that police in Orangeburg, South Carolina, had arrested nearly four hundred Negroes for sitting down at area lunch counters en masse and demanding service. The local news carried continuing coverage of the same kind of events happening right here in Winston-Salem. I had not experienced any of the disruptions written about in the paper. But then, I always carried my lunch to work and rarely visited any of the downtown department stores during business hours. One thing was certain: these protests were gaining in frequency. Nearly every city in the South was now struggling with how to resolve the standoffs. I didn't understand why people couldn't just be content with the status quo. Violence like this benefitted no one.

I quickly flipped pages to find the extended weather forecast. Fay Marian had hoped she'd be able to begin setting some plants as early as next weekend. I wanted to be sure the nighttime temperatures wouldn't fluctuate too much to prevent that.

"Mornin', Miss Esther."

The greeting surprised me. I looked up from the paper to see Nelson standing on the sidewalk in front of St. Philip's Church. He was carrying a garden rake and a battered tin pail.

"Good morning, Nelson." I waved at him. "I saw that you'd been here yesterday. I was sorry to have missed you."

"Yes, ma'am," he said. "There's still a gracious plenty left to do—especially back there by God's Acre."

I smiled at his reference to the small cemetery. "I'm surprised to see you out here on a Sunday."

"Well, the good Lord don't much care how I choose to offer worship. I figure takin' care of His house here is as pleasin' to Him as sittin' on my hind end listenin' to preachin'—especially when it's the same message I done heard twenty-eleven times."

I laughed. "That makes sense to me."

"Now, you enjoy the rest of your Sunday mornin'. I got to get busy before them weeds plumb take hold a this whole side of the street."

"All right. But you give me a holler if you need a second set of hands."

"Yes, ma'am. You know I will for sure." Nelson gave me a respectful nod and continued on his way. I watched his straight back as he climbed the slight hill that led to the old brick church. He paused several times to bend over and pull some stray weeds on his way to the small Negro cemetery.

I loved watching him tend the grounds at St. Philip's. He seemed to take such pride in the work, even though it had been nearly a decade since the congregation had moved out of Old Salem. Nelson seemed to cherish his connection to the place, and to its significance in the life of his community. It had been way back in 1865 that a Union cavalry officer strode to the pulpit inside the old Negro church and told the assembled congregation of slaves that President Lincoln had freed them. After that, the Moravian elders began to sell property to their former slaves, so they might build homes and establish their own community. It never occurred to me to ask *why* the elders had concealed the fact of their freedom from their Negroes— or whether anyone thought doing so had been inconsistent with their Christian beliefs. Since the church had permitted the elders to own slaves, questioning their decision not to recognize President Lincoln's proclamation seemed like an academic exercise. In the end, the right thing had happened—as it usually did.

The settlement the former slaves built across Salem Creek became known as Happy Hill. I had never crossed the creek to visit Nelson or any of his neighbors—my mother absolutely frowned on that. But Daddy had—many times. He would always come home from those visits carrying rolled paper sacks that were chock full of fantastic baked goods. Mother never much cared for the sweet confections, but I shared Daddy's sweet tooth. My favorites were always the thick slices of Brown Butter Buttermilk Pie, and the special fried Sweet Potato Jacks—which Nelson's wife, Ruthie, only made at Thanksgiving. I looked forward to those all year, and usually started pestering Daddy to make a trip across the creek as soon as the leaves started falling.

I'd close my eyes when I'd bite into one of those pies, and my senses would fill up with what I imagined the sights and smells of Ruthie's kitchen were like when she baked. In Ruthie's hands, simple ingredients became magical. To me, the tiny pies tasted like love and hope—like sweet and savory reminders of a storied past. Once I asked Nelson if Ruthie would share her recipe with me so Mother and I could make some, too. He just smiled and said the recipe wasn't written down anyplace—it just lived in her hands. It had come down to her that way, he said. The same way it came to her mama and grandma. "Just like you got your daddy's red hair and that sweet voice."

I knew what he meant, but I was disappointed. "But red hair doesn't taste this good."

Nelson laughed. His voice was low and musical. And the

23

sound of his laughter was always like hearing the bell choir at Christmas.

Nelson had never forgotten my fondness for the fried pies—and always took care to bring me some of the tasty treats every autumn, when Ruthie made them for the church.

Fay Marian had said she and Inez would begin clearing the garden space later that day, and I was welcome to stop over and "bark orders." She made it clear that they didn't expect me to do any of the debris removal—just to supervise. I hadn't planned on going over, but when I was in the kitchen washing up after lunch, I saw both she and Inez hard at work behind the house. After a brief deliberation, I gave in to an uncharacteristic impulse, changed into my gardening clothes, and ventured over to check on their progress.

They both seemed delighted that I'd decided to join them. Fay Marian wore her usual casual combination of garments. But I chose to overlook that because she was engaged in manual labor—an exception my mother would never have allowed for me. For her part, Inez still managed to look tidy and well put together in a pair of dungarees and a lace-up chamois shirt. Even though Fay Marian insisted that she didn't want me to pitch in, I was determined to help out. So I set to work digging up some determined crowfoot grass that had established a good foothold in the rich soil nearest the house. I hadn't been working long when the daughter of Fay Marian's new lodger more or less exploded into the middle of our work zone.

"I'm here," she proclaimed. "What can I do to help out?"

Fay Marian laughed. "For starters, you can go shake hands with Miss Cloud over there."

The young girl swung her head around and saw me kneeling on the ground, pulling weeds. She charged over to where I was working and thrust out her hand.

"I'm Harriet. But you can call me Harrie. We just moved in here yesterday. Where do you live?"

I took off my glove so I could shake her small hand. Her grip was surprisingly firm.

"I'm Esther. But you may call me EJ. And I live right there," I pointed to the back of my small house, "on Church Street."

"Do you live there by yourself?"

"Yes. I do . . . *Harrie*." I wondered about her odd choice of nickname. But something about it did seem to match her demeanor. She was terribly forward for such a young girl.

"My Aunt Rochelle lives alone, too. She works in a department store. Where do you work?" Harrie was still taking in my house—at least as much of it as could still be seen beyond the impressive pile of debris Fay Marian and Inez were creating.

"I work at the post office."

"You do?" Harrie seemed impressed by that. "Do you deliver letters?"

"In a way. My job is to work with letters that get lost or can't be delivered because people move or disappear."

Harrie nodded as if she understood the concept.

"Daddy said my mama departed when I was just a baby. And she didn't leave no forwarding address, neither. My teachers at school all thought that meant she died and called her my dear, departed mama. But Daddy said no. She wadn't dead. Just departed. I wrote her some letters once. But they all got sent back." She gave a wistful-sounding sigh. "I guess them people in the Reidsville post office ain't very good at their jobs."

"I'm sorry to hear that, Harrie." I was, too. It was tragic to listen to a child speak so casually about being abandoned by her mother.

25

"I was, too, at first. But my best friend, Carla Hotbed, told me that some women are just fast and loose." Harrie kicked at a dried clump of red clay. "Carla's older'n me and she knows about stuff like that." Harrie's face was sorrowful. "I sure will miss Carla. She was teachin' me how to roll my own smokes."

Inez cleared her throat. "Harriet? I think it will be much better for you to give up that habit."

"How come?" Harrie seemed baffled by Inez's caution.

"It's not acceptable for young ladies."

I could tell by Harrie's reaction that Inez's logic didn't make much of an impression. She looked at Fay Marian for support. "Ain't ten old enough to smoke?"

"Don't ask me." Fay Marian cleared her throat. "All I can say is it's not much good for us at any age."

I was intrigued that Harrie had quickly tapped into the special relationship dynamic between Inez and Fay Marian.

"Would you like to help me pull weeds?" I was eager to change the subject. "I can show you how."

"Sure." Harrie dropped to her knees beside me. "I didn't know these plants was weeds. Our yard in Reidsville looked just like this. Only we didn't have as many car parts yet."

"Yet?" I asked.

"We only lived there a year," Harrie explained.

"Good collections do take time," Fay Marian agreed.

"So, would you like a pair of gloves?" I had an extra pair in my bag, and I offered them to Harrie.

"What for?" she asked.

"Well, to keep your hands from getting too soiled."

"I ain't worried about that." Harrie showed me her palms. They were already streaked with dirt. "I was just climbin' that big maple tree out front. It's gonna make a great fort. I could see right into the bedroom window of that front apartment."

I heard Inez gasp.

"Which front apartment?" Fay Marian asked with alarm.

"The one where that old geezer with the schnauzer lives." Harrie jerked her thumb toward the west side of the house. "He's pretty weird . . . and he smells like mothballs."

"Mr. Hauser." Fay Marian sounded relieved. "He's . . . *eccentric.* I'm surprised you already met him, Harrie."

"I didn't have no choice. He hollered at me for bouncin' my ball in the upstairs hallway." She looked at me. "He said it made his dog nervous."

"I have heard that schnauzers can sometimes be a nervous breed," I explained, on Mr. Hauser's behalf.

Harrie wasn't buying it. "If that dog's nervous it's probably because it had to listen to accordion music all night."

"Accordion?" I looked at Fay Marian for help.

"Lawrence Welk," she clarified. "It's on every Saturday night. Like I said: Mr. Hauser is eccentric."

"I ain't sure what 'eccentric' means," Harrie insisted, "but it sure don't have nothin' to do with good music."

Fay Marian chuckled.

Harrie was busy trying to uproot a clump of crabgrass. "Damn. This weed is *tough.*"

"Harriet!" Inez issued a warning. "Watch your language, young lady."

"Hey, it ain't my fault. Carla'd say this thing is stuck like shit to a blanket. If I had a screwdriver, I could pry it out."

Inez poked Fay Marian in the side and jerked her head of tight curls at Harriet.

Fay Marian cleared her throat. "Um, Harrie? How about we dial back the cussing? We don't want to offend Miss Cloud."

"She ain't offended." Harrie looked at me. "Are you, Eej?"

Eej?

"Um . . ." I was unsure how to reply. I was reluctant to appear prudish, but I definitely disliked bad language.

"Okay, okay. I'll try. Daddy's always upset about it, too. He says I cuss like a damn sailor. But Aunt Rochelle says that's his fault 'cause I don't have no mama to teach me right. Even though she tells me all that 'act like a lady' jazz is a stupid rule made up by men who ain't smart enough to control their women."

"Your Aunt Rochelle sounds like she's quite important to you." I was eager to change the subject.

"Oh, yeah. She's *really* neat. She lives in Roanoke and drives a bright yellow Thunderbird convertible. She has a *ton* of boyfriends, too. Carla says that's on account of how stacked she is. But Aunt Rochelle says none of them men are worth a flip, and all they're good for is a steak dinner now n' then. She sells cosmetics and gives home perms in her apartment on her days off. I go up there to visit a lot. It ain't too bad once you get used to that rotten egg smell."

"Let me show you an easier way to remove these weeds." I took a trowel and demonstrated how to sink the blade into the dirt and lift the base of the stubborn plant. Once it pulled free, I shook off the excess soil and tossed the weed and its roots into a waste bucket. "See? Isn't that simpler than trying to yank them out? Better than a screwdriver, anyway."

"If you say so." Harrie took the trowel from me to give it a try. "But if you ask me, anything that hangs on this hard oughter be left alone."

"But don't you think this garden will look better without all these weeds?"

"Maybe. I don't know." Harrie stabbed the trowel into the dirt beneath another clump of crabgrass. The plant made popping sounds as Harrie wielded the trowel around its base and its roots were slowly separated from the earth. She lifted the weed intact like a pro and held it aloft. "Poor feller put up quite a fight. Kinda sad." Harrie shook off the dirt and tossed the remains of the weed into the bucket. "What're you gonna fill all these holes with?"

"Vegetables, I think. And maybe some special herbs."

"What kind of herbs?"

"Well, that will be up to Fay Marian. But I think she wants to plant some of the same medicinal herbs we grow in the *hortus medicus* here in Old Salem."

"The hortus . . . *what?*"

"*Medicus*," I explained. "It means 'medicinal herbs,' referring to ancient plants that once were grown and made into cures for medical conditions. The original garden here was started more than two hundred years ago and was designed by one of the first Moravians to settle here: a doctor named Hans Martin Kalberlahn from Norway. We maintain it today exactly the way it was back then, with all the same plants."

"How do you know they're the same plants?"

"Because the Moravian settlers were scrupulous about record keeping. And they kept many diaries and made elaborate maps of their settlements—including the gardens."

Harrie made short work of another cluster of weeds. At the rate we were going, we'd have the entire section cleared in no time. "How come you know so much about these plants?"

It was the second time in two days I'd been asked a variation of the same question. *Strange*. No one else in my life had *ever* questioned my work in the gardens. But then, no one else in my life had ever questioned me much about anything. That was as much my fault as it was due to any other circumstance. I didn't tend to open up to people easily.

Harrie seemed determined to overlook that trait. She all but tapped the ground with her trowel while she waited for me to answer her question.

"Well," I began, "I grew up helping my mother tend gardens. And it was something she did with her mother, too. So, I guess you could say that it's a family tradition—at least for all the women on my mother's side. It's like a sacred obligation."

"What about your daddy?"

I thought about my father's family. The Clouds were not Moravians and had never been keen on gardening. According to my mother, they hadn't been all that keen on God, either. But that wasn't the whole truth. Mother said the war changed Daddy, and that he came home a different man.

That wasn't hard to understand. Daddy once said the mustard gas he took into his lungs in France never went away, and he carried it around inside him like a stowaway. He claimed that extra weight made his mailbag twice as heavy to carry, even on the lightest delivery days. He never talked much about religion, though—just that one time when Mother was home sick with the flu and Daddy walked me to church. When we got there, he said he'd wait for me outside, on a bench in Salem Square.

"I can hear God a lot better out here, in the fresh air," he explained.

When I said I'd rather stay there with him, he told me no—that each person had to work out their own way to worship and that one day, I'd find the best way to hear God's voice, too. The most important thing, he said, was for me to keep my heart and mind open so I could recognize God's voice when He spoke to me. "It may not sound like you think it will," he said, "so that's why it's extra important to always listen for it, even in places you'd never expect to hear it."

"For me," he said, "that happened in a muddy trench in France, one foggy morning in March."

So I went inside the church without him that morning—and I listened for the voice of God. I didn't hear it that day—or on any of the other Sunday mornings I went back with Mother. But I believed what Daddy told me, and I knew with certainty that one day I *would* hear His voice—and that I would know it when I did.

But right then, kneeling in a pile of dirt and weeds with Harrie, I was struggling with what words to use to explain my father's distant relationship to the herbs, and their role at the center of our family life.

Looking at Harrie's earnest face, I knew the simplest explanation would probably be the best.

"He wasn't a Moravian."

She seemed to accept that without question. I would later learn what an anomaly this was for her.

We continued to pull weeds for the next hour. Harrie prattled on about her life in Reidsville and how she'd had to leave school early when her father took the new job at RJR. She also dropped a few more pearls of wisdom from her street-smart best friend, Carla Hotbed. For my part, I thought getting Harrie away from Carla's tutelage was her father's best hedge against his daughter earning a stint in reform school.

A little before 3 p.m., Johnnie Hart appeared in the backyard, looking for his daughter.

"C'mon, Harrie," he clapped his hands, "I gotta scoot. Time for you to head inside." He addressed Fay Marian. "I'm workin' second shift today, so Harrie'll be flyin' solo tonight. Don't worry none about her, though. I got her supper all ready. She's checked out." He glared down at his daughter. "As long as she stays *inside* like she's supposed to."

I was flabbergasted. Mr. Hart was going to leave his ten-year-old daughter at home alone? In a new city, where she didn't have any family to call if she needed help or became afraid?

It was untenable.

Fay Marian seemed to take it all in stride. "No problem, Johnnie. Inez and I will look after her. Won't we, Inez?"

Inez didn't appear too convinced that "looking after" Harrie was the best idea.

"Well . . ." she began.

"She'll do just fine," Fay Marian finished Inez's statement. "And there won't be any tree climbing or any other pastimes that will provoke Mr. Hauser. Right, Harrie?"

It was clear that Harrie was busy trying to calculate all the implied embargoes on behaviors that might be deemed provocative. It was apparently a long list because Johnnie gave up waiting on her to agree to Fay Marian's restrictions.

"You just mind your p's and q's, young lady," he said sternly. "And you listen to Miss Vogler, or I'll take away your Crashmobile."

"Her what?" Inez asked.

"It's some dang car toy." Johnnie waved a hand impatiently. "You wind it up and let it go flyin' into a wall, so it blows all apart."

"It's *super* neat," Harrie explained. "You put it back together and crash it all over again."

Inez looked blankly at Fay Marian. "This is fun?"

"I don't see why not. If my daddy had had one of those, we probably wouldn't be dealing with all these busted-up Simcas."

"*Broken* up," Inez corrected.

Fay Marian ignored her. "You bring the Crashmobile to my place later on, Harrie. We'll eat ice cream and watch Ed Sullivan."

"Nifty!" Harrie was plainly excited.

Johnnie seemed appreciative of Fay Marian's generosity. "I won't make this a habit, ma'am. I promise. This shift is just 'cause I'm new."

"Don't you worry about it, Johnnie. I know what it's like to be the new kid on the block."

He nodded and gave his daughter a quick hug. "Be-*have*." He told her. Then he made haste heading to his car for the short ride across town to the tobacco factory.

"Maybe EJ will join us later for ice cream, too?" Fay Marian suggested.

Harrie looked at me expectantly.

I was flummoxed.

"Um. I . . ." It was obvious I was flailing around, looking for an excuse to decline.

"C'mon, Eej . . ." Harrie pulled out the big guns. "I'll let you crash the car."

I looked over at Inez for support.

She gave me a small smile of resignation.

"I'd call that an offer you cannot refuse."

Rue Graveolens
(Rue)

"And as I gave you the green plants, I give you everything."
                                    —Genesis 9:3

When I arrived at work on Monday morning, Lottie was already there, sorting through the bin of letters that had been sent down to us over the weekend. When I entered our basement warehouse of an office, she looked up at me with a scowl on her face.

"There is no way in hell this many letters piled up in *one* weekend. Them men upstairs are just sandbagging—as usual."

"Good morning to you, too, Lottie."

I deposited my purse inside a locker and stashed my lunch bag in our small fridge before donning Daddy's sweater. I usually carried it with me to work since it was always so cold in the basement of the old post office building. Even on the hottest days of the summer, the space rarely got above sixty-five degrees. That was another reason our postmaster called the Dead Letter Office a morgue. Lottie complained that we could probably hang meat down there. But then, Lottie didn't have much patience for anything she thought was ridiculous or a waste of time. Most people called her jaded. But Daddy always said that was just because Lottie Bean had worked for the post office long enough to have seen just about everything. In fact, it had been Daddy who got Lottie the job working in the DLO.

Back then, the post office wasn't keen on employing married women, and Lottie'd had to quit her job sorting mail after she got married and had her son, Jerome. But things got tight when the Second World War broke out, and businesses everywhere were scrambling to find people to fill the jobs vacated when men went off to war. Daddy went to bat for Lottie, who he'd gotten to know years earlier, and explained that her husband, Marvin, had joined the Army and was off fighting the Japanese in the Pacific theater. He pointed out that the Beans were as much a post office family as the Clouds, and the agency had a responsibility to support the war effort by taking care of our soldier's families—and that included Negroes as well as white people.

So, Lottie got her job back and soon became charged with sorting out the branch's huge backlog of undeliverable mail. Lottie ran the DLO pretty much single-handedly until I had joined her there many years ago, after I withdrew from college—not long before Mother died. We'd worked side by side every day since, and I was used to her zero tolerance for other postal employees who took shortcuts or didn't follow proper procedures.

Like that day.

I walked over to examine the bin of undeliverable mail, affectionately tapping the top of "Uncle Bernie's" elaborate brass urn on the way. The cremated remains of one S. Burnis Orel, 1902-1934, had reposed on a shelf near our processing area, sandwiched between a six-pound package of snuff and a vintage

Colt revolver (sans ammunition), ever since I'd started working in the office. Despite the determined efforts and best resources of the U.S. Postal Service, Burnis Orel had never found his way home. Lottie said he'd probably still be there in that same spot, decades after we both retired.

It made us both sad that no one ever came to claim the man we called Uncle Bernie.

Lottie hadn't been exaggerating about the volume of undeliverable mail. It *did* seem excessive—even for a regional processing center like ours.

"You're right," I agreed. "This is going to take us days to work through."

Lottie shook her head in disgust. "Of all days, I had to pick today to forget my lunch. So now, I'll have to go stand up at one of them damn lunch counters to get anything decent."

I thought about the article I'd read in yesterday's paper. "Aren't you worried about the protests?"

I didn't want Lottie to get caught up in a demonstration that might land her in jail.

"Protests?" Lottie looked at me like I was crazy. "They ain't any protests happenin' in the *back* of the Charles Department Store. Them managers is just *fine* with us slinkin' in through the side entrance to stand up and eat lunch where nobody can see us. They just don't want us sittin' down up front."

I didn't have a response to that. More than anything, I wished I'd brought enough lunch for both of us.

"Well, maybe things will change now that people are paying more attention." I suggested. "They can't keep arresting everybody."

"Can't they?"

"I hope not. It all has to end sooner or later."

Lottie wasn't persuaded. "Seems to me like *sooner* and *later* are terms that don't have much difference when it comes to treatin' people the same." She carried the bin of letters over to our workstation and set it down with a thunk. "This mess ain't gonna end until somebody forces them people to do right."

I wasn't sure if she meant the sit-ins, or the mail sorters upstairs.

Neither one of them was making our lives any easier at the moment.

"Why don't you ask Marvin to bring you something later on? Couldn't you walk up to Fourth Street and meet him?"

Lottie's husband, Marvin, was a driver for the Negro-owned Safe Bus Company, which served the colored neighborhoods in and around Winston-Salem where city buses and trolleys didn't run. City buses were all segregated—but for ten cents, any person could lay claim to any seat on a Safe Bus. But those buses weren't permitted to come any further into town than Church Street.

Lottie laughed at my suggestion. "That man is lucky if he remembers to put on both shoes before leavin' the house."

I knew better than to try to persuade her. Once Lottie had her mind made up about something, there was no changing it. So we set to work sifting through the piles of letters. Lottie had a unique system of separating the mail into piles labeled "good-n-dead" or "merely sick." The sickly variety would be easier to dispatch because they had discernible, partial, or coded markings that would make researching the sender's address easy. The others—not so much. We sorted them all into the separate bins for processing.

Between the two of us, we had a unique combination of skills that kicked in when we'd exhausted our trove of telephone books, city directories, tax listings, atlases, and church bulletins and they'd yielded no results. I had a good reading knowledge of German—which was particularly useful since the city had such a vast German heritage—and I'd been born with a near photographic ability to recall place names and other geographic oddities. Lottie was a whiz at deciphering illegible penmanship, and was also uniquely able to translate the inventive and incomprehensible spellings senders would often employ when indicating a delivery destination.

She held up an envelope. "Look at this. Somebody spelled Pfafftown 'Faffton.' Now wouldn't you think them idiots upstairs would be smart enough to figure this one out? I swanny." She swiftly relabeled it and tossed it into the bin for remailing.

By lunchtime, we'd managed to work through the majority of the merely sick letters. Those, we placed into new envelopes with special labels and loaded into a vacuum tube that connected our office with the main processing area upstairs.

Lottie changed her mind about eating a stand-up lunch and decided to pick something up and bring it back to the office. It was while we were eating that I decided to ask her about the letters Evelyn Haas had given to me on Saturday.

"How many are there?" Lottie asked.

I pulled them out of my bag. "Six, so far."

Lottie took them from me and flipped through them. "What do you mean by 'so far'? Do you think there'll be more comin'?"

"Evelyn said they'd been arriving about once a week, so maybe."

"No return address." Lottie held one of the envelopes up to her face. "They smell good, too. I guess this ain't your perfume?"

"You know not."

Lottie chuckled. "Seems like somebody went to a fair amount of trouble to get these delivered to that garden."

"I thought so, too. But Evelyn insisted there'd never been anyone named Mary Ann Evans working there—not even a volunteer."

"Why didn't you open these?"

"I didn't feel right about doing that at home. In fact, I wasn't even sure I should've accepted the letters back from Evelyn, since they'd been properly delivered."

"Well, they ain't properly delivered if there's nobody by that name there to receive them."

"True."

"Well." Lottie finished her egg salad sandwich and tossed its paper wrapper into the trash bin. "Ain't you gonna open one up and see what's what?"

"I suppose so."

Lottie examined the postmarks and handed me the first letter. I hesitated before picking up the letter opener.

"What's the matter?" Lottie didn't miss much. And she'd been working with me long enough to recognize when I was uncomfortable.

"I can't put my finger on it. Something about this just feels . . . inappropriate."

"How come? You know post office policy as good as I do. That letter's been sittin' around for more than forty-five days. It's past time for us to open it up and look for clues about how to deliver it—or to send it back to," she examined the postmark on one of the other envelopes, "whoever mailed it in Paradise, Virginia . . . wherever in God's creation that is."

"I looked it up in the atlas. It's a small town just east of Roanoke."

"See? That's something useful already. So, either we read the letter for clues, or we ride on up there and follow our noses around until we find somebody who smells this pretty."

"Lottie . . ."

"Oh, for heaven's sake." Lottie thrust out a hand. "Give me the damn thing. I'll do it."

I meekly handed her the letter and opener.

Lottie efficiently opened the sealed flap and withdrew two sheets of pale stationery that matched the envelope. The air between us filled with a more intense hint of the same spicy fragrance.

"Damn. It's even stronger inside." Lottie unfolded the pages and began to read.

Dear Mary Ann,

> *It has taken me this long to become bold enough to confront the reality of my deepest feelings and to rail, at last, against the disappointed hopes you left me with. Why did you open my eyes and heart to beauty—to passion and possibility—only to consign me to a vapid life devoid of love—devoid of promise? You left me alone to endure the bleak prospect of a plodding and predictable existence that holds me hostage in a land of strangers.*

Lottie lowered the pages. "Well, we already know *one* thing for sure."

"What's that?"

"This *has* to be some white woman. Who else would write mess like this? And what in tarnation is a *vapid life?*"

40

"Lottie ..." I took the pages from her. "Don't be silly." I picked up reading where she left off.

> *Every night, I lie alone on a bed of loneliness and sorrow, longing for the sweet touch of a lover who can never be mine. Why did you deign to awaken the first flush of passion within me, Mary Ann, when it was never your design to allow for its fruition? Why were you the author of hope and possibility when you knew that fulfillment would elude me forever? You led me to the stream and allowed me to experience one, brief moment inside the flood.*

> *I remember each sacred moment with her, Mary Ann. How such sweetness and light shone from her eyes! How her intimate touch was like the first bright bloom of Angelica: fragrant, soft and certain. Its slender tendrils reached deep inside and laid claim to all my hidden longing. Together we became one with the garden. Our fresh young bodies twining together amidst the rows of . . .*

I stopped reading and hastily scanned the remainder of the letter. "It's signed by someone named Dorothea." I refolded the pages.

"Why'd you quit reading?" Lottie demanded. "It was just gettin' good."

"Because there's *nothing else* in here that can help us."

Lottie scoffed. "I wouldn't say that."

"What on earth do you mean?"

Lottie sat back and gave me a good once-over. "Child, if you ask me, you need to take this letter on home with you tonight and use it to relieve some of that pent-up tension."

I was baffled by her suggestion. "What tension?"

Lottie dropped her head back and stared at the pipes that crisscrossed the ceiling. Then she sighed. "Lemme ask you somethin': when was the last time you looked in a mirror?"

I had no idea what she was getting at, and my face must've shown it.

"The good Lord gave you that mane of red hair and a good bosom, but you keep them both so covered up that nobody can ever see the gifts you got. And your mama didn't do you no favors by fillin' your head with all them crazy ideas about what a damn lady does and doesn't do. And if that wasn't bad enough, she drug you with her to that damn, worthless garden to dig in the dirt and ruin your nails. Trust me," she thrust the stack of letters at me, "you need to read this. *Twice.* Maybe more."

I did my best to demur and reject Lottie's oddly passionate assessment. But it was clear to both of us that she knew me better than I knew myself.

"I'll think about it," I said, more to end her pursuit of this ridiculous idea.

"See that you do."

The rest of our day passed uneventfully. We spent a frustrating thirty minutes trying to uncover the identity of a letter writer who hadn't bothered to include complete delivery information *or* a return address—and had deigned to sign the letter "Guess Who." Finally, Lottie had had enough.

"Guess Who?" she barked. "Guess *what?*" She snapped the letter out of my hand and tossed it into our discard bin. "You're about to make friends with Mr. Shredder."

We made acceptable headway managing the remainder of the problem letters, and by 5 p.m. we were in good enough shape to feel confident about going home without worrying about what would remain for us to accomplish on Tuesday.

We said goodnight at the street door and went our separate ways. I caught a city bus out front, as usual—and Lottie walked two blocks to the Safe Bus stop on North Church Street, so she could travel across town to her home on Bon Air Avenue, near the airport. During the short bus ride home, I thanked my lucky stars that Lottie had decided to let the issue of the mysterious "garden" letters drop. That actually surprised me. It wasn't like Lottie to give up on an idea so easily—especially when it related to something she felt strongly about.

And one thing I'd learned after working with her for so many years was that Lottie had strong feelings about pretty much *everything*.

I was tired by the time I reached home. That was mostly due to all the extra work and hustle it had taken to process a mountain of dead letters. But more than that, I just felt agitated and unsettled. I knew that some of that anxiety derived from all the social activities of the weekend. I'd found them draining. And they'd resulted in my having next to no time to tend to my normal routines, which led me to feel antsy and frustrated.

I didn't have much of an appetite, so after I changed out of my work clothes, I retrieved a container of vegetable soup from the freezer and sat down to watch the evening news telecast while I waited for the soup to heat on the stovetop. Douglas Edwards was reporting that LeRoy Collins, the segregationist governor of Florida, had given a surprising live address on television and had reversed his position on the lunch counter sit-ins that were sweeping the South. Collins announced that he'd had a change of heart, and now understood that it was wrong to try and stop Americans from struggling to be free. The news showed footage of Negroes being arrested and led away in handcuffs after daring to sit down at white-only lunch counters. And the same thing continued to happen nearly every day, right here in Winston-Salem.

I was surprised to find myself agreeing with Governor Collins. There seemed to be no easy solutions to the present standoff except for people to open their minds—and hearts. I thought about Lottie and her revelation that she'd have to stand up to eat lunch in the back of the Charles Department Store. *It was humiliating. There had to be a better way.*

Surely it should be possible for us all to find common ground over something as uncomplicated as allowing our Negro neighbors the right to sit down when they ate lunch?

Shouldn't it?

And I dearly hoped our city would find a solution soon, before anyone got hurt. Already, too many of the responses to these protests were turning violent.

It was another warm evening, so after I ate my bowl of soup, I went outside to sit on the front porch with my mug of Postum. The feeling of agitation I'd felt when I arrived home had not abated. If anything, it had grown in intensity. I wasn't sure why. But I suspected that some of it derived from the portion of the first garden letter Lottie and I had read.

I still felt embarrassed by the writer's account of her . . . *emotional* interaction with another woman. At least, I assumed

44

the writer was female. The stationery, the scent of perfume, and the tidy cursive handwriting all combined to indicate it. Lottie's brazen suggestion that I would derive some benefit from bringing the letter home and reading it in its entirety unsettled me even more.

What had she been thinking to suggest such a thing? Lottie had to know that I'd never read anything that . . . *pornographic* before. She knew my family and how I'd been brought up. Mama would've sprouted horns if she'd ever caught me reading something that salacious. It was an absurd idea to think I'd choose to do such a thing voluntarily . . . even though I had to admit I'd *thought* about it.

I looked down at my Erle Stanley Garner novel. These books were innocent, guilty pleasures. They hardly constituted anything remotely approaching the graphic content of that . . . *encounter.*

It was clear to me that the letters would have to be destroyed—in accordance with postal regulations that governed the final disposition of dead letters when provenance could not be resolved. It would be up to Lottie to choose whether or not she wanted to open any of the remaining five letters to look for clues. I certainly had *no* intention to risk reading any more of them.

My reverie was interrupted by a high-pitched sound that came out of nowhere. It repeated in several short blasts, followed by a longer report. *What on earth was it?* I could hear dogs barking from several of the backyards belonging to houses lining the street behind mine. Then the sequence of blasts resounded again, repeating the same pattern.

Immediately after that, I noticed a child on a red scooter, speeding around the corner from the sidewalk that ran along Race Street. The rider looked familiar. When she saw me sitting on the porch, she screeched to a halt in front of my house and hollered out.

"Hi ya, Eej! Do you like my new whistle?"

"Harriet? What on earth are you doing out at this time of night?"

"Night? It ain't night. There's about another whole hour 'til dark. Daddy says I'm allowed to stay outside until the gloaming . . . whatever the heck that is."

"It means *dusk*—which will be happening any minute now. You should be at home inside. It's not safe for you to be out on the streets after dark."

"Why? There ain't no traffic on Race Street. How come they call it that when there're never any cars?"

"Because Race Street is named for the old mill that used to be located here. A 'race' was a kind of stream that was diverted to provide power to run the waterwheels inside the mill."

"You mean there weren't no cars?"

"There weren't *any* cars. That is correct."

Harrie looked behind her at the shortest block in the city. "Well, I'll be damned."

"Harrie . . . we discussed this cursing."

"Sorry." She laid her scooter down and advanced toward my porch. "So, do you wanna see my whistle? I just got it today in a box of Cracker Jacks. It's neato. And it makes Mr. Hauser's dog go crazy."

Harrie showed me her tin whistle with great pride.

"Were you blowing this inside the house?" I asked.

Harrie nodded energetically. "Mr. Hauser couldn't figure out why his dog kept getting so upset."

"That's not a nice thing to do, Harrie. The high pitch of this probably hurts his ears."

Harrie looked down at the ground. "I only did it a few times."

"A *few?*" I queried.

"Okay. Maybe ten or eleven times . . . but that was all in the same half hour, so it only counts as once."

I shook my head. Harrie was a handful.

"Hey, Eej . . . look at this. Daddy just unpacked it today." She held up a black eye patch on an adjustable strap. "I have to wear this on account of my lazy eye."

"That's very impressive."

"Yeah. I think it makes me look like a pirate. At first, I liked that—but then kids at school started makin' fun of me. So, I only wear it at home at night. Carla said I should tell 'em all to go to hell."

It made me sad that other children would tease Harrie about needing to wear a patch to correct her eyesight. But Carla's advice didn't sound like it would present a path that would result in anything but a trip to the principal's office.

"What did you think about Carla's suggestion?" I asked her.

"I figgered there was a lot more of 'em than me, and there was no way I could take 'em all on. I already found that one out the hard way."

"What do you mean?"

"I got in a fight one time with some mean kids, and one feller socked me in the eye so hard I had a big shiner for more'n a week. Daddy was *real* mad at me at first, but when I told him why it happened, he just nodded and told me to be more careful. He didn't cut off my TV for a week or nothin'."

I was horrified. "What on earth *did* happen?"

Harrie shrugged. "Some kids were callin' Carla names after school one day, and sayin' she looked like one of them high yellers, you know? And I said 'So what if she is? That don't make her no different from us.' And this big feller started shovin' me back against the fence and callin' me bad names 'cause I was her friend—so I slugged him. But he was a lot bigger'n me, so he tagged me back but good." Harrie looked wistful. "Carla walked me back to her house and her mama held a steak on it and told me I should act more like a lady."

"That was good advice, Harrie."

"I know. I sure did feel guilty about wastin' that steak, Eej. Bein' a lady didn't seem like it was worth messin' up a good supper."

"Well," I struggled with what to say. "It's good that you stood up for your friend."

"Yeah. I thought so, too. Carla always took up for me—so doin' right by her wadn't hard, Eej—even though that shiner hurt like hell."

"Harrie . . ."

"I mean, it hurt real bad. I knew I didn't want another one. So it wadn't long after that I figgered it'd work better just to wear the eye patch at night."

"That seems like a very reasonable solution to me."

"Yeah. Except I can't see as good on the scooter when I have it on. That's why I'm carryin' it in my pocket."

"It's good you kept to the sidewalk, then."

Harrie nodded. "It makes watchin' TV harder, too. I have to turn my head sideways to see the screen good."

"I'm sorry about that."

"It's okay. Lots of people have way worse stuff than this to handle. Did you ever see that kid who lives up on Walnut Street? She has to walk on these two metal crutch things that are hooked to her legs with *spikes*. It's pretty scary lookin'—even without the eye patch."

I smiled at her. "I bet you look quite dashing in your eye patch, Harrie."

She seemed to perk up. "Do you wanna see it?"

I nodded.

Harrie climbed the porch steps and put the patch on so I could view it up close.

"You're right," I agreed. "It does make you look mysterious . . . like a pirate adventurer."

"That's what I think, too. Sometimes I wear it to freak people out. Grown-ups are funny that way. They'll ignore you if they think you're weird. I even got into the movies for free 'cause they thought I looked so pitiful." She paused to think about her successes. "I saw *The Shaggy Dog* eight times. That's the record so far."

"Quite an accomplishment," I agreed.

"Did you ever think about wearin' a disguise to get somethin' you wanted, Eej?"

"Well." Harrie's question took me aback. "Not really." I thought guiltily about the letters Lottie had wanted me to carry home and examine. There was no denying that process would've been simplified if I could've pretended to be someone else, freed from my mother's conditioning.

But Harrie had moved on. "What are you doin' outside?" she asked.

"Just enjoying the warm evening. Is your daddy at work again?"

Harrie nodded. "He won't be home until after eleven. It's the rotten shift he got on account of he's new."

"I'm sorry that means you're at home alone in the evenings."

"I don't mind. He always makes my supper and I'm allowed to watch TV until bedtime."

"Well, I suggest you don't amuse yourself by tormenting Mr. Hauser's schnauzer."

"On account of he's nervous already?"

"And because it just isn't very neighborly," I reminded her.

"Well, *he* ain't very neighborly neither."

"We cannot control how other people behave, Harrie. It's up to us to set better examples."

Harrie was looking at me strangely. I wasn't sure if it was because she thought I was crazy or because of her eye patch.

"Okay," she finally said, digging her toe into the dirt.

"Would you like to come inside and watch my TV sideways for a while?" I suggested. "Then I can walk you back home so you don't have to take off your eye patch."

"Really?" she asked. "That'd be nifty. Can we watch *Cheyenne?* I love that show."

I hardly had time to rethink my impulse before Harrie had pulled open my front door and stood waiting for me to enter the house. Once we were inside, I asked Harrie if she'd like something to drink.

"Do you have any Yoo-hoos?" she asked.

"No. Sorry. I have milk. Or water. Or I could make you some Postum."

"What's Postum?"

I held out my mug. "It's kind of like coffee. But it won't keep you awake at night."

Harrie sniffed what remained of my beverage. "Okay. But can I have it with milk and sugar?"

"I don't see why not. Why don't you go on into the living room and turn on the TV? I'll heat the water—and I'll telephone Fay Marian and tell her you're here, just in case she looks for you."

"Okay, Eej."

Fay Marian was very appreciative that I'd thought to let her know where Harrie was.

"We hadn't gone over to check on her yet," she explained. "But we would've shortly, and I know Inez would've had a cow if Harrie hadn't been in the apartment."

"She's going to watch some TV here and then I'll walk her home."

"You're a good egg, EJ Cloud."

"I'm happy to help out. And she's oddly good company."

"One thing's for sure: that kid knows no strangers."

I rang off as the kettle came to a boil, and fixed Harrie's hot drink. When I carried it into the living room, she was seated in my father's old Morris chair, absently bouncing her feet up and down beneath the ottoman. I noted that she'd chosen to sit in a chair that was at an extreme right angle to the TV, probably so she could see more easily without twisting her neck to the side. I found that to be endearing and sweetly poignant. She was a little girl dealing with big changes, and doing so mostly by herself.

I fetched a coaster and walked over to put her mug on a side table beside her chair when I saw the letter. I nearly dropped the mug.

It was the garden letter that Lottie and I had opened at work earlier. *How on earth had it ended up here in my living room?*

I didn't have to wait very long to find out . . .

"Hey, Eej?" Harrie asked. "Where'd you get this letter?" She reached out and picked it up. I had to fight an impulse to dash over and yank it away from her. Harrie held it up to her nose. "It smells *exactly* like my aunt Rochelle—I mean, when she ain't givin' perms."

"Where . . . where did you find that, Harrie?" I tried to keep my voice calm and neutral sounding.

51

"Over there." She pointed at my leather bag, hanging from its hook on the coat rack in the foyer. "I smelled it right away when we came in from the porch."

I extended my hand to take the letter back from her. I prayed that she hadn't read it.

"It's one I've been working on at the post office. I'm ... trying to find out who it belongs to."

"Is that why you brought it home?"

"Yes. Sort of." The truth was that I had *no* idea how the letter ended up in my bag. Unless ...

Oh, dear heaven ... Lottie. I closed my eyes in mortification. *What had she been thinking?*

"So, it's kind of a mystery?" Harrie asked. "Like *Chevy Mystery Show?*"

"Not exactly like that." I carried the letter back to my bag and securely stashed it in an interior compartment. "But yes. It is a mystery of sorts. We do all kinds of things to figure out who the letters belong to. It's like solving a puzzle when some of the pieces are missing. It can be very challenging sometimes."

"Well, maybe we should ask Aunt Rochelle? She might know who else wears this perfume. I bet it's not very many women 'cause it's pretty expensive."

I remembered something Harrie had said yesterday, when we were all working in Fay Marian's garden. Aunt Rochelle lived in Roanoke—near Paradise. And didn't Harrie say her aunt sold cosmetics in a department store there?

It was a ridiculous long shot ... but why not see if it led anyplace?

"Harrie, are you sure this smells like the perfume your aunt wears?"

Harrie nodded enthusiastically. "Aunt Rochelle tests me on this stuff all the time. She says I have a great nose and could probably find truffles." Harrie shrugged. "I guess that's good. I ain't too clear about what truffles are."

I smiled. "They're fungi. Kind of like underground mushrooms. Very expensive ones."

"Mushrooms?"

I nodded.

"Bummer. I thought they were little troll dolls or somethin'. But I didn't know why you'd need a good nose to find 'em. It ain't like they hide 'em in the stores or anything."

"You mentioned that you visit Aunt Rochelle frequently. Do you think she might help us try to find the person who mailed this letter?"

"Sure." Harrie sounded excited. "She knows everything about this stuff. People come from all over to get her to help them with perfumes and makeup. Daddy said she even got offered a job as a buyer at one of them big stores in Richmond—but there was some kinda problem and her husband didn't wanna go. She ain't married to him no more, though. She said he was a loser and a deadbeat. Course, she said the same thing about the husband that came after him, too."

I had to be in my dotage to think this was a good idea.

I resolved that I'd run it by Lottie in the morning—right after I gave her a good dressing-down for slipping that letter into my bag.

Cheyenne began and Harrie quickly became engrossed in the Western adventure. I tried to pay attention, but my thoughts kept turning to the letter that was pounding away inside my leather bag like *The Tell-Tale Heart*.

It promised to be a long night . . .

After walking Harrie back to Fay Marian's, I resolved to make it an early night. I changed into my nightgown and robe and sat down in Daddy's chair with my book. I had only a few chapters left to read, and I was determined to finish it this evening. But I was finding it hard to concentrate. Every time Della Street appeared in a scene, I thought about Fay Marian's "sultry" comment. And that naturally led me to recall the passage of the letter I'd read earlier.

> Her intimate touch was like the first bright bloom of Angelica . . .

It was uncanny. Angelica was one of the herbs we cultivated in the *hortus medicus*. The Moravians had revered the plant for its numerous healing properties. According to Evelyn Haas, its uses went beyond compounds that treated typical maladies like catarrh, dyspepsia, and insomnia. In his vast colonial-era compendium, Philadelphia apothecary Johann Sauer had noted the herb's special ability to "bring down the menses" for distressed women facing problem—*or unwanted*—pregnancies. Evelyn once winked and confided in me that Angelica was also compounded into a topical cream that proved efficacious for treating premature ejaculation.

"So, one can say the early Moravians had *everything* covered—coming and going."

Evelyn had an almost preternatural fascination with rumors and legends that hinted at a few more lurid aspects to early Moravian communal life—including veneration of homoerotic worship and obsession with the wounds of Christ. And she loved to draw parallels between those whispered stories and the eclectic healing properties of some of the herbs cultivated in the *hortus medicus*.

Angelica, with its explosive globe-like clusters of flowers, was no exception.

Of course, Angelica had *also* been used to ward off witches. In my mind, that attribute went hand in hand with Evelyn's colorful description of the herb's more *prurient* uses.

I forced my attention back to the novel. Della Street was busily engaged using her . . . *charms* . . . to wrangle information out of a distracted travel agent.

> *Its slender tendrils reached deep inside and laid*
> *claim to all my hidden longing.*

In frustration, I put the book aside. It was ridiculous. I drummed my fingers against the big, rolled arm of Daddy's chair. *Reading the rest of the letter would accomplish nothing.* And bringing it home with me, even unwittingly, was a serious breach of protocol. And even if that hadn't been true, giving in to an unseemly impulse would make me no better than . . . than a child, blowing a tin whistle to torment a neighbor's dog.

And yet . . .

Before I could talk myself out of it, I got to my feet and strode across the room to retrieve the letter from my bag. I stood there in the near dark, tapping it against my hand as I deliberated.

Trust me, Lottie had said. *You need to read this.* Twice. *Maybe more.*

Even though I feigned offense, I knew exactly what Lottie had referred to. I *did* withhold myself from the realm of sensual experience. It wasn't something I intended to suppress—it just seemed to happen naturally. I wasn't a prude. *Not really*, I thought. I'd had many friends during my years at Salem College. And I'd learned firsthand about the carnal exploits of some of my female classmates—including the lonely aftermath of nonconsensual sexual encounters, panic-inducing pregnancy scares, and even tales of their occasional Sapphic experimentations with other girls. The more I learned, the less engaged I became. For me, it was tied more to a loss of control than it was to any innate fear of the experience. It wasn't that I was unaware of how vast and prevalent the forbidden realm of sensual experience was: it was more that I passively chose to ignore it.

But now I was finding it impossible to ignore the letter I held in the dim light of my small foyer.

I had two choices. I could return the letter to its resting place inside my bag and go watch *Adventures in Paradise*. Or I could give in to yet another impulse and read the rest of the letter.

It was the irony of the TV show *Adventures in Paradise* that finally tipped the scales for me. I carried the letter back into the living room and sat down to read it. Only this time, I didn't sit in Daddy's chair. That felt vaguely . . . unseemly.

I unfolded the pages and resumed reading from where I'd left off earlier.

> *Its slender tendrils reached deep inside and*
> *laid claim to all my hidden longing. Together*
> *we became one with the garden. Our fresh*
> *young bodies twined together amidst the rows*
> *of young plants, feeling the warmth of the early*
> *summer sun on our backs and inhaling the sweet,*
> *intoxicating fragrance of the White Rose of*
> *York—the sacred smell of heaven. We surrendered*

*the first fruits of our youth, vitality, and promise
to each other. And as I tasted her freshness, laid
bare before me in perfect harmony with all of
nature, I imagined I was at last seeing the face of
God.*

*Why, Mary Ann, would you allow me to know
such completeness—such blissful perfection—only
to deny me its fruition? What possible good can
now be served by the fate you have prescribed for
me? Why withhold all meaning, possibility, and
happiness from me, Mary Ann? Why?*

Sorrowfully,

Dorothea

I carefully refolded the pages and returned them to the envelope before realizing that my hands were shaking. I sat still for the next half hour, waiting for my head to clear and my agitation to subside.

Who was Dorothea? And what power over her did this mysterious Mary Ann have?

None of it made the least bit of sense. The only possible connection between the letter and the garden appeared to be the plants where the two women had . . .

Had what?

I could scarcely allow myself to name what Dorothea had described.

Had had whatever kind of encounter the writer was describing.

Clearly, Dorothea had some kind of unfinished business

with the woman named Mary Ann—and with the other, unnamed woman who'd been her participant in those passionate encounters.

But Evelyn insisted there had never been a Mary Ann affiliated with the gardens. So why did Dorothea send her letter there?

The clock on the mantel chimed. It was a quarter past 10 p.m. I'd been sitting in the living room for more than an hour. And tomorrow was a workday—a workday in which I'd have to confront more of Lottie's shrewd scrutiny. *She'd know I'd read the letter.* And now it seemed inevitable that we'd have to read them all. Just the thought of that filled me with an emotion I couldn't identify. But it certainly wasn't anything approximating ease.

I returned the letter to my bag and turned off the lights before heading to bed.

In the midst of so much confusion, the only thing I was sure about was that sleep would not come easily.

It was unusual for me to arrive at the office before Lottie, but I'd slept so fitfully that I finally gave up and rose before dawn. I made time to detour by Winkler's Bakery and picked up a sugar cake for us to have with our morning coffee. I knew that Lottie was especially fond of the sticky, sweet cake that was a staple of Moravian life. It was hot and fragrant when the clerk passed the flat box to me. I hoped it would stay warm until we got to enjoy it. The tasty treat turned more than one head during the short bus ride to the post office.

Lottie arrived shortly before 8 a.m. and seemed surprised to find me already at work.

"Well, it looks like somebody didn't sleep all that good last night." She stashed her lunch bag inside our ancient fridge and put on her faded blue smock.

"Whatever are you talking about?"

"Your eyes look like road maps. I'm guessin' that means you found the letter in your bag?"

"Lottie . . . I need to ask what on earth motivated you to do something that frivolous?"

"Frivolous?" Lottie shook her head. "We could call it a lot of things, but I don't think frivolous is one of 'em." She walked to the table where we kept our coffeepot and discovered the sugar cake. "Oh, my. What do we have here?"

"I picked it up for us on the way in. I thought we could use a treat."

Lottie laughed at me. "I see I ain't the only one who gets a craving for sweets after certain activities."

I was horrified by her crass insinuation. "Lottie . . ."

"Relax, Esther Jane. Nobody's gonna find out about your smutty little pen pal."

Lottie was busy cutting us each a generous slice of the cake. "So. Did'ja read it? Judging by that blush that's about to burn your face clean off, I'm gonna go out on a limb and say you did."

I gave up trying to pretend I was offended. The effort would be pointless.

"Yes. I read it."

"And?" Lottie handed me a slice of the cake.

"And . . . what?"

"*And* . . . did them girls finish gettin' busy in the dirt?"

"I wouldn't put it quite that crudely."

"Well then, maybe you should read it again," she quipped, "so you can learn *how*."

I dropped into my squeaky desk chair. "Let me know when you're ready to discuss this matter professionally. We have a true mystery to solve."

Lottie perched on the end of her desk to enjoy her plate of sugar cake.

"Child, the only mystery I see is how we can *find* that woman so you can get to know her better."

My jaw dropped.

Lottie cut me off before I could say anything. "Don't go gettin' your britches in a twist. I ain't sayin' you need to take up with them lezzies—but it wouldn't hurt you to get outta your damn head and spend some *other* kind of quality time playin' in the dirt . . . if you get my drift."

I was too stunned to reply.

A buzzer sounded, and Lottie hopped up to open our access door to the dumbwaiter that transported bins of dead letters down to us from the processing area upstairs.

"Looks like a lighter day today." She hauled out the bin and deposited it on our sorting table. "At least that's good news."

I was still feeling stung and indicted by Lottie's comments. And that unsettled me. *Why did her assessment of my relative inexperience annoy me so much?*

We finished our slices of cake in silence before setting to work sifting through the new additions to the letters we had carried over from yesterday's haul.

Lottie held up a standard Number 10 business envelope that looked like it'd been dropped into a mud puddle. The address was nothing but a sea of blurry blue smears. It had a blind-embossed logo in its upper left corner, but no accompanying return address.

"Look at this," she said with disgust. She turned the envelope around so I could see it.

I squinted at the logo. "Isn't that the RJR trademark?"

"Hell to the yes, it is. If them fools upstairs can't tell what the hell post office they're workin' in, they need to wake up and smell the damn cigarettes."

She tossed the letter into our "Return to Sender" basket with contempt.

"Let's just hope the rest of these are as easy to deal with."

Lottie harrumphed. "Nothin' can be worse than that time some fool mailed a box of damn live animals."

I smiled at the recollection. "At least they had applied the correct postage."

"Yeah. That box had as many stamps as air holes."

"Whatever happened to those weasels, anyway?"

"Didn't I tell you?" Lottie stopped sorting to regard me.

"No. I don't think you did. I just recall that they weren't in here the next day."

"Well, you remember how the postmaster told us it was *our* problem to figure out how to dispose of those damn rats?"

"*Weasels*, Lottie. They were weasels—not rats."

"Did they eat trash, have long tails, and slink around the floor on four short legs? In my book, that made them *rats*."

"Regardless. What happened to them?"

"I put feet to my prayers." She chuckled. "I took the freight elevator up to the attic and set them rodents free. That way, they stopped bein' *our* problem and became official tenants of Uncle Sam."

I gasped. "Do you think they're still there?"

"Probably. Thelma up in operations is always complainin' about mouse droppings in all the boxes of forms. I just smile and agree that there's all kind of vermin runnin' around this place, and somebody should ought to look into it."

We continued processing letters until we'd reduced the pile by half. Eventually, I screwed up my courage and told Lottie about Harrie, and the idea about asking Harrie's Aunt Rochelle to help identify the perfume and make any suggestions about where the mysterious sender might have acquired it.

I expected Lottie to look at me like I'd lost my last marble—but she didn't.

"That makes sense to me," she said. "Especially if this kid is right and the perfume is that expensive."

"That's what I thought, too. But would it make more sense just to ask someone here in town to try and identify this mossy, earthy fragrance?"

Lottie thought about that idea. "We could. But it won't help us get a lead on who bought it. If this Paradise is as small a town as you say it is, then this Aunt Rochelle might have a list of customers. And if she does—*bingo*. We're that much closer to identifying the sender."

"I just wish I didn't feel so nervous about letting Harrie take the letter to show her aunt. How do we keep her from trying to read it? Or prevent her Aunt Rochelle from reading it, for that matter?"

"Esther Jane? Have you lost your mind? You can't give that letter to a *child*."

"I *know* that, Lottie. But how else do we get it to Rochelle? We can't risk mailing it again."

"Well, then I suppose, Miss Shirley Temple, you might just have to take that letter up there yourself."

"*Me?* I could never do that."

"Why not? Last time I checked the trains still ran that way."

"But . . ." I was foundering. "I've never . . ."

"Child. If you're gonna start rattlin' off the list of all the things you *never* done, we'll be here all night."

"You don't understand." I was near frantic. "I've never taken a train before."

It was Lottie's turn to be stunned. "Esther Jane Cloud? You are seriously startin' to worry me. Takin' a damn train is about as easy as chewin' gum—which you probably never done either. And at least *you* get to ride back away from the engine noise in the good seats and can get somethin' to eat in the damn club car."

I gave Lottie a withering look. But I knew she was right. Dealing with these letters had become my responsibility, and I was the one with the authority and the means to do it.

The whole situation was becoming outrageous. Ever since Evelyn Haas had passed that box of letters to me, my world had been on tilt. Was I actually considering the prospect of taking a train to Roanoke to meet with a total stranger? And not just with *any* total stranger: with the colorful and, arguably, *loose-moraled* aunt of the precocious ten-year-old who'd exploded into the center of my life like a late-summer storm.

It appeared I was.

But I knew this enterprise was going to require significantly more planning—not to mention permission from Harrie's father. And I'd need to initiate a contact with the postmaster in the tiny Paradise, Virginia, branch to see if he could offer any assistance tracking down our mysterious "Dorothea."

But first, I was determined to reach out to my newest, worldlier acquaintances, Inez and Fay Marian, for advice and counsel. It would be difficult to ask, but I was certain they'd be willing to help me navigate the travel arrangements.

Lottie was still watching me with an amused expression on her round face. Her brown eyes were narrowed—like they always got when she thought she knew better than me about something—which, essentially, was most of the time.

"I'll think about it." I said, before tossing another half dozen letters into our relabeling basket.

Lottie had been right about another thing: the sorters upstairs had gotten very careless.

But at least that made *some* mysteries easy to solve . . .

Fay Marian seemed genuinely pleased that I'd called to ask if she and Inez could help me puzzle through a situation that involved Harrie. It hadn't been my desire to intrude on them on a weeknight—and I certainly never intended to beg for a dinner invitation. But Fay Marian insisted that I walk over to her house and join them for an early supper. I felt sheepish about accepting, but in truth, I did enjoy their company—and it would be good to get their perspective on the idea of traveling to Roanoke with Harrie to visit her aunt. I especially wanted their ideas about the best way to approach Johnnie Hart. The last thing I desired was to appear helpless and pathetic. It was bad enough that I was starting to feel that way.

Fay Marian had directed me to Inez's apartment this time. She explained that it was *her* night to cook, so that meant the meal would be dramatically better. Inez lived in one of the big upstairs apartments, located at the front of the house, overlooking Main Street.

Fay Marian opened the door after I'd knocked and ushered me inside. It was a big, open room with wide-plank hardwood floors, large windows, and thick Persian carpets. Two of the walls were lined with polished walnut bookcases—all filled to the brim with volumes in every size. I recognized the strains of a Bach partita playing from her hi-fi—and something smelled wonderful. Fay Marian noticed me sniffing the air.

"It's her famous New England Bean and Bog Cassoulet." She leaned closer to me. "It's one of those damn Yankee dishes—but it's pretty darn addictive once you get past the cranberries."

"Fay Marian? Don't be scaring EJ with your sophomoric palate." Inez entered the room wiping her hands on a striped dishtowel. "Hello, EJ. We're so glad you could join us. Would you like a cocktail?"

"I'd ... enjoy that. Thank you." It wasn't usual for me to drink alcohol on weeknights—or on any other nights. But tonight seemed like a good time to make an exception.

"I'll fix it." Fay Marian pushed past Inez to approach the chrome drink cart that sat near the entrance to the kitchen.

I didn't miss the affectionate way Fay Marian touched Inez on the arm as she passed her. I was again struck by the special nature of their friendship. Of course, that led me to think about the *other* special relationship I'd read about in the letter last night.

Clearly, there was a great deal about romantic friendships I didn't fully grasp.

Fay Marian lifted a cocktail shaker from the drink cart. "We're drinking Boulevardiers. Inez fell in love with them when she was in Paris. Will that work for you, EJ?"

I nodded. I had no idea what a Boulevardier was, but it sounded sophisticated.

"You have so many books here," I commented, in an effort to cover my discomfort.

"It's an occupational hazard, I suppose," Inez explained. "And I find it hard to part with them after I read them. I know that's silly. Fay Marian is always telling me that I need to give some away. But every time I think about doing that, I get the jitters. I can't believe how many more I've accumulated since moving here."

"How long have you been teaching at Salem?" I asked.

"Nearly five years. I can scarcely believe it. It seems like yesterday that I moved down here from Cambridge."

"Were you in school there?"

Inez nodded. "Radcliffe. I had a job as an adjunct professor for two years after I finished my doctorate. A professor of mine had a contact here and told me about the opening. I jumped at the chance to come to Salem, even though I knew it was a small college and I'd be teaching mostly entry-level English classes."

Fay Marian returned with my martini. It was a pretty, reddish color and garnished with a sliver of orange peel. I was certain I'd like it. But after my first sip, I wasn't too sure. I struggled not to choke.

"Too strong for you, EJ?" Fay Marian asked. She withdrew a cigarette from a box on the coffee table and lighted it. "They're an acquired taste. I acquired *my* taste for them after my first two or three."

"In one night," Inez put in.

"Stop that. She's joking, EJ."

"What's in this?" I asked with a husky voice. I coughed slightly, and my companions exchanged amused glances.

"Rye whiskey, sweet Vermouth and a couple healthy glugs of Campari."

Dear lord . . .

I resolved to drink it *slowly*. It wasn't a good time for me to lose control of my faculties.

"Why don't we sit down?" Inez suggested. "The cassoulet needs another twenty minutes or so before I can add the croissant topping."

We all took seats in Inez's comfortable living room. The music ended and another record dropped into place. I recognized this one: Dvořák's *New World Symphony*. The somber yet agile first movement seemed to fill the room with promise.

"You attended Salem College, didn't you, EJ?" Fay Marian asked.

"I did. I never got to graduate, however."

"That's too bad." Inez sounded like she genuinely meant it. "What happened?"

"My mother became very ill with influenza during my junior year. It was a particularly bad epidemic that season, and many people died. I withdrew to care for her at home. She was sick for several months and passed away in the early summer. Because of my father's career as a mail carrier, I was offered a job at the post office, and I accepted it—just so I could make ends meet." I sighed. "I never went back to school to graduate. I've always regretted it."

"I'm very sorry about that, EJ. I'll bet you were a stellar student."

I looked at Inez with amusement. "Why would you think that?"

"Believe me. I've been teaching long enough to pick one out of a crowd."

"Don't even *think* about arguing with her, EJ," Fay Marian warned me. "It's always a losing proposition." She ground out her cigarette in an amber kidney-shaped ashtray.

Inez glowered at her. "That's only because you're an unrepentant heathen."

Fay Marian bent toward me to whisper. "That's Inez-speak for saying I went to a low-class, state-supported college."

Inez elbowed Fay Marian. "Stop it."

A timer in the kitchen dinged. Inez got to her feet. "Be right back."

Fay Marian watched her leave with a look of unabashed admiration. Observing it made me feel rather uncomfortable. I wasn't sure how to respond or where to look. I wondered why Fay Marian was so determined to express her affection for Inez so . . . *openly*. I wasn't used to such things.

If Fay Marian picked up on my discomfort, she didn't show it.

"It was sporting of you to look after Harrie the way you did last night. Inez and I made sure she stayed in after you brought her home."

"I . . . enjoy her company, actually. She's refreshing."

Fay Marian laughed. "That's one way to put it. At first, I thought Johnnie was making a huge mistake to allow her so much freedom. But you know what? I think the kid can handle it."

"He seems like a reasonable man," I agreed.

"We think so, too. He's had some hard knocks. Raising a child by himself can't be easy. But he goes out of his way to make sure she has what she needs. He cooks her a hot supper every day before he heads off to RJR. I don't know many men who would do such a thing."

That was certainly true. My father had loved me, but I seriously doubted that he'd have been able to cook a complete meal for me. Even the few times he'd tried to make sandwiches were disastrous. There had been that memorable peanut butter, banana, and sardine debacle . . .

I still got queasy thinking about it.

"Yes," I agreed. "Johnnie Hart seems like a good father."

Inez appeared in the kitchen doorway. "Dinnertime you two. Bring your cocktail glasses."

We sat down at Inez's oak trestle table. The cassoulet was bubbling away in a large CorningWare dish that sat on a metal trivet at the center of the table. It looked and smelled divine. Inez had also made a cold salad of cut-up apples, blueberries and strawberries tossed in a tangy citrus dressing to accompany the hearty main dish.

Inez ladled out generous portions of the savory chicken, bean, and cranberry mixture.

"I hope you like this, EJ. It's a New England spin on a French classic."

"I'm sure I will. Thank you again for inviting me. I know it was last minute."

"Don't worry at all about that, EJ." Fay Marian passed me a bowl. "We'd thought about calling you earlier, anyway. I want to book some time on your dance card to get serious about putting in some plants. The rest of the junk out back should be hauled off by the end of the week."

"We don't want to be selfish, though," Inez added. "We know you already have commitments in the town garden."

"I'm happy to help out." I smiled. "I think there's enough of me to go around."

"Well, we thought about asking Evelyn to join us—but quickly thought better of it. She tends to quickly take command of anything she becomes involved in."

Inez agreed. "Sadly, that's also true with our book club. Evelyn has single-handedly selected the last two books we've read. I wouldn't have any issue with that if her tastes were more refined. But the novels of Grace Metalious and Herman Wouk don't truly represent the finest examples of modern literature."

"I just told her to skip the books and go see the movies," Fay Marian added. "I mean, if Lana Turner is starring in it, how bad could it be?"

Inez looked at me for support. "Pretty darn bad."

I laughed. I'd gone to see *Peyton Place* several years ago, when it showed downtown at the Carolina Theater. Even dour Lottie was beyond excited at the prospect of seeing the controversial movie about the scandalous goings-on in a New England small town. I remembered her telling me it was one of the *only* movies that, in her view, was worth climbing the five hundred steps to see—a reference to the flights of stairs that led up the outside of the building to the theater's colored section, located in the balcony. That became Lottie's personal rating scale for movies. And it was noteworthy that not many were deemed worthy enough to warrant climbing the five hundred steps.

"EJ likes mysteries, like me." Fay Marian beamed at Inez. "You're just a stuffed shirt."

"I do enjoy the occasional mystery," I admitted. "But I enjoy other books, too. My only frustration is how long I have to wait to get them from the library. And when they do finally become available, I have to tear through them very quickly to get them returned on time."

"Well, you should apply for a library card at Salem. I'm sure you'd have a better experience there. And as an alumna, you should have no difficulty getting permission to borrow any books you want. I'd be happy to look into that for you, if it's something you'd be interested in."

In fact, I was very interested in Inez's suggestion. "That would be lovely. I haven't been inside the library in years."

"You'll probably find it mostly unchanged, and very quiet. I think the majority of our coeds only spend time there under duress—and that's especially true on weekends. They're much more interested in school-sponsored junkets to Wake Forest or Davidson to 'socialize' with the boys." Inez failed at suppressing a frown. "Sadly, most of our girls are more enthusiastic about earning their MRS degrees than improving their minds."

"Inez? You promised you'd try to stay off your soapbox for at least the first hour."

"It's all right, Fay Marian. What Inez is describing pretty much matches my own experience as a student at Salem. I always felt like a misfit because I honestly cared more about doing my homework than sneaking out of the dorms after curfew—a pastime that was rampant, by the way, even way back in the dark ages."

"Oh, pish posh, EJ. You ain't *that* old. You still exude a certain dishyness to me."

"Fay Marian . . ." Inez warned.

"What? You said the same thing last night after she dropped Harrie off."

Inez blushed. "I apologize, EJ. You must think we're cretins."

"No. I'm . . . flattered. It's not the kind of thing I'm used to hearing."

"Well, that makes *no* sense. You must be running with the wrong crowd."

"Fay Marian . . . *for crying out loud.*" Inez looked like she wanted to stuff a napkin into Fay Marian's mouth.

"You both have already met most of my . . . *crowd.*" The cocktail must have been affecting my demeanor. It wasn't normal for me to be so self-revealing. "Except for my colleagues at the post office, my work in the garden, and a few more neighbors here in Old Salem, I don't tend to socialize very much."

"Don't forget Harrie Hart," Fay Marian reminded me. "I think your new best friend has plans to drag you into every new adventure. And I predict she'll have a limitless supply of them, too."

I was curious about her comment. "Why do you call Harrie my new best friend?"

"Because she talks about you pretty much nonstop. Doesn't she Inez?"

Inez nodded. "For once, Fay Marian is not exaggerating. Harrie seems genuinely fond of you."

That news surprised me. But what surprised me even more was my realization that the affection went both ways. Harrie's easy, unaffected manner and unvarnished candidness were infectious. I found her company curiously refreshing—probably because we were so different.

"Well, apropos of Harrie, I do have something related to her that I'd like to discuss with you. It actually concerns official post office business, so I can't be fully transparent."

"Ohhhh. A real-life mystery." Fay Marian sounded excited. "What is it?"

"As you know, I manage the Dead Letter Office in our main branch downtown. On Saturday, while I was working in the *hortus medicus*, Evelyn gave me a box of letters that she said had been delivered to a nonexistent person, care of the Gardens at Old Salem. Since then, we've been working on determining the provenance of the letters. The only real lead we have came, ironically, from Harrie."

"Harrie?" Fay Marian and Inez exchanged glances. Fay Marian leaned toward me. "Okay. Now I'm truly intrigued."

"All of the letters—there are six of them—were written on

the same uniquely perfumed stationery. Harrie happened to see one of them at my house last night, and she said she recognized the fragrance immediately because it smelled exactly like her Aunt Rochelle, in Roanoke."

"The infamous Aunt Rochelle—a woman after my own heart."

Inez rolled her eyes. "She's talking about the yellow T-Bird."

"It's true," Fay Marian admitted. "They're much classier than rusted-out Simcas."

"So, tell us about how Aunt Rochelle is going to help you solve the mystery of the letters?"

"It's a long shot, certainly," I admitted. "But Harrie says her aunt is an acknowledged expert on fragrances. And since the letters were all postmarked in Paradise, which is a small town just outside Roanoke, I'm hoping she might be able identify the perfume—and to offer some guidance about where it might have been purchased."

"That seems likely," Fay Marian agreed. "I've actually been to Paradise before. There's a hardware store there that still carries replacement parts for all the old Kelvinators in the apartments in this joint. Trust me . . . there's no place in that town to buy fancy perfume. I'm surprised the train even stops there. There can't be more than four or five hundred people still living there, and I'll bet that most of them are well into their eighties."

That didn't sound very encouraging. But it was our only lead. So, it was either pursue this and hope it led someplace or destroy the letters. And something about that latter option just felt . . . *wrong.*

"So," I continued, "my colleague and I both thought that traveling to Roanoke and meeting with Harrie's aunt might prove worthwhile."

Fay Marian agreed. "That makes sense to me. Are you gonna take Harrie along with you?"

I was learning that it was usual for Fay Marian to cut to the chase. "I thought so, yes. But I was unsure about how her father might feel about the outing. I was hoping you both might be able to advise me. And I confess, I might need some pointers on how to arrange the train travel, too."

"Helping you out with navigating the train is no problem. As for Johnnie Hart?" Fay Marian shrugged. "Just ask him. I don't think he'll have an issue with it at all. In fact, I think Harrie goes up there quite a bit—and by herself."

"On the train?" I asked.

Fay Marian nodded. "And it'll be an even easier trip from here. It's a straight shot from Winston. Lots of stops, but no transfers. The old milk run."

Well, that much was reassuring. I was reluctant to admit how nervous I was about making the trip—my very first on a train. Maybe it would turn out to be less of an issue than I'd imagined.

"You mentioned that the letters were addressed to some unknown person." It was evident that Inez was still thinking about the mystery. "Was there any return address?"

"No." I shook my head. "But, in accordance with postal regulations, we *are* authorized to open the letters and read them to try and glean any information that might assist with delivery or return."

"So, have you done that yet?" Fay Marian asked. When I nodded, she followed up. "What did you find out?"

"Um," I demurred. "Not much of any—*consequence*. Just the first name of the writer, who we assume is also the sender."

"You said Evelyn told you the addressee was nonexistent. What was the name?"

I deliberated about disclosing it to Inez. But it didn't seem to be any violation of protocol to reveal a name that we knew didn't belong to anyone affiliated with Old Salem or the gardens.

"A Miss Mary Ann Evans."

"That seems common enough," Fay Marian observed. "A good ole Welsh name. What was the sender's name?"

"It was just a first name," I replied. "Dorothea."

"*Dorothea?*" Inez repeated. "The letter was actually signed, Dorothea?"

"Yes." I was taken aback by Inez's shocked expression. "Does that name mean something to you?"

"Oh, yes." Inez pushed her chair back and got up from the table. "Give me one moment to fetch something." She retreated to the living room.

Fay Marian and I stared blankly at each other.

When Inez returned, she passed a book over to me. It was a leather-bound hardback.

"Look at the title," she directed.

I examined the embossed spine. *Middlemarch.*

"George Eliot?" I asked.

Inez nodded enthusiastically.

"I don't get it." Fay Marian crossed her arms. "What's this tome have to do with this mysterious letter?"

"In the first place, *Middlemarch* is *not* a tome. It's a hallmark of English—and dare I say, *feminist*—literature. And its heroine—a forward-thinking woman who was ahead of her time—was named Dorothea. Dorothea Brooke."

I'd read *Middlemarch* in a college English class. I recalled liking the novel, but feeling vaguely depressed about how Dorothea, a vibrant and idealistic young woman who'd had grand aspirations for a selfless life of philanthropy, ended up being married off to a wealthy but dull and uninspiring older man. I didn't see *any* way the book could shed any light on our mysterious letter writer.

"I remember this book well. We read it in my English literature survey. And I agree the names are similar. But," I regarded Inez, "I don't think that has any real significance for the letters."

"Don't you?" Inez asked. "You say you studied this book in college, EJ. Tell me . . . what was George Eliot's *real* name?"

"It was . . ." I paused in mid-response. *Dear God in heaven. However could I have missed this connection?* I looked at Inez with disbelief. "I cannot *believe* I forgot about that."

Inez smiled knowingly.

"Well, would one of you two scholars mind clueing *me* in?" Fay Marian reached for a cigarette. "I'm feeling pretty left out over here."

"EJ?" Inez asked. "Would you do the honors and enlighten her?"

I faced Fay Marian, feeling as sheepish as I'm sure I looked. "George Eliot's real name was Mary Ann Evans."

Fay Marian's mouth dropped open. "No shit!"

For once, Inez did not chastise her for the unrefined outburst.

I sat struggling with this new information and trying to decide how much more, if anything, I now wanted to reveal about the content of the first letter: Dorothea's lament about the wasted life author Mary Ann, writing as George Eliot, had designed for her. It seemed like an entire world I had to revisit in a moment.

Before I could disclose anything else, a loud, insistent pounding on the door to Inez's apartment caused us all to jump at the sudden disruption.

"What on earth?" Inez laid a hand on Fay Marian's arm.

"I'll go see who it is." Fay Marian ground out her cigarette and got up. "You two stay put."

We heard her cross the living room and open the door. Then we heard a man's voice. He was talking loudly, and he did *not* sound happy.

Inez looked at me with concern. "It sounds like Mr. Hauser. I'll lay you dollars to doughnuts we can guess who it's about."

Oh dear . . . "Harrie?" I asked.

"Who else?"

We could tell by Fay Marian's gentle tone that she was trying to calm Mr. Hauser down. We finally heard her say she'd take care of whatever it was, and that he should go back to his apartment and try to rest. The door closed and she rejoined us in the kitchen. After she'd reclaimed her chair, she took a healthy sip of her cocktail.

"I'm gonna need another one of these. It's gonna be a *long* night."

"What on earth has happened now?"

Fay Marian ran a hand wearily through her frizzy hair. "I gather that Harrie got herself a dog whistle, and according to Mr. Hauser, she's been blowing on it pretty much nonstop for the last couple of hours. He says his dog is having seizures or something, because it's so upset. He's threatened to sue both Johnnie Hart—*and me*—if I don't do something to make her stop."

"Oh, dear." Inez looked nearly as morose as Fay Marian. "What are you going to do?"

"Well, for starters, I'm gonna have to go and confiscate her damn whistle. Right after I finish this." She drained her cocktail.

"I don't think false courage is what you need," Inez offered.

"Please, honey? Let me handle this in my own way?"

I didn't miss Fay Marian's use of the endearment. I uneasily began to suspect that perhaps these two women had more in common with the letter writer, Dorothea, than I realized . . .

Suddenly, *I* was the one who felt like an outsider—*no matter what Lottie chose to imply.*

"Why don't you let me talk with her?" I had no idea where my bravado came from. It may have had as much to do with my desire to flee the emotional energy on display between my dinner companions, as it had to do with wanting to help Harrie mend her problem ways.

Fay Marian looked surprised—and relieved—by my offer. "Are you serious?"

I nodded. "I'm willing to give it a try. We actually discussed this same thing last evening when she stopped by my house on her scooter."

"That'd be *great*, EJ. I can't tell you how much I'd appreciate it."

"Of course." I pushed back my chair and folded my napkin before placing it on the table beside my bowl. "Let me go and try to strike while the proverbial iron is hot—or before Mr. Hauser calls a juvenile probation officer. If you'll both excuse me?"

Fay Marian and Inez both moved to stand, but I stopped them.

"Stay put. I promise I'll stop back by and say goodnight."

"You're certain about this?" Inez sounded unconvinced.

I nodded. "I don't think she's being vindictive. I think she's just bored."

"Okay, then." Fay Marian held up both of their cocktail glasses in a dramatic toast. "Go in peace to love and serve the Lord."

Harrie seemed genuinely surprised when she answered the door and saw me standing there.

"Hi, Eej. What are you doing out after dark?"

It was difficult not to smile at the irony of her question. But I was there on a serious errand, and I needed to maintain my composure.

"May I come in?"

"Sure." Harrie held the door open for me and I stepped inside from the hallway.

The apartment was a near duplicate of Inez's, but not quite as large. And the windows overlooked the backyard. Harrie and her father also had a nice view of the rear of my house.

I noticed a few small branches on the roof that I'd not been aware of. I'd need to ask Nelson if he'd be willing to help me remove them. I had a ladder, but I wasn't good with heights, and hadn't been since I'd once climbed a tree in Salem Square and gotten trapped because I'd gone too high and panicked when I couldn't figure out how to get back down. I'd been stuck there for more than two hours and when Mama found me, she was furious. She'd had to get the fire department to get me down and said the experience was an embarrassment for our family.

The Harts's apartment was sparsely furnished—only a tattered-looking sofa with sagging cushions, and two mismatched chairs. The room also contained a braided rug that had seen much hard use and a coffee table made from two wooden crates with a varnished plank top. The only artwork appeared to be a faded painting of Jesus in Gethsemane in a chipped wooden frame. That was hanging above their television. I noticed two wads of aluminum foil stuck to the tips of the rabbit ears. An overhead light and one massive pole lamp provided all the ambience the room had.

To be fair, the Harts had only just moved in. I could see cardboard boxes stacked against the wall that backed up to their small kitchen. I presumed they simply hadn't had time to fully unpack. I noticed a partially completed jigsaw puzzle on the coffee table. I wondered if Harrie and her father worked on it together. Her black eye patch lay curled up beside it.

Harrie had been watching TV. The remains of her supper sat on a folding metal tray beside the chair she'd been sitting in.

"Were you visiting Fay Marian and Miss Inez?" Harrie asked.

"I was. They were kind enough to invite me over for dinner."

"What'd you have?"

"A cassoulet. And it was very delicious."

"I like casseroles, too. Aunt Rochelle makes them a lot. My favorite is the noodle one with Velveeta cheese and Ritz Crackers on top."

"That does sound good. However, this was a *cassoulet*—it's a French stew made from beans and meat. Miss Inez also added cranberries to hers."

Harrie made a face. "That sounds icky. Cranberries taste like sour rocks. That's a French thing?"

I nodded.

"What'd you call it, again?"

"Cassoulet."

"What's that mean in English?"

"I think it means . . . casserole."

We both smiled at that.

"Do you wanna watch TV with me? *Bugs Bunny* is almost over—then *The Rifleman* comes on."

"I can only stay a little while. I stopped by to talk with you about Mr. Hauser's dog."

Harrie's face fell. "He ratted me out, didn't he?"

"He stopped by Miss Inez's apartment to express his concern about your dog whistle."

Harrie sighed and dropped into her chair. "I know I said I wouldn't do it anymore."

"So, why did you change your mind?"

"I don't know." She shrugged her narrow shoulders. "I guess I got bored."

I sat down on the sagging sofa. I had a better view of the puzzle from there. It looked like a battle scene. I could make out most of the word "Combat" in the partially completed title.

"Harrie? I know that Mr. Hauser can be challenging sometimes. But intentionally doing things that make his dog unhappy isn't a nice way to behave. And it's not fair, either. His dog hasn't done anything to deserve being tormented—and even if it had, being cruel or spiteful doesn't make any situation better."

Harrie was staring down at her feet. "I know."

"Do you remember telling me how you felt when other children at school teased you because of your eye patch?" She nodded. "Don't you think that's how Mr. Hauser's dog feels when you blow your whistle? It's not his fault that he lives inside the apartment next door with a . . ." I searched for the right word to describe Mr. Hauser. "Curmudgeon."

Harrie looked up at me. "Is that another French word?"

"No. I don't know what language it comes from, actually."

"What's it mean?"

"Um." I decided that with Harrie, honesty was always the best course. "I think it usually references a cranky old man."

Harrie looked over at the common wall their apartment

81

shared with Mr. Hauser. "Well, that sure does sound like him."

"But not his dog, Harrie."

"No. I guess not." She met my eyes. "Is he gonna tell Daddy?"

I nodded.

"*Great.* No TV for a week."

I realized that Johnnie Hart would have to trust Harrie to abide by his predicted punishment order. But strangely, I believed Harrie would respect his restrictions. Her conduct toward Mr. Hauser's schnauzer notwithstanding, Harrie seemed . . . *honorable* to me.

"Would you like to think about apologizing to Mr. Hauser? I think he would appreciate it."

Harrie's expression was a mixture of moroseness and frustration.

"Do I have to? He's really *weird*—and he doesn't like me."

"Then maybe you could apologize to his dog?"

Harrie gave that idea some thought. "I guess I could do that."

"Good girl."

"Will you stay here until I get back?"

"Of course."

Harrie glanced at the TV. It appeared the Bugs Bunny adventure was reaching its denouement.

"If you hurry, you can return before *The Rifleman* starts." I suggested.

"Yeah." Harrie stood up dejectedly. "Okay. I'll be right back."

She started for the door. I didn't care for the obvious slump to her shoulders. It didn't suit her.

I got an idea . . .

"Harrie?" She turned around to face me. I picked up her eye patch and held it out. "Aren't you forgetting something?"

Harrie's smile was like seeing the sun come out.

Her errand didn't take long. I heard the sound of her footsteps pounding back along the hallway, and met her at the door. Her face was animated.

"I didn't think he was gonna let me in at first," she blurted while ripping off her eye patch. "But when I told him I was real sorry about the whistle and wanted to tell his dog, he let me in. And he wadn't weird when I apologized neither." She lowered her voice. "But it *really* smells like mothballs in there. I think he needs one of them perfume testers like Aunt Ro Ro gave me." She flopped onto the sofa. "I wonder if there's one that's good for gettin' rid of that—and maybe cooked cabbage, too?"

I told her I had no idea.

"I promised his dog I wouldn't hurt his ears no more. Mr. Hauser seemed real happy about that. And guess what else, Eej."

"I don't think I *can* guess, Harrie."

"He's gonna let me play with him—as long as I promise not to let him out of the yard!"

"That's wonderful news. Aren't you glad you went over there?"

She nodded. "Apologizing sure takes it outta you, though. I wish I had a Postum."

I reached out and smoothed a shock of her unruly hair. "How about you come by my house tomorrow and we'll make some?"

Harrie gave me a blinding smile. "It's a date."

My conversation with Johnnie Hart about having Harrie accompany me on the train to visit her aunt in Roanoke was much less awkward than I expected. Johnnie seemed relieved—and pleased—that I'd expressed any interest in spending quality time with his daughter.

"To tell you the truth, Miz Cloud, that gal could use some gentlin' up. Rochelle does a good job tryin' to help look after her, but she lives too far away to give Harrie more'n a spit shine now-n-then. Harrie told me as how you got her to apologize to Mr. Hauser about that damn tin whistle of hers." He shook his head. "I swanny . . . that gal just has a head for mischief. I think she takes after her mama."

"I enjoy spending time with Harrie, Mr. Hart. She's not a burden to me at all. And she'd be doing me a big favor if she accompanied me on the trip to meet with your sister."

"Well, I dunno about that. But she's done made the trip a hundred times by herself, so she'll know the ropes about gettin' there. I can give you Rochelle's phone number so's you can set somethin' up. She works ever day but Sunday and Tuesday, so either one of them would be the best time to go up there."

"Thank you, Mr. Hart. That would be lovely."

"Call me Johnnie, ma'am. Nobody calls me Mr. Hart. That makes me sound like my granddaddy."

"All right—Johnnie." I smiled at him. He was a gracious man, and it was obvious he cared a great deal about his daughter. "Please call me EJ."

"Yes, ma'am. Lemme git that phone number for you so you can call Rochelle. And you pretty much have to call her late at night or pretty late in the mornin' to catch her. She's kinda more . . . *socialized* than a lot of women."

"I understand."

"Now, Miz Cloud . . . *EJ* . . . don't you let Harrie push herself on you more'n you want. I know she gets lonely, and I feel real bad about her spendin' so much time alone, 'specially when I had to take her outta school so early."

"I enjoy Harrie's company, Johnnie. She's not a burden at all."

"Thank you for that, ma'am. And thank you for gettin' her to apologize to that Mr. Hauser. She wouldn't never a done that all by herself."

He wrote his sister's phone number down on the back of an old envelope and handed it to me.

"Thank you, Johnnie. I look forward to meeting her."

I took the envelope from him gratefully and headed home. I'd waited until Saturday morning to seek Johnnie out. It was the only day besides Sunday that I knew I could catch him at home. I was hopeful that Rochelle would be able to meet with me on a day next week, and that it wouldn't be too intrusive if I had to call on her at work. I wanted to be sure the trip to Paradise occurred on a day the post office in the small town would be open.

I still had to ask Harrie about our excursion. I didn't have much doubt that she'd be open to the idea of an outing. I hadn't been back at home long when I heard her voice, calling out to me from my front porch.

"Hey, Eej? Are you home?"

"I am! Come on in, Harrie. I'm in the kitchen."

I heard the door open and close. Harrie roared into the kitchen with the speed of her Crashmobile.

"Daddy told me we're going to Roanoke to see Aunt Rochelle! When can we go? Tomorrow?"

"I'm glad you like the idea, Harrie. But if your aunt agrees to meet with me, I'll need to go on a workday."

Harrie's face fell. "How come?"

"Because I also need to meet with the postmaster in Paradise, and the office is only open on weekdays."

"Rats. When are you callin' her?"

"Probably later this afternoon."

"Yeah. She's probably still in bed right now."

I looked at my wall clock. It was nearly 12:30. Johnnie hadn't been kidding about his sister's esoteric schedule.

"Have you had lunch yet?" I asked her. "I'm just making a sandwich before I head downtown."

"Why're you goin' downtown? Can I go, too?"

"You didn't answer my question about lunch. Would you like a sandwich?"

Harrie shook her head. "Daddy already made us lunch. Can I have some of that Postum?"

"*May* I have some Postum? And, yes. You may."

I put the teakettle on to boil.

"Are you workin' in Fay Marian's garden today? Can I help?" I cocked my ear toward her. "*May* I help?" she corrected.

I cut my ham sandwich in half and transferred it to a plate. "I'm working in the town garden today, Harrie. But, yes, you may accompany me there if you like." It wasn't hard to agree to allow Harrie to join me. I thought that being outside and productive was a better activity for her than watching TV or working on her G.I. Combat puzzle. And even though we'd had a minor breakthrough with the dog whistle, I didn't doubt Harrie's ingenuity when she was left too long to her own devices. "That's why I have to go into town. I need some new rolls of twine and some plant stakes."

"Are you takin' the bus?"

"I am. Do you like to ride the bus?"

"Yeah. It's nifty. I like to ride up front by the driver and watch people throw their coins in that slot. Sometimes they miss and the driver gives me a nickel if I crawl under the seats and find them." She dug into the front pocket of her pedal pushers. "I got my allowance today." Harrie showed me her two shiny quarters.

"Can I . . . *may* I go with you and get some new comics at the drugstore?"

The kettle started to boil, and I fixed our two mugs of Postum. "I think we can do that. I might look for a new book to read while we're there, too."

"Neato." Harrie watched me add milk and sugar to her beverage. "Maybe I can find a ball for Mr. Hauser's dog? He doesn't have any toys."

"That's a nice idea, Harrie."

"I felt kinda sorry for him. I know what it's like not to have anything good to play with. All I had in Reidsville was a busted wheelbarrow and some old croquet mallets. They don't work as good when you had to use rocks instead of balls. After a while, the top parts got busted up and we got splinters. So, me'n Carla tried to set 'em on fire with kerosene and threw 'em on the train tracks to see if they'd burn up them wood ties. But we got caught and some old geezer chased us halfway back to her house. She kept tellin' him to go to hell. We got lucky he was outta shape and we could run faster."

Yes. Gardening was going to be a much better hobby for Harrie . . .

"We'll look for some dog toys," I agreed.

We sat together on my front porch and drank our Postum. After I'd finished my sandwich, we walked together to the corner of Church and Academy Streets to catch the bus. The driver seemed to recognize Harrie right away. I was amazed how much she'd managed to get around in just one week. There were quite a few passengers waiting on the bus—most of them were colored people, who were boarding through the back doors. Harrie waved energetically at a woman wearing a bright red coat and carrying several shopping bags.

"Hey, Miz Peebles! We're goin' to Woolworth's to get some

special dog toys."

The woman waved back and smiled at her. "Somebody must've got their allowance early this week."

"Yes, ma'am. I'm gonna get some new comics, too."

"Well, that's awful nice to hear. Now you be a sweet girl and do right for that fine lady, you hear?" Mrs. Peebles nodded at me politely before boarding the bus and claiming a seat.

I never ceased to marvel at how easily Harrie made friends.

Once we got off the bus downtown, we walked straight to Woolworth's. I wanted to get my twine and plant stakes first because I had a feeling the trip to Walgreen's would take longer. *They carried dozens of comic books.*

After we'd entered the store, Harrie asked if she could go and check out the pet supplies. I made sure first that she knew how to find me if she finished before I did. She assured me that she knew her way around the store. After the experience on the bus, I had no reason to doubt her. Two seconds later, she'd darted off in search of a toy for Mr. Hauser's beleaguered schnauzer.

The twine was on sale, so I bought four large rolls. Evelyn was good about reimbursing volunteers from the garden's small supply budget, but I was always happy to contribute what I could in these small ways. After I'd paid for my purchases, I set off to find Harrie.

The pet department was easy to locate. I just followed my nose until I turned a corner and saw the hamsters, playing on their beds of cedar chips. The space contained a large display of bubbling fish tanks, and about a dozen parakeets kicking up a ruckus from inside their small cages. I walked up and down the two aisles of the department to no avail. Harrie was not in sight.

Wonderful. Why did I think she'd stay put?

I had no choice but to peruse the entire store until I found her. I just hoped she hadn't decided to leave the premises and head on to Walgreen's without me.

That would've been a bridge too far.

I did find her . . . eventually. She was sitting at the lunch counter like she'd had all the time in the world. I didn't realize what else was taking place until I walked over to retrieve her.

Harrie was seated next to a young Negro man. Two other Negroes sat at the far end of the counter. The waitresses stood clustered together near the entrance to the kitchen. They all had worried expressions on their faces.

My heart rate accelerated. *Good grief . . . Harrie had managed to plant herself in the middle of a sit-in.*

"Harriet?" I walked up behind her. "What on earth are you doing?" I whispered with urgency.

She swiveled around on her chrome seat.

"Hi ya, Eej. I'm gettin' some apple pie. Do you want a piece, too?"

I glanced nervously at the young man beside her. He met my gaze.

Dear Lord . . . It was Lottie's son, Jerome.

"Miz Cloud?" he asked. "What are you doin' here at the lunch counter?"

"Jerome?" I was too surprised to know what to say. "Does your mama know you're here?"

Before he could answer, Harrie chimed in again. "Me'n Jerome are gonna split my pie. Ain't we, Jerome?"

Jerome met my eyes. "I didn't know she was with you, ma'am. She just came up and sat down here beside me."

I laid a hand on his shoulder. "I know that, Jerome. But you shouldn't be here." I looked around nervously. "I don't want you to get arrested."

"Why's anybody gonna get arrested?" Harrie demanded. "It ain't against the law to eat pie, is it?"

I closed my eyes. "Harriet . . ."

A waitress approached and deposited Harrie's order. She glared at me before hastily retreating to the service area. I noticed that Harrie's thick slice of pie was topped with a big scoop of vanilla ice cream. Harrie pushed the plate toward Jerome and handed him her fork. "You go first. But don't eat all my ice cream." She looked up at me. "I like that part best."

Jerome's expression conveyed a multitude of emotions. It was clear he wasn't sure what to do. Frankly, I wasn't sure either. I *had* to do something. After deliberating for what felt like an hour, I impulsively sat down on the other empty stool beside him.

He looked at me with surprise. I met his eyes.

"Save me some ice cream, too," I said.

Jerome gave me a small, nervous smile and bravely lifted a forkful of the pie to his mouth. Less than ten seconds later, a balding store manager appeared and angrily told all of us that the lunch counter was now closed, and we all needed to leave before the police arrived.

"I don't want no trouble with you people," he warned. I could see bright beads of sweat glistening on his broad forehead. He kept shifting his weight from one foot to the other. It made his stocky form wobble in place like an agitated metronome.

"You go on now, Miz Cloud." Jerome said quietly. "This ain't your fight."

I laid a hand on his arm. "Your mama would never forgive me if I stood by and let you get arrested."

"My mama would never forgive *me* if I let anything happen to you and that child," he admonished. "You two go on now." He turned to face Harrie. "Thank you, young lady. I believe that was the best bite of pie I ever tasted."

I reluctantly got to my feet and extended my hand. "Come on, Harrie. We need to go on and finish our errands. You thank Mr. Bean for watching out for us."

Harrie looked back and forth between the two of us. The fuming store manager continued to stand nearby, rocking on his feet and shooting anxious looks back and forth between us and the street door, plainly willing the police to make a hasty appearance.

I was beyond relieved when Harrie laid her precious coins down on the counter before climbing down from her stool and joining me.

"Okay," she said. "But I still want to get some ice cream." She smiled hugely at her new friend. "Bye, Jerome."

"Good-bye, young lady. It was real nice sharing this pie with you."

I took hold of her hand and we walked toward the exit. Before we left the store, Harrie turned around and hollered, "Pie ain't illegal!"

Harrie never did find a toy she liked for Mr. Hauser's schnauzer. I suggested that maybe we should just pick up a box of dog biscuits. That way, whenever she saw him, she could give him a special treat. So we bought a bright yellow box of Ken-L Treats.

I had a harder time convincing her to put back the Muriel cigars . . .

"I wonder if these things taste good?" Harrie had opened the box and kept sniffing the dog biscuits during the bus ride back to Old Salem.

"I don't suggest finding out," I replied.

I was still shaken by the lunch counter experience in Woolworth's. *How could I have been so shortsighted to take Harrie there?* Especially when I *knew* what had been happening in the city for weeks.

And I was desperate to find out if Jerome had gotten away safely. I was tempted to call Lottie at home to ask—but I wasn't sure if Jerome wanted her to know about what he'd been up to by joining in the protests.

"Are you still upset about that pie?" Harrie was looking at me with concern.

"Not about the pie, no. But what you did could have ended very badly, Harrie."

"Why? All I did was share some pie with Jerome. Why was that a bad thing?"

"It wasn't a bad thing at all. But right now, the city is . . . trying to figure some things out about . . . about all of us finding ways to get along better. Sometimes, that becomes difficult and ends up getting people into trouble. We need to be more mindful about how we behave and try not to do things that will make the process worse for others."

"So, we shouldn't order pie anymore?"

"Well . . . no. That's not exactly what I meant."

I was out of my depth on this one. I knew the reason I was struggling so much with an explanation was because I didn't understand it either. I'd never had to think deeply about any of these issues because they had never involved me. *Not until today.* Before, it had all just been something distant in the news—like stories about the plane crash in Indiana, or that awful Sharpeville massacre in South Africa where police had opened fire on unarmed Negro protestors. These were just horrible events that kept happening *someplace else*. Not here—and *never* to me.

And Jerome wasn't some rabble-rouser or Yankee agitator, here in the South to stir up trouble. *He was Lottie's son.* Lottie's son: who'd come tearing into our basement office at age twelve, proudly showing off his very first Scout badge. Lottie's son: who taught Sunday school at Shiloh Baptist Church. Lottie's son: who worked two jobs to pay his tuition at Winston-Salem Teacher's College. Lottie's son: who today faced arrest for daring to share a piece of apple pie with a ten-year-old white girl.

No. I didn't have a vocabulary that could explain any of this to Harrie.

"Is it like blowin' my whistle to pester Mr. Hauser? And how that ends up hurtin' his dog, instead?"

I looked at Harrie with amazement.

"Yes. I think it's very like that."

"Then I'm glad we got him some treats."

"Me, too."

The bus stopped at Academy Street, and we collected our bags so we could get off for the short walk home.

"I think I'd be nervous, too, if I had a weird name like his."

"The dog, you mean?"

Harrie nodded.

"What *is* his name?"

Harrie looked up at me.

"Mortimer."

"Oh, my . . ."

"Yeah," Harrie agreed. "I bet he got beat up at dog school."

I did not disagree with her.

"What's this one called?"

Harrie was pointing at a spiky cluster of scrambling plants that were just beginning to sprout tiny, translucent flowers.

"That's fumitory. Sometimes called 'earth smoke.'"

We'd been weeding in the sorrel bed, and the fumitory stalks were notorious for grabbing onto weeds and other neighboring plants. It was difficult to separate them from the weeds without damaging other herbs.

"What was it used for?"

"That one was used mostly for digestive complaints—liver diseases, primarily. And it was also used to treat the French pox." I regretted the words as soon as they'd left my mouth. I prayed that Harrie wouldn't pay any attention to them.

No such luck . . .

"What's the French pox?"

"Um . . ." I was very glad Evelyn wasn't working in our section. She'd been busy weeding near the rows of salsify and wormwood. I'd have *never* lived this one down if she'd overheard our conversation. "It was a kind of a . . . skin disease . . . that people sometimes got through close . . . um . . . *contact* . . . with open wounds or sores on others."

"Yuck. Why would anybody ever want to do *that?*"

"I honestly don't know."

"How come there are so many French things buried in the dirt around here?"

I wasn't sure what she meant. "What French things?"

"Well. These fuma-plant things—and all them cars in Fay Marian's backyard."

Oh. "The cars didn't *grow* in Fay Marian's yard, Harrie. They were just parked there."

"They're really creepy. I wouldn't want to have close contact with any of them rusted-out things, neither."

"I'd agree that it would be wise to stay away from them."

"Them French have some strange ideas. Just like that funny casserole thing with the weird name and the sour cranberries."

She sat back on the ground and sighed.

"What's the matter?" I asked. We'd been weeding for about two hours, and it was hot in the sun. I was thinking it was about time to wrap it up for the day. I was sure Harrie was tired. I knew I was.

"It's this whole garden here," she said. "I don't get it. Them old-timers planted all this stuff to make medicines for a bunch of weird diseases—like that pox thing. And everybody works hard to keep growin' the same plants in here, just like always. But how come they didn't grow nothin' that made people treat each other better? Ain't there any plants for that?"

I'd never thought about the *hortus medicus* quite that way. But she was right.

"I don't have an answer for that, Harrie. I wish I knew."

"Me, too. If there was a plant like that in here, I'd pick it and take it down to that mean man at Woolworth's. Maybe then he'd stop havin' people arrested for wantin' to sit down and eat pie."

"Maybe so." I got an idea. "Harrie? Fay Marian asked me to help her come up with ideas about plants to put into her new garden space. Would you like to help me find out if there are any herbs that might have the kinds of positive effects you're talking about?"

Harrie brightened up. "Do you think there are some?"

"I'm betting there are."

"Okay, Eej. I say, let's *find* 'em."

"It's a deal." I got up and brushed off my knees. "Now let's collect our things and head home. I've got some work to do—and I still need to call your aunt Rochelle."

"Daddy is takin' me out to Staley's for barbecue. He said after that, we could stay up late and watch *Have Gun–Will Travel.*"

"That sounds exciting."

"It's a lot better'n that accordion stuff Mr. Hauser watches."

We'd finished packing up our supplies and left the garden, heading down Main Street toward Harrie's apartment building. It had been a long day, full of surprising encounters and stark revelations. I had much to think about. And as if the events of the day hadn't been enough, I knew that once I was alone, I'd have to contend with the second letter that Lottie had insisted I take home with me for the weekend.

I said goodbye to Harrie, who promised to let me know how Mortimer liked his Ken-L Treats. I told her I supposed he would like them very well and reiterated how proud of her I was for her magnanimous decision to turn away from acts of torment to embrace understanding.

As I rounded the corner on Race Street and drew closer to my bungalow, I had an eerie premonition that I was on an inevitable collision course with the *pièce de résistance* of an already overwhelming day. But I knew with certainty that I could no more change course or reverse direction than the captain of the Northwest Orient flight could've forestalled that catastrophic explosion over Indiana.

I was fortunate to connect with Harrie's aunt Rochelle on my first try.

I'm not sure exactly what I'd been expecting, but the woman who answered was altogether softer-sounding and less abrasive than what Harrie's descriptions had led me to imagine. Rochelle said she'd be delighted to try and help me identify the fragrance and would do her best to help me isolate the handful of places near Paradise where someone might go to procure it. We agreed that Harrie and I would travel there on Tuesday, because Rochelle had that afternoon off and could fetch us from the train station. She also suggested that since the train made a stop in the tiny town of Paradise, it would be easy for us to walk the short distance from the station to the post office, so I might meet with the postmaster there. It was a long shot, but since I was fairly certain that the letters had to have been mailed *at* the post office, perhaps the branch manager would recall something about their provenance.

It was clear that I'd have plenty to discuss with Lottie on Monday morning—most notably, my surprising encounter with her son at the lunch counter in Woolworth's. I had no idea what reaction to expect from her—or even whether Jerome would have said anything about it to her.

The radio broadcast no local news on Saturday nights, so I knew I'd have to wait for Sunday's paper to discover whether there'd been any arrests in the wake of yesterday's protests. I dearly hoped not.

With each passing day, my general sense of unease increased. I felt that real events had conspired to crack the glass dome that preserved and protected the small life I led in Old Salem. Since childhood, the village's quaint rituals and traditions— its symbolic liturgies and professions of faith, combined with perfectly preserved buildings and public spaces—had sustained me. I'd always felt a harmonious connection with a community ethos that venerated simplicity, faith, and a commitment to industry. These were the values that had been passed down by generations and presented to me without question or discussion.

Only my father had ever dared to question the infallibility of the Moravians and their idealized living experiment. And his doubts were only ever expressed indirectly, without rancor and always in a manner overlaid with nuance.

But I was learning that there had *always* been troublesome undercurrents—as Inez had pointed out on our first meeting. How had she characterized them? *Awkward contradictions.* She'd said there were disturbing things implicit in a reverence for the preservation of "old-world traditions" that "failed to change with the times."

I'd found that pronouncement unsettling at first. *But now?*

Now it was impossible for me to deny all the ways this community had failed to change with the times. And not simply Old Salem, the town within a town—but our entire city. Our state. Region. Country. *All of it.* The tectonic plates of history were shifting, moving us all into different states of being—into better ways to respect, honor, and understand one another. Why were so many of us desperate to inveigh against it? To cling to our old ways out of fear and desperation?

The Bible taught us that when the scales fell from our eyes, we could no longer see the world as it had been. Today, when the scales had dropped from my own eyes, I could no longer deny that every person was imbued with the simple right to sit down and eat a piece of pie.

"Out of the mouths of children you have ordained strength."

It was that simple—like most great truths so often were. But moving this, or any community forward? That was shaping up to be the work of several lifetimes.

My own existence had been like one of my grandmother's needlepoint compositions: tidy, ordered, and perfectly constrained by its frame. I had never ventured beyond its simple parameters. But lately, the silken threads that had defined my known world were beginning to unravel. And I was terrified about what might be revealed when everything I thought I knew fell away.

The second of the remaining garden letters reposed inside my leather bag. Lottie had wasted no time pointing out to me that this letter had passed the mandated forty-five-day hold requirement, and now could be opened and read. I had intentionally put off doing so until tonight. And even when the appointed time had arrived, I was still ambivalent about confronting whatever expression of disappointed hope and untethered passion the writer had chosen to unleash on her unknown recipient.

But I owed it to myself and to the sacred commission of my office to examine the document for any clues that might assist in our proper disposition of the letters.

That was still true . . . wasn't it?

I asked myself that question as I carried the letter into my living room. It was early evening, but darkness had yet to fall. Daylight saving time was still a way off, but it seemed to me that the days were already growing longer. I chose not to light any lamps. I liked the way the low angle of the light shining in through the windows cast geometric patterns across the walls and floor. I'd made numerous changes to the room during the score of years that had passed since my mother's death. I'd painted the walls a brighter color and had taken up the faded carpet, patterned with cabbage roses. Gone, too, were the heavy draperies and the lace armchair doilies my mother had tatted by hand. It had been a considerable expense, but I'd also removed the behemoth electric heater my parents had installed inside the fireplace opening. Now, on the coldest nights, I burned logs that Nelson salvaged from neighborhood elm, poplar and linden trees, and carefully stacked inside a timber shelter he'd built beside my back door.

I sat down and briefly held the letter to my face before opening it. It was remarkable that the perfumed scent was still so pronounced. That had to be a testament to . . . *something* extraordinary about the fragrance. I eagerly anticipated discovering what Aunt Rochelle (I still wasn't certain about her last name) would reveal to me about the perfume.

It was with no small amount of trepidation that I opened the envelope and withdrew the letter—three pages in length this time. The stationery and handwriting were identical to the first letter.

Dear Mary Ann,

> *Tonight, I find myself despondent and newly bereft of hope that any aspect of my insipid situation might change.*

> *I long for release from this torture. And I appeal to you, once again, to take pity on me in my misery and explain why you will not release me from this life of unremitting dullery. What offense did I commit, Mary Ann? To what account can you hold me other than that of being a character cursed by the circumstances of her birth? I live the life you crafted for me—a life so*

very different from the one you allowed yourself.
When every grand possibility once existed for
me, when my world was opened and my mind
improved by access to the grand teachings of
the classics—you decided, instead, to withdraw
from me all considerations of a nobler life, freed
from convention and constraint. I labored as
your unwitting handmaiden in a lush garden
of promise and gained the knowledge of good
and evil. Little did I understand that such
enlightenment would result in my banishment
from true paradise and consign me to live out my
days in a macabre imitation of tragedy. You held
the keys to all of this, Mary Ann. You alone had
the power to pen a different ending for my story.
But it pleased you to withhold from me the same
sweet freedoms you claimed for yourself.

And she, who once was fresh and unspoiled
as the soft, spring rain, was made to grow dry
and withered on untended vines of lost hope. The
whispered endearments of our first expressions of
passion, our sweet and untutored explorations,
will forever abide as secret harbingers of a cruel
fate—as sweet remembrances of past truths that
may never be spoken aloud.

How fragile and dearly bought were our
beliefs that we might accede to lives of purpose
and accomplishment? How vain were our hopes
that the fullness implicit in the marriage of true

*equals might one day be ours? How altruistic
and resolute were our determinations to throw off
the chains of male authority and fashion a world
predicated on just principles and purity of intent?
How foolishly did we trust that your steady hand
would guide us toward the percipience you taught
us to seek?*

*Were these promises no more than a litany of
pious falsehoods, Mary Ann? Was it never your
goal to allow our roots to take hold in the soil
of fertile imagination and flourish like the first
young plants of spring? Or like Moses, was your
design always to lead us to the boundary of the
Promised Land, only to deny us entry at the last?*

*With ineffable sadness, I offer this plaintive
appeal,*

Dorothea

Dorothea's second letter had not been punctuated with as much *graphic* content as her first missive, but the emotion it conveyed was every bit as unsettling. *Who was she?* And what aspect of her present circumstances had led her to pour so much sadness and disappointment into letters that could never reach the eyes of her intended audience?

Harrie had been right. These letters were becoming every bit as arcane as an episode of her beloved *Chevy Mystery Show.*

I had been sitting in the living room for so long I hadn't

realized that darkness had finally overtaken the light. The room had descended into shadows and everything in it had dissolved into shades of gray. Its contours were familiar, yet strangely unfamiliar.

My mug of Postum no longer steamed from its resting place on the table beside my chair. The murky liquid had grown tepid and drained of its flavor.

In that moment, still holding the pale, scented sheets of paper in my hands, I realized that I shared an unhappy kinship with the mysterious Dorothea. With each passing day, more meaning and vibrancy seemed to drain from my own sheltered life. Dorothea's lament had become part of my own rude awakening to the hidden realities of the life I lived in an inhospitable community that seemed bent on denying the dignity of authentic experience to so many of its people.

My small world was becoming a puzzle, missing pieces from its center. And there was no roadmap to guide me to the place where the missing pieces could be found.

And even if it were completed, what kind of picture would the puzzle reveal?

I continued to sit quietly in the dark for hours, contemplating a new universe of questions, and not finding any answers.

Melissa officinalis
(Lemon Balm)

"Truly I tell you today, you will be with me in Paradise."
                                                        –Luke 23:43

When I arrived at the DLO on Monday morning, Lottie didn't bother waiting until I'd hung up my bag and donned my sweater to launch into a spirited tirade about how I'd taken leave of my senses by joining her son, Jerome, at the lunch counter sit-in on Saturday.

"What in the world kind of foolishness was that?"

"I gather this means Jerome told you about seeing me there?"

"Not just *you*—that infernal child who's turned into some kind of damn shadow of yours. It don't make *no* kind of sense. What in tarnation did you *think* would happen by sittin' down there like you were almighty Esther the Queen—and orderin' him a damn slice of apple pie that could've landed *all* a your behinds in jail?"

I hadn't seen anything in yesterday's paper to suggest that

Jerome, or any of the other protestors, had been arrested. Lottie's hypothetical declaration seemed to indicate that all of them *had* escaped being taken into custody. That much was a huge relief.

"It wasn't like that, Lottie." I knew it was a weak defense, but I didn't have a better one to offer.

"*No?* Then what in thunder *was* it like?"

"It just . . . *happened.* Harrie had accompanied me to Woolworth's because I needed to pick up some gardening supplies, and she disappeared to go look at pet toys for a neighbor's dog. I had no idea she'd decide to make a detour and head for the lunch counter to use part of her allowance to buy dessert."

Lottie looked unconvinced. "Yeah. *Just* desserts, if you ask me." Her brown eyes blazed. "Lord knows I can't control what that boy of mine does. But I expect you to have better sense. Your daddy didn't raise you to go off half-cocked and act like a crazy woman."

"Oh, Lottie . . ."

"Don't you 'Oh, Lottie' me." She wagged an index finger at me. "Stop actin' like one of them damn suffragettes, *Miss Cloud.* This ain't your damn fight."

"That's what Jerome said, too."

"Well, hallelujah and amen. Maybe that boy still *does* have some of the sense he was born with."

"He was very brave, Lottie. And he tried to protect us both." I gave her a nervous smile. "He said you'd kill him if anything happened to us."

Lottie didn't reply. I could see most of her umbrage retreat to less volatile territory.

"And he was very sweet with Harrie, too," I added. "I was . . . proud of him."

Lottie gave a curt nod of assent. "He told me that child has less fear and more gumption than any of the damn men runnin' this city."

"He's right about that. I don't think it ever occurred to Harrie that *any* person would be denied the right to sit down at a lunch counter and order a slice of pie. So, she just refused to accept it. And when I saw her sitting there on a stool next to Jerome, I had no real choice." I met her eyes. "It became my turn to refuse to accept it, too."

Lottie slowly shook her head.

"Y'all are just crazy. None of this is ever gonna change."

"Why do you say that? It can't stay this way. Not forever."

"No? *Why not?* You think finally bein' allowed to sit down at a damn dime store lunch counter to order a plate of bad food is suddenly gonna make the world a more just place? *It ain't.* That's only gonna happen when people change their hearts and realize the God they worship expects them to start livin' up to them so-called Christian values they all love to preach about in their segregated churches. And that'll probably happen on the same day hell freezes over, and we start earnin' the same pay as them men upstairs who can't tell shit from Shinola—*or* how to recognize a damn R.J. Reynolds logo on the front of a so-called dead letter."

Lottie strode off angrily to retrieve our bin of mail from the dumbwaiter.

Her words had found their mark. I knew she was right.

But I still didn't agree that what Jerome was doing was a waste of effort. Doing nothing for so many years had gotten us . . . nowhere. Lottie was probably right that small changes didn't amount to much. But small changes had a better shot at changing hearts than *no* changes had. I was now certain about that.

When Lottie returned with the overflowing bin of mail, I resolved to say as much to her.

"Lottie?"

She looked at me with a gaze that contained an implied question.

"I'm . . . sorry."

"You're sorry? Sorry about what?"

"About . . . about *all* of this . . . the arrests. The injustices." I waved a hand in frustration. "Jerome and that awful manager at Woolworth's. *All of it.* It's just wrong—and it's never been right. And I have no defense for not . . . for not speaking out about it sooner—or even noticing it before now. It's . . . it all sickens me."

I didn't know what kind of response to expect from her. Lottie didn't suffer fools lightly. In fact, Lottie didn't suffer most people lightly.

That day, standing in our bleak basement office with the pipes humming overhead, was no exception.

"Don't be lookin' to me for absolution."

"It isn't *that* . . . I just . . ." I met her eyes. "I don't know what to do anymore. About *anything.*"

Lottie actually laughed. "Well, you're in luck, Esther Jane. That part is easy."

I wasn't sure what she meant, and the distress on my face must've shown it.

"*Do better.*" She picked up the mail bin and carried it to our sorting table.

I was more confused than before. "That's it?" I asked her.

Lottie glared at me. "What'd you *think* I was gonna say? Do penance and go climb the five hundred steps on your knees?"

"I don't know." I managed a weak smile. "Maybe?"

"Lemme ask you something: how many years we been workin'

together down here in this damn basement?"

I blinked. Lottie knew the answer to that question as well as I did. "Nearly twenty, of course."

"Twenty. Twenty damn years. And in all that time, have you *ever* thought about the fact that we've never so much as gone out for lunch together? Or visited each other's houses? Or sat beside each other on the same damn bus? Or have you ever wondered, *even one time,* if I get paid the same amount of money as you for doin' the same damn day's work, year in and year out?"

I couldn't answer her. I was too humiliated to admit that *none* of those things had occurred to me before that moment. I lowered my head. "I'm . . . truly sorry, Lottie."

"*White people . . .*" Lottie shook her head. "I don't know why some of y'all think you need to be damn martyrs to prove you ain't as bad as everybody else. Just sweep your own damn corner. And for god's sake, open your damn eyes and at least *see* the real world that's boilin' over all around you—not just that damn fairy tale you been livin' in." She slammed the bin she'd been holding down. "And while you're at it, keep that child away from them damn lunch counters until this whole sit-in mess is settled."

"Yes, ma'am." I knew better than to push her.

"Now get over here and grab a stack of these letters. We ain't gettin' paid no time and a half, and I wanna be outta here on time tonight."

I regretted putting her in such a mood.

Lottie and I didn't talk much the rest of that morning, other than to share insights on some of the mail pieces. By my calculation, we'd already spoken volumes. By lunchtime, Lottie had cooled off enough to ask me for details about the content of the second letter.

"Any more of them *Spring Fire* stories?"

"What on earth are those?" I had no idea what she was referring to.

"Never mind." She waved a floppy stack of letters at me in frustration. "I shoulda known you've never heard of it."

"I've never heard of half the things you bring up, Lottie."

"Don't I know it? And that's a damn shame, too. But forget about *Spring Fire* . . . was there anything good in the second letter?"

"By *good*, do you mean any information that helps us identify the sender?"

"*No*. By 'good,' I mean anything *good*. You know . . . *juicy*."

I finished applying new labels to a handful of letters and carried them over to the vacuum tube.

"Honestly, Lottie. You have the strangest ideas sometimes."

"I know I do. I keep hopin' maybe one day you'll acquire a few of your own."

I loaded the processed letters into the tube and shot them upstairs for re-mailing.

"No." I faced her. "Nothing you would call *juicy* was in the second letter. Neither was there any more information to help us locate the sender. I did reach out to the post office in Paradise, to ask if I could meet with the manager there on Tuesday."

"What'd they say? Did they have any ideas about who mailed the letters?"

"I didn't share any specifics over the telephone—only that I was bringing up some undeliverable mail that I needed help processing."

"Well, let's hope they got somebody workin' in there who's more on the ball than them jokers we got upstairs in this place."

I agreed with her sentiment. "I also hope the branch manager is a tad more helpful than the window clerk who answered my call."

"What was his problem?"

"*Her* problem. She didn't seem to be very engaged or interested in our predicament."

"Typical. You'd be better off askin' for help from one of them civil service rats in the attic of this place."

"*Weasels.*"

"Don't be sayin' that too loud, *Miz* Cloud. You don't wanna get busted for wanton destruction of federal property."

"I'd prefer not to get *busted* for anything."

"What time does your train leave tomorrow?"

"Nine-twenty. I'm grateful I got permission to go so soon. I just wish I wasn't so nervous about traveling."

"Well, don't be. All you gotta do is sit down on your pampered behind and wait for them to tell you where to get off." She smiled conspiratorially. "So to speak."

I chose to ignore her innuendo. "I wish it were that simple."

"We got nothin' to lose. Either you come up with a lead and figure out how to find your pen pal, or you don't. And if you don't, we bag 'em up with all these other 'Guess Who's,' and send them speedin' right along to Uncle Sam's Franklin stove. Unless," she waved a hand impatiently to encompass the shelves lining walls that were filled with letters and parcels we'd been unable to resolve, "you're feeling *sentimental,* and you'd rather let 'em join their soul mates over there to ride out eternity right here, in post office damn purgatory. It's that simple. Or . . ."

"Or what?"

Lottie shrugged. "Or you wait to see if she keeps right on spillin' her guts to that dead author you told me about."

I hadn't thought about that possibility. Evelyn hadn't mentioned anything about additional letters arriving when I'd seen her in the garden on Saturday. But then, she'd earlier acknowledged that she only checked the garden's mailbox about twice a month.

Maybe there were already more letters waiting in the Old Salem town office?

I didn't recognize the wizened volunteer who was filling in during the lunch shift in the Old Salem office, which meant that she didn't recognize me, either. That made my errand exponentially more difficult. Evelyn was the master gardener, so she, by rights, was the only person authorized to collect mail for the gardens. But I knew it was highly unlikely that Evelyn would bother checking the mail anytime soon—and I desperately wanted to know if more letters from our mysterious sender had been delivered. If so, having access to examples of more recent correspondence might serve to better jog the memory of the staff in the tiny Paradise, Virginia, post office. It was worth a shot, anyway.

But the officious volunteer seemed suspicious and appeared unwilling to accede to my request.

"I'm not at all sure about this." She cast about the small space to see if anyone else was still on hand in the office. But apparently, everyone had already departed for lunch. "This seems highly irregular, and I don't even know where they keep the mail for the garden."

"Mrs. Haas told me it's dropped into a box for retrieval. I suspect that might be located someplace near the spot the regular mail is delivered?"

She sighed and reluctantly began to search beneath the counter that separated us where we stood. I could hear her shifting items around before she muttered, "This must be it."

She stood up holding an oversized shoebox. Someone had stenciled the word "Gardens" on the side of it with a black Magic Marker pen. I could tell the box contained some items, but wasn't sure how many, or what they were.

"That's super," I said optimistically. Then I resorted to obsequiousness. "I can't thank you enough for finding it. You've been extremely accommodating."

The persnickety woman appeared unmoved. Our standoff continued.

Inspiration struck. I withdrew my official Postal Inspector Identification Card from my bag and showed it to her.

"These are my credentials," I explained. "I am here on official United States Post Office business. The garden has been receiving some correspondence that should not be delivered because the recipient does not exist. It's my responsibility to collect the letters to process them downtown in our Undeliverable Mail Division."

That seemed to do the trick. She reluctantly passed the box across the counter to me so I could quickly examine its contents. I felt my heart rate accelerate. Mixed in among a smattering of seed catalogs and store circulars was another one of the letters—same stationery, same handwriting, and same addressee. I carefully withdrew it, realizing it was imbued with the same intoxicating scent, too.

"This is precisely what I was looking for." I had to fight not to show the emotion I felt, standing there holding it in front of the near-scowling woman. "Thank you for your assistance. I'll leave these other things for Mrs. Haas to collect."

I placed the letter and my ID card back into my bag and made haste to leave the office before the humorless volunteer could change her mind. I wondered vaguely why she didn't apply for a window agent position with the postal service . . . she certainly had the requisite disposition.

Once outside, I walked to Salem Square and sat down on the same bench where my father had waited on me that day he'd walked me to church. It was a lovely Carolina spring day. I was amazed at how much the cherry and tulip trees had leafed out in just the past week. This had always been my favorite time of year—probably because it dovetailed with the beginning of work in the garden. Few things were more gratifying for me than the hours spent setting new plants and clearing away the detritus of winter to allow fledgling perennial herbs access to sunlight and space to grow.

It was most unusual for me to be outside like this during a workday. Sitting there on a low bench along the perimeter of our town square—enjoying the warmth of the sun on my face and listening to a musical choir of birds mixing with the laughter of students, hurrying to and from class—I realized what a mistake that had been.

I took a few moments to examine the newest letter I'd successfully managed to purloin from the unwilling volunteer. Its *Paradise, Virginia* postmark read *April 15*. Because the sender knew enough to include a zone code on the address, the letter had probably reached Old Salem on or before the 19th—well before Lottie and I notified the area carrier not to deliver any more of the correspondence to the garden. Any successive letters would be intercepted in the main branch and dispatched directly to the DLO.

The letter seemed similar to the others in heft, leading me to surmise that the contents would be roughly approximate in length to the others. I noted that the perfumed scent that permeated it was stronger and sweeter smelling than on the first letters—an obvious indication that it had been written more recently. Unfortunately, it would be a minimum of another three weeks before Lottie or I could legitimately open the newest letter to look for clues about the identity of the sender.

Unless I suspended that part of the protocol—which I knew Lottie would remind me was within my discretion as a postal inspector.

I resolved not to give in to that impulse until I knew for certain that the trip to Paradise would yield no results. I returned the letter to my bag.

I had the better part of an hour remaining on my lunch break and I was deliberating about whether to head straight back to the post office to eat my packed lunch, or to take advantage of the unseasonably warm day and stop into a nearby eatery to procure something I might enjoy in the park. I decided that I'd walk to Mayberry and get a sandwich. The ice cream shop was a popular hangout for Salem College students, and it was close to a bus stop. I'd eaten countless meals there when I'd been enrolled, and I knew the service was fast and dependable. Just as I approached the restaurant, I heard someone call out my name.

When I turned around, I was surprised to see Inez Bell.

"How wonderful to see you, EJ." Inez joined me near the entrance. "Are you going in for lunch?"

"Hello, Inez. I had an errand to run over here so I thought I'd grab a quick sandwich before heading back downtown."

"I'm between classes, myself. Would you like some company?"

I told her I'd like that very much, and we entered the small shop together. We were lucky to be seated at a table right away. There were quite a few coeds inside, and most of them were laughing and eating ice cream. Several of them recognized "Dr. Bell," and greeted her with enthusiasm. I was happy to see that

Inez appeared to be so genuinely liked—although I wasn't at all surprised.

"I have to admit, I was surprised to see you," Inez shared, after we'd ordered our sandwiches.

"Why was that?"

"I don't know. Going out to lunch didn't seem to me to be something you'd probably do very often. And certainly not over here, so far away from your post office."

"That's true. It is an anomaly for me."

"Which part?" she asked. "Going out to lunch, or being so far away from the post office during business hours?"

"Yes," I replied. Inez laughed. She was a very pretty woman. Today she was wearing a smart linen suit in a vibrant shade of fuchsia that set off her complexion perfectly. It wasn't difficult to imagine why Fay Marian held her in such high esteem . . . *to say the least.* "To be honest," I continued, "I visited the town administrative office to see if any more letters to our friend, Mary Ann Evans, had been delivered."

"Oh." Inez's eyes grew wide. "And had there been?"

"Yes. One." I shifted around on my chair to withdraw the newest letter from my bag. "As you can see. Same stationery, same handwriting . . ."

"And the fragrance you mentioned," Inez observed. "I can detect it from here."

"It is very . . . distinctive."

"That's putting it mildly. Fay Marian would be far less . . ."

It was my turn to finish her statement. "Circumspect?"

She smiled. "You took the word right out of my mouth."

"She is quite a character."

"She is. And she's so grateful for your help starting her garden—*and* for your intercession with Harrie. That was going the extra mile."

"Well," I demurred, "Harrie is hardly a burden. I find her company to be surprisingly . . . refreshing. I'm actually looking forward to our outing tomorrow."

"That's right," Inez recalled. "You're going with her to Roanoke, aren't you?"

I nodded.

"So, you're going to get to meet the infamous Aunt Rochelle?"

"Yes. She was very kind to offer to pick us up at the train station—and to do what she can to help isolate the fragrance. With luck, we may even be able to figure out where someone from a town as small as Paradise could buy it."

"You'll get to ride in the oft-cited yellow Thunderbird. Fay Marian will be green with envy."

I smiled. "I don't expect it to be all that dramatic. But I am very much looking forward to Rochelle's help identifying the perfume."

"What will you do then?" Inez leaned forward and propped her chin on her hand. "Suppose you *are* successful in identifying the writer of the letters. Is there some protocol in place for that?"

"There is, actually. We return the letters to the sender and explain that the phantom addressee could not be located."

"But in this case," Inez raised a finger didactically, "we know the addressee has already *been* identified as a fictional character, and could *never* be located. And we can intuit that the sender was likely aware of that when the letters were mailed."

"True . . ."

"Doesn't that alter the process? Even a tiny bit?"

I struggled with how to answer her. "Not as far as the U.S. Postal Service is concerned."

"Oh, come on, EJ. There *have* to be exceptions. What about

the thousands of letters children write every year and mail off to Santa Claus? Doesn't the post office bend the rules for dealing with those?"

I gave her a shy smile. "I'm not at liberty to discuss top secret particulars governing holiday deliveries to the North Pole."

Inez didn't buy it. "So, if you cannot answer *that* question, I'll pose another one: what if the mysterious sender doesn't *want* to be identified? What if this mysterious 'Dorothea' intended for the letters to end up precisely as they have—knowing that someone affiliated with the gardens would eventually open and read them?"

"You mean with no idea that the postal service would ever become involved?"

"Correct." Inez nodded. "In that case, exposing who she is might end up being most unwelcome for her. In fact, I'd venture to guess that the very last thing our Dorothea desires is to have the letters handed back to her."

I found Inez's suggestion to be worrisome *and* intriguing in nearly equal measure. And I was keenly aware that something about her hypothesis carried an eerie ring of truth.

What *would* I do if our investigation resulted in the exposure of someone who'd intended, all along, to remain anonymous?

But I was an agent of the United States Postal Service. And it wasn't my job to make assessments, pass judgments, or develop exceptions based on the motivations of customers who used our services. The simple act of placing a stamp on an envelope and inserting that envelope through a mail slot constituted an implied contract—and demonstrated a belief and an expectation that the letter would be delivered to its rightful, intended recipient. *Period.* So, in that sense, any regrets the sender might later entertain became irrelevant.

Didn't they?

I had no idea how to communicate any of this in a coherent way to Inez, who was regarding me with a look of such intensity that I could easily imagine the consternation of her students when they didn't complete their assignments on time.

"That would, indeed, be an unhappy outcome," I agreed, belatedly.

I could tell that Inez was prepared to press her point further, but our sandwiches arrived, and I was saved by having to concentrate on dispatching my lunch in the short amount of time I had left, before hurrying to catch a bus back downtown.

But we parted on very cordial terms, and Inez made me promise to report back to her and Fay Marian as soon as Harrie and I returned from Roanoke tomorrow evening.

Johnnie had been right about Harrie being an experienced traveler.

We arrived at the train station about thirty minutes before our boarding time. The bus trip across town had taken longer than I'd anticipated. I was unaware that I'd been fidgeting—opening and closing my bag to repeatedly count my cash to be sure I had enough money on hand to pay for our tickets, and obsessively checking the time on my watch. But Harrie noticed my agitation and took pains to reassure me.

"Don't worry, Eej. They say it always takes longer on this bus on account of it's the one that goes to the airport. But we'll get there on time."

I wasn't persuaded that Harrie's confidence in the city transit system was well placed. By my calculation, she hadn't made the trip to Roanoke since moving to Winston-Salem. But I decided to trust her assessment. Sure enough, we arrived at the station in plenty of time.

"Did you get any breakfast at home?"

Harrie nodded. "Daddy had cereal and a banana out for me."

"Well, we'll find a place to get a nice lunch in Roanoke."

"Aunt Rochelle will take us someplace in her car. She eats out all the time."

I wasn't surprised, based on reports about the schedule she kept. "It's very generous for her to meet with me on her day off."

"Yeah," Harrie agreed. "It's good we aren't going up on one of her perm days."

I had to agree with her about that. I remember how the house always smelled after my mother got her biannual perms. Daddy always complained that the house smelled like a vat of egg salad that had gone off.

Harrie marched us up to the ticket window to purchase our tickets. I noticed that she took time first to put on her eye patch.

"Two returns to Roanoke," she bellowed. She cast her uncovered eye at me. "That means round trip."

The agent passed the tickets beneath the grilled window. "That'll be $19.50."

I passed him two ten-dollar bills. "May I have a receipt, please?"

After I'd collected our tickets and the receipt, Harrie took my hand and led me toward the platforms.

"This way, Eej."

I followed along dutifully, and we reached the small waiting room. It contained three rows of seats and two long benches. About six other passengers sat on the chairs, reading newspapers or sipping from paper cups of coffee. They appeared to be business travelers. Through a set of double doors, I could see—and hear—the train waiting for us. The big diesel locomotives also hauled freight and mail in cars that sat forward of the passenger compartments. I noted with a twinge that the green passenger car closest to the engine was designated for colored passengers.

I shouldn't have been surprised to discover that those travelers had a separate waiting room from ours, too. But I was. And I felt a surge of embarrassment about why I'd never considered it. It was true that I'd never traveled by train before. In fact, I'd rarely ventured far enough away from Winston-Salem to travel by any means other than car or bus. But that didn't excuse my lack of thoughtfulness or curiosity about how complete and pervasive these social restrictions were.

When we were instructed to board, a bespectacled conductor wielding a large brass punch took our tickets and waved us toward the first passenger compartment located behind the colored car.

Harrie boarded with excitement and quickly claimed an upholstered bench-style window seat that was emblazoned with a large "Norfolk & Western Railway" logo across its high back. Other travelers boarded with less dispatch. It seemed clear that they were used to making this journey. Only one or two passengers appeared to be carrying any luggage. I surmised that meant we'd probably see quite a few of the same riders on our trip back home later that day.

I have to admit that it *was* thrilling for me when the big locomotive jerked forward and began its slow departure from Union Station. Traveling north through the area of East Winston locals called Reynoldstown, and along the planned route of the new North-South Expressway, I saw for the first time a part of the city I had never visited—but where so many people I knew had always lived. These depressed and forgotten neighborhoods hugged inhospitable, sloping stretches of terrain or wound along bottomland areas near ponds that appeared to be filled with rainwater or runoff from the nearby tobacco plants. It was a shocking tutorial on just how divided life in our city was.

Along a wide bend, where the tracks crossed North Liberty Street, I saw a young woman heading toward what plainly was an outhouse, located in a backyard that was filled with flattened cardboard and other trash. Visible in the hazy background behind her—just beyond an expanse of overgrown field—I could clearly see the distinctive outline of the downtown R.J. Reynolds Tobacco Company skyscraper.

If Harrie had noticed anything different about the landscape, she didn't comment on it. I knew her life in Reidsville had not been on a par with her new situation in Winston-Salem. I recalled her earlier observations about the condition of Fay Marian's backyard, and how it had not been that dissimilar from her previous home. My mother had always been loath to part with clutter, too. It had taken me the better part of a year to discard all the buttons, rolls of string, irregular bits of fabric, and folded stacks of brown paper she had stashed in virtually every drawer and closet. I knew that in the Harts's case, that same proclivity to allow things to pile up probably derived from a belief that one day, an old tire or rusted car bumper might become useful. It was a simple difference in scale. My unwillingness to embrace that axiom showed how firmly enmeshed in the confines of my picture-perfect, snow globe world I'd become.

It occurred to me that this trip to Paradise would push me beyond my boundaries in other ways I had not even thought about.

The train made several short stops in Walkertown, Salem Chapel, Pine Hall, Mayodan and Stoneville before crossing the state line and pulling into the tiny station in Paradise, Virginia. Fay Marian had been right when she'd winked and told me the city limits sign had "Welcome to Paradise" written on each side. It did appear to be a very small town. I wondered why the train still stopped there. No one got off or on. It was more like a rolling stop. Harrie and I would stop there on our way back to Winston-Salem, to visit the post office. I dearly hoped that, as predicted, we'd be able to walk to the post office easily from the station.

The train pulled into Roanoke closer to 9:45 than 9:20. I hoped Harrie's aunt hadn't been too inconvenienced by our late arrival. The station was exponentially busier than any of the previous stops. People seemed to be darting in all directions. But Harrie appeared unfazed by the beehive of activity.

"This way, Eej." She strode off toward the street exit and I followed her meekly.

Aunt Rochelle was easy to spot. I should say that Aunt Rochelle's *car* was easy to spot. The immaculate, bright yellow Thunderbird was parked—illegally—in a clearly marked loading zone. Its white convertible top was up, probably because it was at least fifteen degrees cooler there in the Roanoke Mountains. I pulled my sweater more tightly across my chest.

"There she is. Aunt Ro-Ro!" Harrie took off running toward a tallish woman standing near a painted balustrade. The woman was altogether . . . *provocatively* attired for 9:45 in the morning, and clearly was engaged in deep conversation with a good-looking man wearing a form-fitting business suit.

"Hello, you little Munchkin." Aunt Rochelle turned away from the man and faced Harrie with her long arms extended.

"Come and give your auntie some sugar."

The two of them embraced while I approached at a more sedate pace.

Rochelle stepped back and faced me. "You must be EJ. I'm Rochelle." She extended her hand. The color of her nail polish matched her bag and shoes perfectly. "Welcome to the Star City."

I shook her hand gratefully. "Miss Hart, I cannot thank you enough for being willing to meet with me today."

"Don't be silly." She put an arm around Harrie and hugged her close. "I won't pass on any opportunity to spend time with my favorite rug rat. Oh. Pardon me for being rude." She gestured toward the businessman, who was watching our interaction with great interest. Something about the directness of his gaze made me feel slightly uncomfortable. "EJ, this is my good friend, Hal . . ." She hesitated.

"Wilcox," the man added. He extended his hand to shake mine. "A pleasure. Are you going to be in town for long?"

"Don't be ridiculous, Hal." Rochelle swatted his arm. "EJ is here with my *niece*—just for the day . . . on official business."

"Oh." The man withdrew his hand and winked at me. "A pity. Perhaps another time?"

I was uncertain how to answer.

Rochelle clapped her hands together. "And we're *off*. You have a nice trip, Hal. I'll see you next . . ."

"Friday," he supplied.

"Friday it is." Rochelle leaned toward Hal and pecked him on the cheek. "Thanks for breakfast, doll."

I began to rethink this entire idea . . .

Harrie was already climbing into the back seat of Rochelle's car.

"Can we put the top down, Aunt Ro-Ro?"

"Not yet, sweetie. It's still too chilly." Rochelle waved me toward the front passenger seat. "Hop in, EJ. We'll head straight over to the store. I do my best work there."

Given her recent interactions with Hal, I doubted the veracity of that statement. But I complied with her request, and moments later we were on our way. The dashboard radio had roared to life when Rochelle started the car, and an earsplitting refrain from The Zodiacs filled the air.

Harrie began singing along in the back seat. "I waaaanttt you, stay-ay-ayyyy . . ." she crooned.

I wasn't very keen on popular music and the only reason I'd recognized the selection was because I'd heard it playing so many times on the transistor radio that Lottie kept in our office.

"How was the trip up?" Rochelle hollered over the music.

"Fine," I replied—then repeated it at a louder volume after Rochelle cupped her ear.

"Hang on," Rochelle yelled. "I'm gonna take a shortcut and skip some of this traffic."

She yanked the car's steering wheel sharply to the right and the Thunderbird bounced up over a curb and shot down a narrow alley between two buildings.

"Woo hoo!" Harrie called out. "Can we do that again, Aunt Ro-Ro? My head bounced off the roof!"

Rochelle exited the alley onto another street without stopping or slowing down. Brakes squealed, car horns blared, and at least one traumatized pedestrian shouted obscenities at us.

I was very happy I hadn't eaten much for breakfast. I don't think I'd have held onto very much of it after the ride from the train station.

Rochelle simply waved them all off. "I've never understood

how so many people can be that cranky this early in the morning," she declared. "It's a mystery to me."

She made another abrupt turn—without signaling—and squealed into a parking lot, screeching to a halt inches in front of the attendant's kiosk. He seemed to take her entrance in stride.

"Mornin' Miz Rochelle." He doffed his blue cap. "Why you comin' in to work on a Tuesday?"

Rochelle didn't bother lowering the volume on the car radio.

"Hi there, Willy," she yelled. "I've got my niece and a special visitor with me." She tossed her head toward the back seat.

Willy bent down to look inside the car and beamed when he saw Harrie. "Why there's little Miz Harriet. How're you doin' young lady?"

"Hi Willy! We're here on official post office business."

"Is that a fact?" He straightened up and pointed toward some vacant parking spaces. "Well, you all have a nice day takin' care of your business, Miz Rochelle."

"Thanks, Willy."

Rochelle hit the accelerator and we shot across the lot at a ridiculous rate of speed. I had no idea how she'd missed running over Willy's feet—or crashing into the brick wall of the Heironimus Department Store.

She shut the engine off. The sudden onset of quiet seemed unnatural after the din of our wild ride across town from Roanoke Station. I wasn't sure my legs would support me when I tried to stand up.

"Follow me, girls." Rochelle led the way toward a large metal door. "We're taking a shortcut. It's quicker than going around front to the street entrance."

I'd had just about enough of Rochelle's shortcuts. But Harrie and I dutifully followed behind her, like obedient lemmings.

Rochelle's "shortcut" led us through a loading zone to a massive warehouse that was packed to the gills with merchandise. Boxes were piled about a mile high on all sides. The dimly lighted space was like a retail canyon, and I had no idea how Rochelle navigated the space so seamlessly. Before I knew it, we'd passed through a set of double doors onto the sales floor of one of the most exclusive department stores in the city of Roanoke. A large plaque dominated the wall above a gleaming black concert grand piano. It proclaimed that S.H. Heironimus was committed to hiring "ethical, moral, hardworking, and religious people" who went on to serve its customers with "respect and dignity."

Following along behind the insistent swish and sway of Rochelle's leopard-print swing coat, I wondered just how long the Heironimus mantra had been emblazoned above the piano.

After passing through a half-dozen departments, we arrived at the cavernous area that housed the cosmetics counters.

Rochelle led us to an office that was discreetly tucked behind a massive fragrance display. Once inside, she shed her coat and stashed her handbag inside a locker.

"Welcome to my home away from home." She waved us into chairs. "Now show me your wares and let's get busy."

It occurred to me to wonder how often she used that very line in her social engagements . . .

I was immediately horrified by my thoughts.

Harrie immediately plopped down on a shopworn settee like she had not a care in the world. I was impressed by how easily she seemed to roll with whatever came her way. I envied her that trait.

I sat down on a straight-backed chair and withdrew the stack of letters from my ubiquitous leather bag. I saw Rochelle's nostrils twitch and flare immediately. She didn't even wait for me to pass the letters across the desk.

"That's *Vol de Nuit*," she gushed.

"Well, I know it may seem a tad unorthodox . . ."

"No," she insisted. "The letters. It's *Vol de Nuit*."

In desperation, I looked at Harrie for . . . what? Support? Solidarity? Some sort of confirmation that I had the legal right to ask for Rochelle's help identifying the scent on the stationery?

"What I mean to say is that I have the legitimate authority to examine these letters—in detail—to look for clues about the sender. It's the only way we can hope to return them to their rightful owner."

Rochelle looked at me quizzically. Then she got up from her chair and said, "Hold on a second. I'll be right back." She left the office and went out to the sales floor. I looked over at Harrie.

"What am I missing here?"

Harrie shrugged. "Don't worry. Aunt Rochelle always knows what she's doin'."

I wasn't so sure I shared her point of view.

I heard the door open and close, followed by a soft, whooshing sound.

A cloud of something fragrant—and familiar—wafted past my face.

My eyes widened and I swiveled on my chair to face Rochelle. She was holding a perfume tester bearing a spritz nozzle.

"Is that . . . ?"

"*Vol de Nuit*?" she repeated. "Yes. That's the name of the perfume. I recognized it immediately. I even wear it myself sometimes. We sell it, but it's expensive and a special order. And I'm certain we're the only store between here and Richmond that can even get it."

"I told you, Eej," Harrie chimed in from the settee.

"That kid's got a nose." Rochelle nodded toward her niece. "She could have a real career in this game—but I don't think it's in the cards."

I wanted to ask why not, but didn't get the chance. Harrie beat me to it.

"How come, Aunt Ro-Ro? You said I could find mushrooms."

"Truffles," I reminded her.

Rochelle narrowed her eyes. "How long have you two been spending time together?"

I chose to overlook her question. "You're absolutely certain this is the same scent that's on these letters?"

"I'd stake my T-Bird on it." Rochelle reclaimed her seat and looked at me thoughtfully. "You know, EJ . . . that fragrance works for you. I think you should consider taking a tester home and trying it out." She thrust the tiny bottle into my hands.

"What? Um. No . . . I don't think so."

"Why not? Wear it to your next cocktail party and see if it nets any positive results."

Cocktail party? Rochelle did *understand that I was a postal inspector, didn't she?*

"I appreciate that. But I think I'd like to stay focused on one mystery at a time."

"You *do* know what Guerlain says about the fragrance?"

I confessed that I had not the slightest idea.

Rochelle retrieved a shiny Guerlain brochure from a drawer and read the description. *"Vol de Nuit* is a fragrance dedicated to adventurous women who nourish their passion for risk-taking, and know how to claim their place in a man's world without losing their femininity."

How well that description suited Dorothea was without dispute. I did not, however, believe it described me at all.

Rochelle was still regarding me with interest. "Do you always wear your hair that way?"

Instinctively, I raised a hand to my hair. "What do you mean?"

"She means that ol' bun, Eej. It is kinda tight."

I looked over at Harrie. "My . . . *bun?*"

Harrie nodded. "It's kinda like Miss Kitty's hairdo, Eej."

"Without the rest of her assets," Rochelle added drily.

"Wait a minute . . ." I looked back and forth between them. "This trip is *not* about me, my hairdo, *or* how I smell. And furthermore, I don't *go* to cocktail parties."

"That's true. She don't go to parties," Harrie assured her aunt. "She drinks a lotta Postum, though."

Rochelle stood up. "Tell you what. How about we go up front and discuss the likelihood that your missing person probably special orders her *Vol de Nuit* here? You'll be more comfortable up there and we can chat up some of the other girls at the counter. They'll have information about special-order customers, too."

I was relieved that we finally were getting someplace.

"That would be wonderful."

It wasn't until I was seated in the "more comfortable" chair—with a black cape draped over my shoulders—that I realized what Rochelle had in mind.

I tried to object, but it was futile. Rochelle gently pushed me back against the chair.

"Trust me," she said.

My thoughts swung back to "Hal" at the train station.

Right then, *trust* seemed like a foreign land—one with a closed border. I was trapped in makeover hell, and no passport in the world could free me from my predicament.

"What are you going to do?" I asked. My voice sounded small and defeated. I didn't recognize it.

Rochelle bent close to my face. "Only what God intended."

"Want a Yoo-hoo, Eej? I know where the break room is."

I looked over at Harrie, who stood beneath a towering ad for Guerlain perfumes. A slogan was emblazoned above her tousled head. *Vol de Nuit. Are you her type?*

I decided to give up.

"Why the hell not?" I told Harrie.

It turned out that for Rochelle, what "God intended" for me included unpinning and brushing out my long red hair, shaping my eyebrows, lengthening my eyelashes, and applying base and powder coats to my face.

I felt like a ski slope . . .

While she worked, she queried her colleagues about any women they knew who special ordered *Vol de Nuit*. Since all the women picked their special orders up in the store, none of the perfume was mailed to any home addresses. But Rochelle pointed out that we were lucky: there had been only eighteen special orders for the fragrance last year—and only four since January. She noted that there had been enough interest in the product that the cosmetics manager planned to add the perfume to the store's inventory in the next quarter.

"That'll bring the price down out of the stratosphere." Rochelle was brushing my cheeks with some kind of pale pink powder. "Special orders are always about twice as expensive as things we carry in the store—and this one already costs more than a new set of snow tires."

"Is there any way I could get a copy of the names of the women who have ordered the perfume within the last year?" I knew I was treading on thin ice, but without the names, the information was next to worthless.

A salesclerk who was restocking lipsticks in a glass case spoke up. "It's not just women. Some of those orders came from men."

"Probably gifts for their wives," another clerk chimed in.

"In your dreams, Darnelle," Rochelle said with disgust. "I doubt *any* of it went to their *wives*."

"You'd know better'n me about that." The woman named Darnelle stood with her hands on her shapely hips and admired Rochelle's progress with my . . . transformation. "I swanny, Rochelle. She's starting to look like Rita Hayworth."

"That was the idea."

I wanted to steal a look, but I was too terrified. I wondered how long it would take me to scrub off my second face when I finally got home.

I needed to remember to pick up a jar of Noxzema before we left the store.

"Hey, Aunt Ro-Ro?" Harrie had been sifting through a box of closeouts displayed at the end of a counter. "Would any of these perfumes work on a dog?"

"A dog?" Rochelle sounded intrigued. "Did your daddy finally let you get a dog?"

"No . . ." Harrie was dejected. "I wanted to get some for Mr. Hauser's dog."

"Mr. Hauser lives in the apartment next door to Harrie and her father," I explained.

"Try not to talk for a minute. Okay, EJ?" Rochelle bent closer. "I'm going to paint your lips."

Paint my lips . . . with what?

"Why does this man's dog need perfume?" Rochelle asked.

"He kinda stinks." Harrie made a face. "Like mothballs

and rotten cabbage."

Rochelle laughed. "It sounds like what he needs is a bath, Munchkin—not twenty-dollar perfume."

"A bath?" Harrie brightened up. "Hey, Eej? Do you think Mr. Hauser would let me give Morty a bath? I could use Fay Marian's hose. Not them ones out back with all the rips in them. There's a pretty good one I found under the front porch when I was checkin' the area for blasting caps."

I looked up at Rochelle with raised—and newly arched—eyebrows.

"Go ahead." She stepped back.

"I think you could ask Mr. Hauser," I said. "Very politely. See if he would like for you to give Mortimer a bath."

"I don't know why he wouldn't." Harrie looked confused. "Who wants a dog around that smells that bad?"

"I'd leave out any references to mothballs or rotting cabbage," I added. "I think Mr. Hauser would be more sympathetic to your cause if he thinks you're just trying to be neighborly . . . and nice."

"Okaaaayyyy." She stared at her sneakers. "Who knew bein' a neighbor had so many rules?"

"And, Harrie?"

She looked up at me.

"Why on earth were you looking for blasting caps?"

"Carla told me she saw a commercial about 'em on TV. She said they could blow your hand clean off. She said they were slicker'n snot, and would probably work a whole lot better takin' out them train tracks than settin' old croquet mallets on fire."

"Well, I don't expect you'll find any under Fay Marian's porch." I decided to ignore the latest evidence of Carla Hotbed's express trajectory toward prison. "And if they're that dangerous, you shouldn't be looking for them in the first place."

"I told Fay Marian about 'em, since she's still diggin' in the backyard. And how Carla said they could be disguised as ordinary stuff . . . like cement squirrels."

I was intrigued. "What did she say?"

"She said it was good to know, and that them things could really jack up your car."

I sighed.

"Listen to EJ, toots." Rochelle was standing back to admire her handiwork. "You don't want to end up in reform school. It's bad for the skin. Besides," she reached out with a soft brush and touched an area of my cheek that still wasn't to her liking, "if you blow up all the train tracks, you won't be able to come up here to visit as often."

Harrie considered that consequence. "Okay. But at least we know the porch is secure."

"That is good news," I agreed.

"All right," Rochelle announced. "I think my work here is through. Ready to take a look, EJ?"

I wasn't at all certain I was. But Darnelle and another salesclerk named Paula were exclaiming over her progress.

"Dang, Rochelle . . . you should sign this."

"It's one of your best jobs ever."

"But . . ." the woman named Paula pointed at the crown of my head. "Don't you think a tad more loft on the hair would add more magic? I'd tease that up a little."

Rochelle disagreed. "The trick to a great makeover is work like a sculptor: your job is to take things *away*, not add more than you need."

She's right, Paula," Darnelle agreed. "It's like Coco Chanel said: before you leave the house, take one thing off."

Rochelle swung my chair around so I could look in the mirror.

I was . . . speechless. I didn't recognize the face of the woman looking back at me. It wasn't that she looked bad—or even cheap, which was what I had feared. She just looked like a stranger. I felt . . . *exposed*. As if the makeup had revealed me—not covered me up.

"You look great, Eej." Harrie gave my transformation a ringing endorsement. "Wait'll Fay Marian sees you."

"I am *not* letting Fay Marian see this," I declared.

"Why not? You're a *dish*. Fay Marian says that to Miss Inez all the time."

I looked at her with surprise.

"Miss Inez is gonna love this cause she *really* likes your hair. She says it's good enough to make wigs. Expensive ones."

I sighed. "Well, at least she didn't say cheap ones . . ."

"Trust me, honey." Rochelle fluffed my hair and pushed one side of it off my shoulder. "There's nothing cheap about how you look. We just need *one* finishing touch."

Oh, dear heaven. What was she going to do next? Add an artfully placed, two-inch beauty spot?

Rochelle retrieved the bottle of *Vol de Nuit* and spritzed the air above me, before rotating my chair through the mist.

"Now you're ready," she declared.

Ready? "Ready for what?" I asked with wonder.

Paula spoke up. "I'd say ready to take on all comers."

"And goers," Darnelle added. Paula laughed merrily.

"Just let me get up that list of names," Rochelle said, "before we head out for lunch. You girls need to be back at the station by 1:45 to give you time for that stop in Paradise."

Rochelle walked off to compile the list for me. I realized that I needed to thank her for her . . . *efforts* on my behalf. But words were eluding me right then.

Harrie approached my chair and stood beside me so she could look at my reflection in the mirror.

"Face it, Eej," she observed. "It ain't every day you get a good comb-out and a Yoo-hoo."

I narrowed my tastefully shadowed eyes and regarded her.

"Are you sure you're only ten years old?"

Rochelle returned bearing her coat and both of our bags. She handed me a folded sheet of paper. "That should be enough to get you started. Now some of these people special ordered other things, too. But all of the *Vol de Nuit* purchasers will be included on this list. Maybe you'll have luck checking these names out at that post office in Paradise."

I took the paper from her gratefully and stashed it securely in my bag. If the post office didn't yield any useful results, I could always visit the town library and consult the city directory. *If Paradise even* had *a public library* . . .

"Rochelle," I began. "I don't want to seem ungrateful. You're obviously very . . . *accomplished* at your craft. I'm . . . flattered that you took the time on your day off to . . . tend to me in this . . . in this special way."

"Honey?" Rochelle laid a manicured hand on my arm. "A new face is no different than a new pair of shoes. You have to try it out for a while to see if it fits. If you decide it does? Well, you just come on back up here and I'll fit you out with everything you need. Okay?"

I gave her a small smile. "Okay."

"Now." She clapped her hands together. "Let's go get some lunch. I don't know about you, but I could use a little hair of the dog."

"Oh?" Darnelle observed. "Big date last night?"

135

"Maybe." Rochelle fluffed her own auburn locks.

"Who was it this time?" Darnelle asked. "That Coty salesman?"

"Really, Darnelle. He *has* a name."

"Oh, yeah?" Darnelle asked Rochelle. "What is it?"

"It's . . . *Hal*. Hal . . .?" She looked at me for help.

"Wilcox," I supplied.

"He comes back on Friday," Harrie added.

Rochelle explained that we were having lunch at the Ponce de Leon Hotel, which was less than a ten-minute walk from the store. We made our way toward the street entrance.

Harrie got distracted by a colorful kitchen appliance display near the Jefferson Street exit, and stopped to look over the newest products. Rochelle hadn't noticed that her niece had been lagging behind, so I hurried back to fetch her.

"Come on, Harrie. We don't want to get lost."

"Did'ja see these Osterizers, Eej? They're *really* nifty. We could make Yoo-hoo milkshakes."

"Yes, they are. But what *won't* be nifty is if we lose Rochelle. So come, on. We need to hustle."

Harrie was still caught up in her retail trance. "They have a 30-cup coffeemaker, too." She looked at me with amazement. "You could fix us enough Postum to last a whole *week*."

"Harrie?" I grabbed hold of her hand, "We have to go, *now*." I whipped around to steer her back toward the exit, precisely in time to slam, full speed, into a female customer who had just entered the store.

It was humiliating. The woman grabbed hold of me in a desperate attempt to prevent herself from falling and ended up getting tangled in the shoulder strap of my leather bag. We stumbled sideways and nearly upset a tower of Enna Jettick shoes. I'd never been more embarrassed.

"Oh, dear . . . I'm *so* sorry," I gushed and tried to help the woman regain her balance. "Are you all right? I cannot apologize enough for my clumsiness."

"I'm fine." The frustrated shopper finally succeeded in freeing her arm from the strap of my bag. "No harm done." She took a step backward and looked at me. I saw her blink a few times and a strange expression suffused her face. I couldn't tell if it was shock or annoyance. "Are you . . . is that . . .?" She didn't finish her question.

"I am so terribly sorry," I repeated. "Please forgive me. We were just in a rush to catch up with our friend. She's taking us to lunch and we're not local—so I was in a hurry to not lose sight of her."

"It's fine." The woman was still eyeing me strangely. "You'd better run on if you want to stay with her." She gestured toward the street door.

"Yes. You're right." I reached out for Harrie. "Come on, Harrie. Let's get going so we can try and catch up with your aunt."

I glanced back at the woman who continued to stare at me with an unreadable expression.

"Thank you, again, for your understanding."

We promptly continued on our way to catch up with Rochelle. We'd nearly reached the door when I dared to sneak a last look back behind us. The flustered woman still stood in the same place, watching us leave.

"Hey, lady?" Harrie called out to her. "Check out them Osterizers. *They're on sale.*"

I didn't think it was possible for our day to get any stranger. It would be a couple more hours before I realized how wrong my prediction was.

Our train back to Winston-Salem was running about thirty-five minutes late, but I assured Rochelle that we'd be just fine waiting on our own in the station.

"We've already taken up too much of your day off," I apologized. "But I cannot thank you enough for your help —and for your . . ." I struggled to find the right word to characterize my metamorphosis. "For my *improvements*. It was very unselfish of you, and most unexpected."

"Just do me a favor and live with it for a little while? Before you crack into that jar of Noxzema you didn't think I saw you buy?"

I blushed. "I'll try. Thank you again."

"Don't worry about it. I'd do anything for this kid." Rochelle hugged Harrie. "And it's obvious that you're now part of *her* family—so that makes you part of *my* family, too."

I was very moved by Rochelle's pronouncement. "Thank you, Rochelle."

Rochelle wished us luck with our detour to the Paradise post office, waved good-bye, and disappeared in a swirl of leopard.

"Hey, Eej?" Harrie nudged me. "Those men over there keep staring at you."

"What men?" I cast about the waiting room. Sure enough, I saw several bored-looking businessmen seated on a row of chairs, all pretending to read newspapers. I could see them continuously taking surreptitious looks in our direction. I wasn't sure how I felt about that. I was used to being invisible, and I liked the freedom that went hand in hand with it. This? This was something altogether different for me.

"Let's sit down over there." I indicated some chairs that were out of the direct sight line of the business travelers.

"You can't blame those men, Eej. It's not their fault you look like a dish."

Dish? I hardly thought my conservative gray travel suit rendered me the least bit . . . *dishy.*

I closed my eyes. "Harrie? That's not helping."

"How come?"

"I'm not sure this sort of presentation is truly representative of who I am."

"That don't make sense, Eej."

I looked down at her. "*Doesn't* make sense."

"Okaaayyy, already," Harrie said with chagrin. "*Doesn't* make sense. Rochelle didn't change nothin' about you, Eej. It's still your same face and hair. Carla always said only tramps and country-western singers look cheap, on account of they don't know how to do makeup right. But Aunt Rochelle is a professional, and she did everything perfect on you." Harrie sat back and looked me over. "It all looks real good, Eej. Just like you was born this way."

I thought about correcting her grammar, but decided that doing so would only make her double down on her observations. "Thank you, Harrie. I appreciate that."

She nudged me. "That ticket man keeps starin' at you, too. I bet they think you're a movie star."

"I don't think so."

Harrie had moved on. "Do you think Mr. Hauser will let me give Morty a bath?"

"I'm not sure. I hope so."

"He loves them Ken-L Treats. That whole box is mostly gone."

That surprised me. We'd just purchased them on Saturday. "How many are you giving him at a time?"

"I don't get to see him very much, so I have to make sure he gets enough to make it worth it. So, I stick 'em under their apartment door at night when Mr. Hauser is watchin' TV. Morty likes that a lot. I hear him sniffin' around on the other side of the door."

"Why don't you ask Mr. Hauser if he'd like you to take Mortimer for longer walks?"

"Do you think he would?"

"I think he might. Exercise would be good for him."

"Yeah," Harrie agreed. "He is kinda fat."

I bent toward her. "All those extra treats probably are not helping."

The conductor entered the waiting room and announced that our train was arriving. All the assembled travelers collected their belongings and moved toward the door that led to the platform. When Harrie and I approached, all the men who had already queued up quickly stepped aside and waved us to the head of the line. Their appreciative stares felt like a hundred pinpricks as we walked past them. I had a difficult time keeping my composure.

I'd never experienced a power dynamic quite like that before. I was both charmed and appalled. It was so transparent and yet so unexpectedly . . . flattering. If I hadn't been so timid, I'd have tried an experimental hair flip, like I'd seen Rochelle demonstrate earlier with poor Hal, the besotted Coty salesman.

But what would be the point? That kind of power was wasted if you didn't have anyone you cared to impress. I wondered idly if the same dynamic would work as effectively with other women—and if I'd have had an easier time with that crusty volunteer in the Old Salem administrative office . . .

Probably not.

On the other hand, Inez certainly seemed to use her feminine wiles to great advantage with Fay Marian.

But I was pretty sure that whatever was transpiring between them wasn't typical.

Unless one considered the type of encounters Dorothea had described in her letters . . .

The platform doors opened and Harrie grabbed my hand to lead us toward the passenger car where we'd find seats for the short trip to Paradise.

Harrie and I exited the one-room station building in the tiny hamlet of Paradise, Virginia, and asked a porter for directions to the post office. He pointed across a rather bleak-looking landscape toward a two-lane road that ran past what looked like a boarded-up service station.

"You walk one block past that ol' Esso station there and take a right. The post office is the second white buildin' on the left, right past the garden. You can't miss it. Just look for the flags out front."

We thanked him and struck out on the last leg of our epic journey.

"Y'all make sure you're back by no later'n 3:50," he called after us. "They ain't no more trains to Winston from here after that."

We'd be cutting it close—especially if the postmaster were in an accommodating mood and tried to help us cull through the list of *Vol de Nuit* customers to identify the ones who might live in Paradise.

It was a tall order.

During the short train ride from Roanoke, I'd managed to

rewrite the list of names in alphabetical order on a clean sheet of paper. I thought that might help expedite our search.

The town of Paradise appeared to be made up of no more than five or six city blocks, filled mostly with ramshackle houses and swaths of mostly empty storefronts. What few businesses remained open appeared to tilt toward low-end retail establishments and public service agencies. I saw one bank, an old movie theater, and, to my amazement, a small public library. The porter had been right, and the Paradise United States Post Office was easy to spot. It was a square, white frame building with a gravel parking lot. It had a wooden picnic table set up on a narrow swath of grass that ran along one side of the lot. A large hickory tree towered over it and probably cast welcome shade on hot summer days.

Only one car sat in the parking lot. I was glad for that. It meant the place was probably not very busy. Hopefully, we wouldn't have to wait too long to meet with the postmaster.

I noticed Harrie digging something out of the front pocket of her pedal pushers. It was her eye patch.

"Do you think you'll be needing that here?" I asked.

She put it on. "You never know."

I held the door open for her. "Good thinking."

Once inside, I took a deep breath. This place had the same distinctive smell that all rural post offices had. It came from that jumbled confluence of paper, leather, adhesive, cardboard and mildew. I'd never set foot inside one of these outposts that didn't smell exactly this same way. Daddy always told me it was the sweet scent of promises kept.

I prayed his words would prove prophetic.

We approached the small counter, but I didn't see anyone working. Harrie noticed a hand-lettered sign that read, "Ring bell for service." So, I took hold of the battered hand bell that sat atop the counter and gave it a tentative shake. I heard a door open and close, and a woman appeared from behind a bank of shelves. She stopped dead in her tracks when she saw me.

It was the woman I'd nearly knocked over while hurrying out of the department store.

"Oh, my," I blurted out. "It's *you*."

"Small world," she finally said. She was carrying a bin of mail, and she set it down atop an old oak desk that was nearly covered with other bins and wire baskets before approaching the counter where we stood. She noticed Harrie standing beside me. I could see her eyes narrow as she did a slow double take.

It had to be the eye patch. It was rather unsettling at first.

"Did you buy one of them Osterizers?" Harrie asked enthusiastically.

"No," the woman said drily. "I managed to resist temptation."

"Too bad." Harrie shook her head dejectedly. "I wanted to make Yoo-hoo milkshakes."

It was quiet for a moment. Then the woman said, "Those *would* be pretty good."

"Well, I know this is awkward," I began. "But my name is EJ Cloud and I'm a postal inspector from Winston-Salem. I called the other day to speak with the postmaster here."

"*You're* a postal inspector?" The woman sounded incredulous.

"Yes." I had my ID card at the ready, and I handed it to her. "I manage the area's regional DLO."

"I remember you." The woman handed my card back. "I mean, from *before* you nearly knocked me over. I was the person with whom you spoke."

Just my luck . . .

"Oh. So, then, could you tell me if the postmaster is here today?"

"You came all the way up here from Winston-Salem," she eyed Harrie again, "with your . . . assistant . . . to talk with the postmaster about *what*, exactly?"

I was reluctant to disclose more than necessary to this . . . most unaccommodating person.

"I'm sorry. It's a matter of some sensitivity. Would you kindly connect me with the postmaster, please?"

Our standoff continued.

The woman was about my age, as near as I could tell. She might even have been considered attractive, if she'd been able to summon up an expression that wasn't a scowl. I was about to channel my inner Lottie and try to pull rank on her when she reached behind an adding machine and slid a wooden nameplate across the counter to rest in front of her. It read: *B.L. Troy, Postmaster.*

I met her gray eyes. "*You're* the postmaster?"

"Surprises seem to be going around."

I was flustered. "Why didn't you tell me so in the first place?" When Troy didn't reply, I hurriedly asked, "Is there a place we might go to discuss the reason for my visit?"

She looked dubious and cast a look at Harrie.

"Don't worry about Harrie. She's . . . self-sufficient."

"I'll go hang out at the picnic table. I brought a book to read, didn't I, Eej?"

I looked at B.L. Troy, Postmaster. "She brought a book."

"All right." Troy sighed. "But you'll have to make it quick. I don't have anyone else to staff the counter."

"Fine." I swung my bag around and pulled out the book Harrie had picked up at Walgreen's on Saturday. I saw Troy eyeing the bag with curiosity. Probably she recognized it as a mail carrier's satchel.

Harrie had first selected *The Cricket in Times Square* by George Selden. I'd been dubious about the reading level of the book when she showed it to me, but she was sure she could manage it.

"I can ask you about any words I don't know, right, Eej?" she'd asked. Harrie then said she was already pretty sure I would, since I always corrected most of the words she *did* know.

I'd told her of course I would help her, but suggested maybe it would work better as a book we read together. Harrie was very enthusiastic about that idea. In the end, I'd bought the Selden book and helped Harrie select another book to read on her own. She ended up with *Beezus and Ramona*, by Beverly Cleary. I was convinced the wild exploits of the precocious and untamed Ramona Quimby would hold Harrie's interest.

I handed the Ramona book to her. "Now, Harrie? You take this book to the picnic table, and you *stay* there. No wandering around. No exploring. *No changing plans.* Understood?"

She nodded. "I promise, Eej."

"Okay. I'll be out to meet you in just a few minutes, and we can head back to the station to catch our train home."

Harrie nodded and lifted her eye patch. "Bye, Postmaster." She waved at Troy.

"Goodbye . . . *Harrie*. Meeting you was an experience."

"See you in a bit, Eej." Harrie made a beeline for the door and headed straight for the picnic table at a determined lope.

I faced the dour postmaster . . . *postmistress*.

"So." She replaced her nameplate with a neatly hand-lettered sign that read *back in 15 minutes* before impatiently waving a hand to suggest I should meet her near the door at the end of the counter.

I obeyed her directive, and she unlocked the door to admit me to that holiest of holies—the sorting and processing area. Once she'd closed and secured the door behind me, she indicated that I should follow her into a small, private office.

She did not invite me to sit down, but I chose to, anyway. I had decided I no longer wished to be intimidated by this inhospitable public servant.

"I'll get right to the point of my visit," I said and placed the alphabetical list I'd created on the short train ride from Roanoke on her desk. "About two weeks ago, I received a packet of letters that had been wrongly delivered to a nonexistent addressee, care of the gardens at Old Salem." I withdrew the letters from my bag and handed them to Troy. "You can see that they all are very distinctive. Written by the same person on the same stationery, and all postmarked here, in Paradise, Virginia."

Troy flipped through the letters quickly, with what appeared to be a singular lack of interest.

"Why bring them back here?" she asked. "They appear to have been properly delivered."

"Well. 'Properly delivered' is not exactly accurate. There is not, and has never been, an individual by that name affiliated with the gardens."

"How do you know that?"

I was taken aback by the directness of her question.

"Because the letters were returned to us by the current master gardener, a woman named Evelyn Haas. She stated that no one engaged with the gardens had that name."

"I reiterate: why bring the letters back here?" She held one up. "They have no return address. I can't do anything with them other than send them right back to your office."

"That would normally be true," I agreed. "But in this case, we have more to go on."

Troy actually seemed intrigued. "What is that?"

"You may have noticed that the letters all bear a distinctive fragrance?"

"Not really," Troy replied. "I assumed that scent was *your* perfume."

I fought to stifle a blush. "Well, that part is complicated—and unrelated. But believe me: when considered on their own, the letters all carry the same fragrance."

Troy sat back in her creaky oak desk chair and folded her arms. "I fail to see how that has any relevance."

"Miss Troy? You may not realize that my job entails following *any* leads or clues that might assist with the rightful delivery, or return, of dead letters. The United States Postal Service takes this process *very* seriously, and we are charged with exhausting all possibilities that might assist with carrying out the sacred commission that defines the mission of the DLO."

She stared back at me for a moment before replying, "It's Mrs. Troy."

"My apologies."

"What would you have me do, Miss Cloud?"

I picked up the list of names I'd received from Rochelle. "I was able to get a successful ID on the fragrance at the department store in Roanoke where I ... *ran into you* ... earlier." I passed the list to her. "The perfume is available by special order only. This is the list of area customers who have ordered the perfume, called *Vol de Nuit*, within the past year."

Troy scanned the list of names. "I don't see *your* name on this list." She looked up at me. "Or do you buy yours in Winston-Salem?"

I was finding it difficult to maintain my composure.

"*I* don't wear the perfume," I explained, "or haven't, until today. As I said . . . that part is *complicated*."

"So far, everything about your errand seems complicated."

I sighed in frustration. "It would be supremely helpful if you would, please, look over the list and identify for me the names of any customers you recognize who live in Paradise."

Troy scanned the list again. "Are there any names in particular you're looking for?"

"None in particular. Well—perhaps anyone named Dorothea?"

Troy laughed. "Miss Cloud. This is a small town. Population 567. Most of the residents are female and quite elderly, and at least a quarter of them have names that are derivatives of Dorothy."

I withdrew a pencil from a cup on her desk and handed it to her. "If you would be so kind?"

Troy took the pencil. I saw her go through the list of names and make small tic marks next to a couple of them. She passed the paper back to me.

"Those are the only names I recognize."

I looked at the names she'd indicated. "And do you know where these people live?"

"You mean street addresses?"

I nodded.

"No. Everyone in this town gets their mail from a PO box inside this building. We have no home delivery." I noticed her glance at my father's old mailbag again.

It seemed like my best hope for solving our mystery had reached a dead end. Unless . . .

"Do you have a copy of the town's City Directory?" I asked.

I saw something flicker across her face. It was probably just impatience with my errand. We'd been sitting in her office long enough to have heard at least three patrons enter and exit the lobby.

"Nope." She checked her wristwatch. "If that's all, Miss Cloud, I do need to get back up front."

I sighed and returned the letters and list to my bag. "Of course. Thank you for your time."

"Sorry I wasn't more help." To my thinking, she sounded anything but sorry.

"Would you do a me one last favor," I asked, "and give me one of your cards? Just in case I think of anything else that might be useful."

Troy gave a bitter-sounding laugh. "The government doesn't supply us with any *cards* up here."

She retrieved a notepad and jotted down her name, telephone number, and the post office hours. She tore off the sheet and handed it to me. "This is the number for the phone that rings back here. When I'm up front working, it's harder for me to be social."

I wanted to tell her that I'd already discovered that.

"Thank you. You've been very . . . *helpful.*"

"I doubt it." Troy got to her feet. "But you're welcome, just the same."

She did not offer to shake my hand, and that, strangely, relieved me. I turned to leave, but she stopped me before I reached the door.

"Miss Cloud? I do have one question."

"All right," I asked. "What is it?"

"I noticed that only two of the letters have been opened. Why not all of them?"

"We have strict procedures governing the disposition of dead letters, Mrs. Troy. They may only be opened and examined for any clues that might assist in delivery forty-five days after receipt."

"And who does that? You?"

"That's correct."

She nodded but didn't ask any other questions.

I let myself out and exited the small building to go and find Harrie.

What a colossal waste of time. In my mind, people like Mrs. Troy were precisely the kind of people who gave career civil service employees a bad reputation.

Predictably, I did not see Harrie seated at the picnic table when I crossed the parking lot.

What was it with this child? Why could she not follow the simplest instruction?

In frustration, I began to cast about for her. I sighed with relief when I caught sight of her, over near the opposite side of the garden, engaged in conversation with an elderly couple.

That kid knows no strangers, Fay Marian had observed.

She'd certainly been right about that. I walked toward where they stood.

"Harriet?" I called out. "Are you ready to head for the train station?"

"Hey, Eej? Come over and meet Mr. and Mrs. Truitt. They've lived here *forever*."

The Truitts watched me approach with unbridled curiosity. I blamed Rochelle for that. I was sure I made quite a spectacle crossing the gravel lot. And I was equally curious about what tale Harrie had spun about the reason for our visit to their town.

Maybe she'd told them we were there to look for blasting caps?

"How do you do," I said. "I'm EJ Cloud, and am up here for a spot of post office business. Harriet here was kind enough to accompany me on the trip."

"I already told 'em that, Eej."

"Howdy." Mr. Truitt seemed to have a great economy with words.

Mrs. Truitt didn't say anything at all.

"They live two streets back," Harrie explained, "by the sawmill. They came in to get their mail, but there wadn't any. Miz Truitt was upset 'cause her sociable security money was supposed to be here today."

I was amazed that Harrie had been able to extract even that much information from these two stone-faced residents of Paradise.

I wondered if Mrs. Truitt's first name was Dorothy . . .

"I'm very sorry about that." I felt the need to apologize for the sins of the United States Postal Service. "Sometimes, federal mail can take longer to reach a destination when it arrives by train." I was fairly certain this was how Mrs. Troy received all the branch's mail from the Roanoke distribution center. *And* I had noticed a canvas bag of mail being unloaded when Harrie and I were in the station.

Mr. Truitt nodded at me. "At figgers." He took hold of his wife's elbow. "Come on, Dottie. Let's head on home. We can come back and check fer it later on."

"Bye." Harrie waved at them. "Thanks for talkin' with me."

"You take care now, young lady." Mr. Truitt waved back. "We enjoyed our little chat."

The Truitts turned around and shuffled off in what I guessed was the direction of the sawmill.

"Did you get to read any of your book?" I asked Harrie.

"A little bit. Did you know Ramona's aunt has a yellow convertible, too?"

I smiled at her. "I did, actually. That's why I thought you might enjoy the stories."

We started to make our way back to the train station.

"I wonder if the book has any men named Hal?"

I told her I didn't imagine it did.

It had been a long day, and Harrie was yawning by the time we claimed our seats for the ride back to Winston-Salem. I calculated that we'd likely arrive at Union Station sometime after 6 p.m. I worried about keeping Harrie out so late and knew that her father would be at work by the time I dropped her off at home. I didn't know if Johnnie Hart would've thought to prepare Harrie's dinner or not, so I resolved to fix her something to eat at my house before taking her back to their apartment.

I didn't expect Harrie to object. After all, it was Tuesday night, and I was pretty sure Harrie would want to watch *Wyatt Earp* on TV.

One thing I had learned about Harrie was the depth of her devotion to TV Westerns.

She was sound asleep and drooped against my arm within a few minutes of the train leaving the station. I didn't blame her. The rhythmic clacking sound made by the train rolling along over rail joints was hypnotic. If I hadn't been so keyed up, I probably would've dozed off myself. But my mind was just too active.

I took advantage of the quiet and the chance to think over everything that had occurred that day. There was much to consider—and most of it had nothing to do with the official reason for the errand.

Harrie's Aunt Rochelle had proved to be consistent with what I'd been led to expect. Her eclectic social engagements were, indeed, eye opening. But even with that, she proved herself to be a shrewd businesswoman with sharp instincts and a no-nonsense approach to relationships. I envied her that. Rochelle exuded confidence and independence. And it was evident that she adored her niece. Harrie's fondness for her aunt had not been misplaced.

I decided that I liked her.

Although I was still extremely uncomfortable with the liberties she'd taken with my appearance. Rochelle had instructed me to "live with it" for a while before deciding it wasn't "a fit" for me. *Could I do that?*

I raised a hand to smooth the length of red hair that now lay across my shoulder. I was positive my mother would've taken one look at me and declared that I looked like a floozie. But I was equally sure that if Lottie could see me, she'd clap her hands with joy.

It was my own opinion that mattered. And I honestly had no idea what I felt—except awkward.

I glanced down at Harrie's face, relaxed and at peace—like she had not a care in the world.

After Rochelle had completed her handiwork, Harrie had told me I looked "like a dish."

But then, Harrie also thought Carla Hotbed was a reliable arbiter of polite society.

It was clear I wouldn't solve this part of the mystery anytime soon.

My thoughts shifted to a consideration of my frustrating interactions with that awful postmistress, Mrs. Troy. What on earth had led that woman to be so irksome and unhelpful? It didn't make any sense to me at all. And why had she made that overtly sarcastic remark to me about the *Vol de Nuit*? *That* had been entirely inappropriate—and unprofessional.

I decided that I didn't like her.

Which didn't matter much because she'd shared next to no information that was helpful. The only thing I'd managed to get from her was confirmation of the names of customers from Paradise who'd special ordered the perfume at Rochelle's store in Roanoke.

I looked over the list again, and the tiny checkmarks Mrs. Troy had placed beside the names she recognized as belonging to women in Paradise. There were only two—and it was worth noting that neither of them was named Dorothy:

Darlene Boitnott

Brooke Casaubon

I supposed that for a town the size of Paradise, even boasting *two* residents who special ordered the exotic perfume was some kind of a claim to fame. But without knowing anything more about these two women, I was still pretty much stuck back at square one.

I'd have to wait and see what Lottie thought about it all in the morning.

I spent the rest of the trip back to Winston-Salem thinking about the remaining letters and wondering if they would offer us any more clues. Lottie had been encouraging me to go ahead and read them without waiting the full forty-five days required by our procedures. She'd insisted that this formality was pointless because it was abundantly clear that no one would mysteriously show up to claim the correspondence. And I now knew from Inez that the addressee, Mary Ann Evans, was never intended to be the actual recipient.

Maybe Lottie was right. What good purpose would be served by waiting another two to three weeks to examine the remaining letters for additional clues?

As carefully as possible, I withdrew the stack of letters from the bag at my feet. I didn't want to risk waking Harrie, who now was softly snoring. I selected the third letter by the date on its postmark and carefully opened its flap. It contained two sheets of paper. I unfolded it and began to read.

Dear Mary Ann,

A full week has passed since last I opened my heart to you about events I would wish not to recall. But as much as I try, I cannot rid myself of those powerful memories that threaten to consume me. They have become my unwelcome, constant companions; especially as I lie awake during the deepest part of night, touched by a faint breath of spring that parts the curtains and enters my lonely chamber.

Was it only yesterday, Mary Ann, that I lived a carefree life filled with the resiliency of youth and a naive belief that true love, once found, would never desert me? Was it not you who afforded me access to the rich and timeless lessons of art and literature, and taught me to appreciate how the fullness of the cycle of life is contained in the simple cultivation of the earth? I lived and learned at your feet, Mary Ann, and I carried the weight of the lessons you taught me within my heart like noble talismans.

You designed us for one another, Mary Ann.
You were the author of our youth and freshness.
Yours was the voice that whispered sweet promises
of the perfect bliss of passionate connection. It was
you who scripted the path our journey would take.
Beneath your pen, we were transformed from
wide-eyed, single sisters engaged in a scholarly
experiment, to hungry participants in a sublime
awakening that clothed us both in the glorious
raiment of sensual experience. And when you led
us first to drink at the font of perfect beauty, the
bed of tender young plants upon which we lay
opened to make us one with the earth. Our young
lives were that day forever changed.

All of this, you planned. All of this, you
allowed. All of this you set into motion, Mary
Ann, before withdrawing your favor and
condemning us to lead separate lives—lives bereft
of hope, possibility, passion, or fulfillment. This
endures as the harshest example of the cruelty of
your betrayal.

I remain, as ever, alone and adrift.

Dorothea

Until I'd read the letter I held between my hands, I hadn't known whether I felt more fear—or hope—that it might contain another reference to the writer's passionate connection to a lost, great love.

Now, as the train slowed for its approach to Union Station, I uneasily began to comprehend my answer.

And that was a revelation greater than anything I could name.

Harrie had no objection to dining with me before we made the short walk to Fay Marian's house on Main Street. I'd been correct that she'd been looking forward to getting home in time to watch *Wyatt Earp*, which was telecast directly after her beloved *Rifleman*. I didn't worry that she'd get into any mischief after that. She still seemed unusually tired to me. I predicted that she'd be sound asleep long before the famous marshal had cause to draw his coveted Buntline Special.

We'd rounded the corner from Race Street and had nearly reached Fay Marian's apartment house when Harrie grew excited and took off running toward something up ahead. Night had fallen by then, and I couldn't make out anything clearly—so at first, I thought Harrie might've seen Mortimer, Mr. Hauser's dog. But when I drew closer, I heard a familiar voice calling out my name.

It was Fay Marian. Apparently, she and Inez had been out, and were approaching the house from the opposite direction.

"Hey there, EJ," Fay Marian greeted me as I joined them beneath the streetlight. "We're so glad we got to . . ." Her voice trailed off.

I heard Inez gasp.

Oh, no . . . I'd completely forgotten about my hair—and the rest of Rochelle's efforts on my behalf.

Before I could offer any explanation, Harrie blurted out, "She's a dish, ain't she? Aunt Rochelle worked her over."

"I think it's called a *makeover*, Harrie." I looked at Fay Marian and Inez apologetically. "It *wasn't* my idea, I assure you."

"I don't know why in the hell not." Fay Marian had found her voice again. "You look *fine*."

Inez elbowed her in the ribs. "She means you look lovely, EJ."

"*Lovely* is what you call your grandmother's wrist corsage. EJ looks more like a tasty hunk of hot wax." Fay Marian had the sense to lurch away before Inez could sock her again. "Will you *please* quit doing that? It's gonna leave a bruise."

"Can we go inside?" Harrie pleaded. "I wanna watch *Wyatt Earp*."

"Sure. Let's all go to my place. You can watch it there, Harrie."

"Okay, Fay Marian." Harrie took off running for the house.

We followed along more slowly.

"So, I guess we don't need to ask you if *your* day was uneventful?" Fay Marian chuckled. "I take it you got along swimmingly with Aunt Rochelle?"

"In a manner of speaking." I looked at Inez. "She did positively identify the perfume on the letters. And she also provided me with some other useful information."

"Like how to apply eye shadow like a pro?" Fay Marian quipped.

"I'm sincerely going to clock you if you don't knock it off and start behaving," Inez warned.

"And yet," Fay Marian held up an index finger, "the College and Academy both frown on the use of corporal punishment."

When we got inside Fay Marian's apartment, Harrie was already settled into a chair and had the TV on. It was clear that she'd done this same thing more than once.

"Need anything, Harrie?" Fay Marian asked.

"No, thanks." Harrie didn't take her eyes off the screen. A posse was chasing after some ne'er-do-wells. I was sure Harrie would not be stirring from her seat for at least half an hour.

"We'll be in the kitchen if you think of anything."

"Okay, Fay Marian."

We moved into Fay Marian's small kitchen and took seats at her table.

"We just had dinner with friends at Salem Tavern," Inez said. "But we were hopeful we'd hear from you this evening. I know I've been dying to find out if you were able to solve the mystery of the letters."

"Before you get started," Fay Marian asked me, "would you like anything to eat or drink?"

"No. Thank you, kindly. Harrie and I ate a light supper together at my house after we got back from the train station."

"In that case," Fay Marian pulled out a chair and sat down, "fire away. I'm all ears."

"And *mouth*," Inez added.

"Hey, I can't help it. I mean . . . *look* at her."

"Please." I held up a hand. "I'm already terribly uncomfortable about this . . . lapse in judgment. I should never have come out tonight looking like this."

Fay Marian tilted her head and squinted at me. "I think you have that backwards, EJ. This right here," she waved her hand in circles to encompass my visage, "would be what we call the *perfect* look for going out at night."

"Fay Marian . . ." Inez warned.

I began to wonder if the Salem Tavern served Boulevardiers . . .

"Did I mention you *smell* great, too?" Fay Marian glanced at Inez. "Doesn't she smell great?"

Inez ignored her. "I did notice that, EJ. I'm assuming it's the same scent as the letters?"

I nodded. "Harrie was correct. Her aunt successfully identified the perfume immediately and proceeded to douse me with a store sampler. I have *no* idea why."

"Well, at the risk of offending, I have to say it does rather suit you. I daresay, not many women could pull it off. What's it called?"

I sighed. "*Vol de Nuit.*"

"Night Flight," Inez translated. "Of *course*, it is."

"It's only available by special order," I added.

"Did Harrie's aunt have any information about who might have purchased it?" Inez asked.

"She did, actually. She wrote up a list of the names of customers who'd special ordered it within the last year."

"That's exciting." Inez's eyes grew wider. "And did you find the name and address of our mysterious Dorothea?"

"Not exactly. Rochelle's list only included customer names— no addresses. Apparently, special orders have to be picked up in the store. So, I took the list with us to the post office in the town of Paradise, and asked the postmistress there if she recognized any of the names."

"Well?" Fay Marian demanded. "Did she?"

"Eventually. She was not very disposed to be helpful initially."

"Sounds like every small-town post office *I've* ever been in," Fay Marian quipped. "No offense, EJ. But your employer doesn't have the best track record for hiring people with winning personalities."

"Fay Marian . . . *really*. Do I need to make you stand in the corner?"

"Not unless you promise to send me there with another one of those French cocktails you're so partial to."

"*That* will certainly not be happening." Inez looked at me apologetically. "EJ, I can understand if you'd rather discuss this

160

all another time." She shot a disapproving look at Fay Marian. "Some of us seem incapable of behaving like grown-ups."

"How do *they* behave? You'll have to remind me again later . . ." I was eager to change the subject.

"As I said, the postmistress in Paradise did eventually review the list of names for me. She indicated which ones belonged to residents of the town."

"Any candidates?" Inez asked.

"I don't have any idea. I'll have to research their contact information before I'll be able to reach out to them."

Fay Marian nodded. "How many are there?"

"Only two."

"Hmmmm." Inez seemed intrigued by that. "Do you remember their names, by chance?"

"Oh, yes. Darlene Boitnott and Brooke Casaubon. I have no idea, either, if they're married—or if so, what their husband's names might be."

"Wait a moment." Inez touched a hand to her forehead. "Did you just say *Brooke* Casaubon?"

"Yes. Why?"

"EJ. *Think*. It's a reference to *Middlemarch* . . . again. *Brooke.* Dorothea Brooke."

I closed my eyes. *How had I missed that association a second time?*

"I feel like a dunce," I said morosely.

"Join the club, sister." Fay Marian successfully dodged Inez's retaliatory poke.

My mind was racing. *What was the name Casaubon a reference to?* Finally, enlightenment struck.

"Casaubon was the name of the man Dorothea married!" I blurted out.

Inez was nodding. "The *first* man she married—the dull,

repressive old landowner."

My head was spinning. Suddenly, I wanted to join Fay Marian and drink another one of those crazy French cocktails.

The good news was that I'd successfully pinpointed the person in Paradise who'd been mailing those letters. The bad news was that I was even further away from identifying her because the writer was so determined to keep her true identity concealed.

"What are you going to do now?" Inez asked.

"I don't have the first idea," I answered.

A thin, strident voice piped up, "Why don't we go back to the store and ask Aunt Rochelle and them other clerks what this Brooke person looks like?"

None of us had seen her appear in the doorway of the kitchen.

"Is your program over?" Inez asked her.

"Yeah. *Dobie Gillis* comes on next. There's commercials right now."

"Not for you, young lady." Fay Marian got up. "Your daddy said you needed to be in bed by nine o'clock."

"He won't care," Harrie complained. "Today is special."

I stood up, too. "Today *was* special. But *you* are sleepy, and so am I. I think we both need to go to bed early."

"Are you leavin', Eej?"

"I am. How about I walk you to your apartment?"

"Okay." Harrie's tone was one of dejection. "Can we give a dog cookie to Morty?"

I considered Harrie's request. "Maybe just one. Morty needs his sleep, too."

Harrie yawned. "I think he sleeps most of the day already."

"Now, there's a life *I* want," Fay Marian added.

"Let us walk you both to the door." Inez pushed back her chair.

162

"No need." I held up a hand. "We know the way. Don't we Harrie?"

"Sure do, Eej."

"Goodnight you two." I addressed the women who had become my surprising confidants. "Thank you for the conversation."

"Goodnight, EJ. Call me tomorrow if you'd like to brainstorm some more."

I smiled at Inez. "I will."

"See you on the flip side, EJ." Fay Marian gave us each a wave.

Harrie and I were nearly out the door when Fay Marian emitted a low whistle.

"Hey, Harrie?" She hissed. "You're right . . . *EJ is a total dish.*"

Tanacetum vulgare
(Tansy)

"For advice comes from the deep waters of the heart;
those with understanding can draw it out."

—Proverbs 20:5

Lottie didn't have much wisdom to impart about what next steps we could take to resolve the mystery identity of the letter writer. I'd filled her in on the information I'd been able to gather on the trip to Virginia, and how what had initially looked promising had turned out, instead, to be another frustrating dead end.

"So, you're sayin' that whoever lives in that town and special ordered that perfume used a *fake* name?"

I nodded.

"And it was *another* fake name from that same damn book that's a hundred years old?"

"Yes."

"White people." Lottie shook her head in disgust. "Don't y'all ever watch television?"

"Now why would that make this mystery any easier to solve?"

"It wouldn't. But at least it'd be more interesting."

"As much as I hate to admit it, I think we've reached diminishing returns on this one. Whoever the sender is, it's clear they don't want to be discovered. That makes our part in this drama moot."

Lottie didn't seem quite ready to cut bait. "Shouldn't that postmistress up there know every damn person in that town?"

"One would think so."

"So why ain't she helpin' you figure out who the hell lives there that smells pretty enough to be writin' these damn letters?"

"It wasn't a question I felt like I could ask her."

"Why the hell not? Ain't she on Uncle Sam's payroll just the same as us?"

I hadn't shared any details with Lottie about my disturbing session in Rochelle's "comfortable" chair. When I'd dressed for work that morning, I'd put my hair up in exactly the same way I'd done it for the past twenty years. I wasn't ready for any repeat of Fay Marian's rhapsodies about my transformation—mostly because I knew that Lottie's would be the loudest voice in a chorus of celebration.

"There had been an . . . *accident* . . . with the perfume at the department store," I explained, "and I ended up wearing some of it. A *lot* of it, actually," I added. "That made it difficult for me to press her for assistance she seemed unwilling to offer on her own."

Lottie wasn't buying my explanation. "It sounds to me like this woman needs to be workin' upstairs with that crop of lazy jokers we got mannin' the front counter."

I didn't make any reply.

Lottie watched me in silence for a moment. "Why do I feel

like there's somethin' else you ain't tellin' me?"

I looked at her guiltily. I never could keep secrets from her.

"I read another one of the letters on the train."

"Well, glory be to God on high. And what'd you discover?"

"Nothing of any consequence—certainly nothing that could help us resolve our issues with them."

"Uh huh. And how about anything that could help resolve your *own* issues?"

"*My* issues?" I was tempted to ask her to define what she thought my "issues" were, and how they could possibly be related to the letters, but I refrained. I refrained because I knew if I asked, she'd tell me—and I wasn't in any kind of state to hear it.

"You want me to give you a list?" she offered with a wry smile.

"No." I held up a hand to stop her. "I do not."

"So, what are you gonna do with these?" Lottie picked up the stack of letters from my desk. "Burn 'em? Put 'em in a box and stick 'em on one of them shelves over there so they can gather dust until they're as old as that damn book that holds the key to this mess?"

"I honestly have no idea."

"Well, at least go ahead and read the rest of 'em. What kind of harm could it do at this point?"

I supposed she was right. There wasn't much point in parceling them out. And my job did give me the discretion to override regular process. The trip to Paradise yesterday had been proof of that.

"I'll think about it," I said.

"That's what you said the last time," she reminded me.

The bay door buzzer sounded. Lottie crossed the room to collect our daily accumulation of undeliverable mail. She carried the bin to our sorting table and we set to work.

It was an unremarkable assortment. Most of the items were misdirected or damaged pieces of business correspondence that should've been redirected upstairs. The bin also contained a dozen or so letters with incomplete addresses and a smattering of postcards that were torn or had been water damaged to the extent that the address information was not readable. I extracted one small, paper-wrapped parcel that had been tied up with so much string it resembled a miniature mummy. It appeared the adhesive address label had been torn off. Only the rounded corners of one side remained stuck to the box, revealing nothing about the intended recipient.

I held it up to show Lottie. "What on earth do you think this is?"

"Does it rattle?" she asked.

I shook it gently. "Yes. A little."

"My guess is a ring. Judgin' by the size, it's probably in a jeweler's box. We might could track it down that way."

Lottie truly was a genius at this work.

I set the box aside. We'd open it later, after we'd dealt with the easier cases.

"Well, well. Look what the cat drug in."

I looked over at her quizzically. Lottie had a smug expression on her face. She was holding up a familiar-looking letter.

My heart sank. "You have *got* to be kidding me."

"Not so much, Inspector Cloud." Lottie fanned the thing toward me so I could inhale its unmistakable perfume. "Looks like your little pen pal ain't quite finished with you yet."

I dejectedly took the letter from her. The postmark read April 20—just *five days* after the last letter had been mailed.

So, Dorothea was sending them faster now. Why?

I sat down on a stool and faced Lottie. "Whoever said *April*

167

is the cruelest month?"

"Don't ask me. But they must not've lived in Paradise, Virginia."

"No," I agreed. "That was a *different* person named Eliot."

"Seems to me like you already got one too many people named Eliot playin' in your sandbox. I wouldn't be lookin' to add any more."

I looked at her miserably. "What am I going to do, Lottie?"

Lottie was busy searching a drawer for more re-mailing labels. She looked up at me with impatience. "How about your job?"

I was unprepared for the brusqueness of her response. My face must've shown it.

"Don't be givin' me that Camp Fire Girls look of yours," she declared impatiently. "This here is a merit badge you're gonna have to work for."

I was lost. "I have no idea what you mean."

"Don't you? Then how about you reread that damn procedures manual you claim to live by? See if you can get reacquainted with all them whys and wherefores that explain why you don't have to give a rat's ass about some low-level stamp-jockey's reasons for refusin' to do her own damn job? Maybe then, you'll figure out you need to make another trip to Paradise, and remind that damn woman she doesn't get to *choose* whether or not she gives you the help you need to close this case." She slammed the drawer shut. "*That's* what I mean."

I got up and walked to my desk to add the newest letter to our stack.

And I resolved that when I got home that night, I'd read them all.

Fay Marian called me a little before 7 p.m. to apologize for her irreverent behavior the night before.

"I'm pretty embarrassed," she said. "I'd had a couple of cocktails with dinner and was feeling more uninhibited than usual." She hesitated. "Okay . . . maybe a *lot* more uninhibited than usual. I hope I didn't offend you, EJ."

I tried to set her mind at ease. "I wasn't offended at all. Please don't worry about it."

"Honest?" she asked. "It was just a shock to see you looking so . . ."

"Loose?" I suggested.

"Well. No. That wasn't the word that occurred to me. More like . . . glamorous."

Glamorous? That seemed like a stretch to me. "Thank you, but I think you're overstating the change."

"No." Fay Marian disagreed. "I'm really not."

I was eager to change the subject and talk about something less personal.

"I hope Inez wasn't too hard on you."

Fay Marian laughed. "You're kidding, right? We should turn that woman loose on Mr. Hauser's schnauzer."

"Why?" I joked. "Does he have behavioral issues, too?"

"*Touché.* I honestly don't know what Inez sees in me. I know I drive her crazy." She sighed. "Maybe I'm just a project—like one of her problem students?"

"Fay Marian. You know that's not the case."

"I wonder sometimes."

"I hope you're not serious, because I don't need to wonder. Inez sees in you what we all see in you: a delightful, spirited companion with a heart of gold."

"You make me sound like a horse." Fay Marian laughed merrily. "On the other hand, she *does* enjoy riding me."

I wasn't certain if she'd intended her remark to be a double entendre—but the possibility she *might* have completely flummoxed me. I was grateful we were talking on the telephone, so she couldn't see my face. I was sure it was a study in prudishness and mortification.

"Are you still there?" Fay Marian asked.

I realized I'd been silent too long. "Yes. I'm sorry. I got distracted by . . ." I frantically searched the room. "It's my dieffenbachia. I seem to have overwatered it."

"Your *what?*"

"It's also called 'Dumb Cane.'"

"Oh! Inez has one of those, too. She says sometimes it was named after me." Fay Marian laughed. "I won't keep you any longer, then. Thanks, EJ, for not being annoyed with me."

"Of course. You have nothing to apologize for, I'm sure."

"Hey. One last thing before I let you go. We're having a cookout for all the tenants on Saturday night—if it doesn't rain again. We'd love it if you'd join us. It'll be very casual. And I promise there'll be *no* Boulevardiers."

I smiled. "I'd love to join you. Let me know what I can contribute."

"I'll have Inez call you. She's in charge of the particulars."

"All right. I'll look forward to hearing from her. Thank you both for including me, Fay Marian."

"Don't thank us. We have a purely selfish motivation."

I knew better than to ask, but I did it anyway. "What's that?"

"We're hoping you'll let your hair down again and class things up." She laughed and rang off before I could reply.

While I finished tidying up my dinner dishes, I tried to divert my mind from thinking too deeply about the relationship dynamic between my new friends.

I wasn't very successful.

It was abundantly clear to me that Fay Marian and Inez were engaged with one another on a level that transcended the customary modes that defined friendships between women. I wasn't a complete prude—even though Lottie loved to tease me and suggest I was. I'd known girls in college who'd openly shown affection for one another, and had heard of others who'd carried those demonstrations of attachment even further. There had even been one girl who'd paid special attention to me in ways I began to question and grow wary of. I recalled the times my mother had sternly warned me to be on the lookout for lesbians, as if they were some predatory pack of wild animals that preyed on the flesh of young girls. Her warnings gained in intensity after I enrolled at Salem College, precisely because, as an all-girls school, it suffered from an unearned reputation as a Sapphic enclave.

But that was a typical and dismissive characterization of all women's colleges—including Ivy League schools like Radcliffe, where Inez had studied.

True . . . there were so many exceptions, the rule seemed pointless—but, still, the stereotypes persisted. I did my best to stay above all of it. My focus was my coursework and not on any of the innumerable opportunities that existed to allow me to explore my sexual . . . *tendencies.*

Early on, I had allowed some of my friends to coerce me into joining them on junkets to socialize with boys from Wake Forest and Davidson. Those trips invariably descended into hurried, dark-corner or back seat fumblings that didn't produce edifying results for any of the participants—at least, not from my perspective. After the first few outings, I began to wonder why the administration continued to sponsor what essentially were school-sanctioned lessons in debauchery. My distaste for the practice soon earned me the nickname "Sister Cloud"—a reference to the early Moravian practice of keeping the sexes separated. It had been that same practice that in 1722 had led the early church Brethren to establish Salem Academy as the country's very first school for young women—called Single Sisters.

I didn't know if my ideas would have changed if I'd been able to complete my education there. My mother's lengthy illness had forced my early withdrawal from college—and after her death, I became too absorbed with my work for the postal service to spare much thought about dating or romantic entanglements. It wasn't that I didn't have opportunities. I did. But none of them were tempting enough for me to consider materially changing the comfortable confines of my daily life. I'd never second-guessed or questioned my determination to remain single until very recently, when I met Fay Marian and Inez, and got to observe their easy and affectionate camaraderie firsthand. It didn't much matter to me to find the right way to characterize the true nature of their relationship. What I admired, irrespective of any labels, was the comfort, respect, and genuine companionship they seemed to share. Their relationship appeared to me to represent a true association of equals—not something I'd ever believed possible to achieve within the traditional roles society defined for women.

Yes. Sister Cloud was quite content with the choices she'd made.

Until recently . . .

And I couldn't deny the part the letters from Dorothea were playing by prompting an unscripted and disturbing reexamination of my solitary life.

I had earlier resolved to sit down this evening and read the remaining letters. I felt I owed it to myself to do so before I closed the book on this unfinished chapter. And for once, I chose not to overthink my decision.

I sat down in my favorite chair and laid the letters out in order on the table in front of me.

Three of them I had read. Five I had not. Two of them had arrived just within the past week.

And how many more were already en route to me?

Because I no longer shied away from admitting that the letters now belonged to me. Somehow, throughout the course of working to resolve them by undertaking fruitless actions intended to fulfill my responsibilities—somehow, I'd stopped ignoring the shocking immediacy of how their contents laid bare the wasteland of my own "vapid life." I'd been forced to confront the unhappy truth that the story Dorothea was telling was *my* story—at least in spirit, if not in essentials.

It even made sense to me that Dorothea's identity would probably never be discovered. Her identity, like my own, inhabited an unknown country. It would always be just out of reach. She was as unfamiliar to me as the woman I had seen reflected in the cosmetics department mirror yesterday. Both women were strangers. Yet each shared connections on some alternative plane.

Now that I had discovered her, I struggled with how to integrate her into the rest of what I'd pieced together in a clumsy effort to understand who I was becoming.

I picked up the fourth letter and opened it. After carefully withdrawing its single sheet of paper, I began to read.

Dear Mary Ann . . .

It was nearly midnight before I finished reading the remaining five letters—and then had reread them all a second time. When I could, I forced myself to consider them literally, and as dispassionately as possible.

It had been an effort. But doing so allowed me to make several important observations.

In essentials, the remaining letters had been much the same as the first: heartrending laments over an indifferent life lived without hope, fulfillment, or the promise of passion. However, more details about Dorothea herself had been revealed. It became clear that she'd first met her beloved—and later consummated their relationship—while working in a garden. That offered some clarity about her motivation to send her tales of passionate remembrance to the gardens at Old Salem.

And other clues emerged, too. Dorothea referenced being part of a "community of single sisters" more than once. I began to suspect that perhaps Dorothea herself had once been a student at Salem College. That, in conjunction with her stated reverence for working in a garden, could help establish Old Salem as the setting for her narrative.

But that only got me as far as it went.

I tried to sleep that night, but it was pointless. My dreams were too filled with images of Dorothea and her young lover, discovering the fullness of life—and each other—while twined together in a lush garden filled with the heady scent of healing herbs.

On Saturday, Harrie joined me on Salt Street to do another spot of weeding and planting in the town garden.

She had much news to report. Mr. Hauser had agreed to allow her to walk Mortimer twice every day—but only as far as Salem Square. And she announced proudly that Fay Marian was allowing her to help cook the hamburgers that night, provided she promised to be careful and not toss any kerosene-soaked objects into the grill to help the fire along.

Harrie had expressed confusion about why Fay Marian would think she'd want to do that. She explained that kerosene fires were only good for burning up things like railroad ties—not hamburgers.

She said she thought that difference was obvious.

She also asked me if I'd thought any more about going back to Roanoke to ask Aunt Rochelle, Paula and Darnelle for details about the woman from Paradise who'd bought the perfume.

"If she bought it from them, they'd know what she looks like, Eej."

I told her I supposed that was true. But I wasn't sure another trip up there would be happening any time soon.

"How come? Didn't you have a good time?"

"I had a very good time, Harrie. But I don't think I'll ever be able to locate the mysterious woman, even if I do find out what she looks like."

"Why not? If that post office lady don't know her, we can ask the Truitts. They know everybody in that town."

We'd finished clearing weeds from the last rectangular patch of sorrel. A gentle rain had fallen last night and had softened the ground enough to make our work much easier. Evelyn would now follow along behind us and cover the area with fresh mulch. It was time for us to move on and begin to set the tiny fumitory seedlings.

Harrie and I picked up our buckets and tools and moved along the central pathway to the garden's designated spot for fumitory. Evelyn already had the shallow trays of seedlings in position for us. Harrie was immediately filled with questions about the herb, and why it needed to be in exactly the spot where we were preparing to set the plants. I did my best to try and explain the ethos behind the way the *hortus medicus* was laid out.

"The early settlers here believed that God created a plant to cure every kind of sickness. The ancient Greeks and Romans called this idea the 'Doctrine of Signatures'—meaning the plants themselves often looked like the diseases they were cultivated to treat." I stopped to show her the spotted leaves on some Lungwort plants. "These leaves are said to resemble the appearance of diseased lungs. Another plant, Milkweed, was used to promote milk production in new mothers because its sap resembled spilled milk. These plants," I pointed at the flats of fumitory, "were used to rid the air of unhealthy toxins. The leaves were often burned like incense."

"If nobody uses them to make medicines today, why do they still want to grow them?"

"I think because preserving our connections to the past helps us remember where we came from."

"I came from Reidsville. But I don't think I need to plant busted car parts in the front yard here to help me remember that."

Harrie had a point.

"That isn't exactly what I meant. I was thinking more about remembering the good things we learned along the way. How our ancestors lived and worked to make better lives, and how we can learn from the things they got right and from the mistakes they made along the way. If we don't remember, we run the risk of making the same mistakes all over again."

Harrie seemed to get it. "I guess if Aunt Rochelle had remembered why she divorced that first deadbeat husband, she might not've married the second one. Is that what you meant?"

"Yes," I answered. "That's exactly what I meant."

"Well, if any of these special plants can keep her from marryin' a third one, maybe she could think about plantin' a few of 'em out in her yard, just like that lady in Paradise done."

I'd been using my trowel to make a series of small holes so we could set the fumitory seedlings. Harrie's words brought me up short.

"What was that?" I asked her to repeat her observation. "Where'd you see the plants?"

"In that garden up there beside the post office. I was walkin' around in it lookin' at plants and I saw some of them same ones we have in this one."

To say that Harrie's pronouncement stunned me would be an understatement. "Are you absolutely sure about this, Harrie?"

She nodded energetically. "I saw that angel plant with the little umbrella things on it."

"Angelica?"

"Yeah. That one. And there was some of that yellow one, too . . . that one that helps people not to get so mad."

Yellow one?

"Do you mean Lemon Balm?" I asked.

"Yeah. There was a *bunch* of that one," she added.

I hardly knew what to say. It appeared my thinking that there had been some connection between the letter writer and the *hortus medicus* may have been accurate.

"Are you okay, Eej? You look kinda worried."

"No. No, Harrie. I'm fine. Just surprised you found some of these herbs up there."

"I would'a looked around for more, but that was when Mr. and Mrs. Truitt came out. So, I started talkin' to them. They said the garden belongs to the lady that lives next door, but it's more of a whole town thing, like ours. I guess lots of people grow stuff in there. Mr. Truitt said they have tomatoes and things there in the summer, and the lady is real good about sharing them with folks."

"Did Mr. Truitt tell you who the lady is?"

"No. But he said she lives in that big white house right beside the garden. I guess it belonged to her husband's people. He said it was real fancy inside and has one of them big theater-type pianos."

I was stunned that Harrie had been able to glean this trove of information from Mr. Truitt, who'd barely strung three words together when he'd spoken to me. And Mrs. Truitt hadn't uttered a single syllable.

"I'm impressed that you were able to learn so much about the town, Harrie."

"It's the eye patch, Eej." Harrie spoke like an accomplished grifter sharing trade secrets. "People tell you stuff when they feel sorry for you."

I began to wonder if I should invest in one . . .

While Harrie and I worked setting the fumitory plants, I thought about where these new clues might lead us.

But was I still invested in the process enough to want to try?

I didn't know the answer. But there was one thing I did know without a doubt: *Lottie* would be one hundred percent in favor of following up on this new information without delay.

Harrie must've anticipated the direction of my thoughts.

"So, are we goin' back up there, Eej? Aunt Rochelle said we could come *anytime*—especially since we need to go to the store. So, it don't matter if it's on her day off." Harrie seemed to recall something else. "But she might be busy on Friday, since Hal's gonna be back."

I agreed wholeheartedly with Harrie's theory about Friday.

"Have you already asked your aunt about another visit, Harrie?"

"Yeah. She called last night to see if we got home safe."

That made sense. I immediately felt guilty for not thinking about contacting Rochelle myself. I had no acceptable excuse for my recent level of distraction.

"Maybe we *can* go back," I told Harrie. "I'll ask your father about it."

Fay Marian's cookout was a big success. Not only had all of her tenants been invited, but several of her friends from town were also in attendance. I was surprised to see Evelyn Haas there— and a few of Inez's colleagues from the college had also been invited. One of them I recognized from my own years as a student.

Professor Lydia Ogletree, who'd taught both sections of my English literature survey and several other courses, including Chaucer and The British Novel, had been the one who'd assigned *Middlemarch* as required reading. I quite liked her. She'd had a quiet demeanor, but for all her acuity, had always been very genteel in her approach to the material. I took as many courses with her as possible, and it was because of her that I'd declared English as my major.

I remembered how disappointed she'd been when I'd been forced to withdraw.

"Promise to come back," she'd entreated me. "You have a good mind, and you owe it to yourself to continue your studies. Many girls come through here, but few have the sense and application you possess to make good use of the gifts they've been given."

Sadly, I'd never returned. And I'd never been able to summon enough courage to seek Professor Ogletree out and explain to her why I hadn't. I'd been too shy and embarrassed about my change in circumstances. Seeing her today was both gratifying *and* upsetting. It was upsetting because I knew my time had come to face the music.

I wondered if Inez had known about my special connection with her.

It wouldn't have surprised me one bit. Inez seemed intuitive about most things.

I decided to take the bull by the horns and approach her myself.

"Dr. Ogletree?" I gently touched her elbow. "I don't know if you'll remember me . . ."

"Why Esther Jane Cloud," she interjected. "Of course I do."

I noticed that she still had the same penetrating blue eyes. She had to be well into her seventies now, but she appeared to be as sharp as ever. I felt all over again that same sense I'd always had that she could see right through me—and I knew in an instant the same thing would apply to any vague excuses I offered up today for why I'd never returned to school.

"I'm so happy to see you here," I said. "I had no idea you'd be attending."

"Oh, yes. Dr. Bell invited me. She lured me by hinting that I'd be able to renew acquaintance with a former student. I had no idea it would be you." She smiled. "I'm very happy to see you, Esther. Although I have to say I wouldn't have recognized you right away with your hair down like that." She dared to reach out a small hand and touch it. "The way it reflects the sun is quite striking."

I tried not to blush. It had been a last-minute impulse to give in to Fay Marian's entreaty that I adopt the more casual hairstyle for the cookout. I hadn't thought anyone would actually notice, but apparently I'd been mistaken. I'd already observed several of the other attendees eyeing me strangely, too.

"I'm very glad to see you, too. I've only gotten to know Inez recently. I can imagine what a fine addition to your department she is. She seems like quite a scholar."

"I'm not surprised you've already discovered that about her. Yes, we were very fortunate to get her. She's an excellent teacher and has quite a good academic pedigree."

"Oddly enough, she's been hugely helpful to me in trying to make sense of a mystery I've been struggling to unravel at work. Ironically, it involves characters in *Middlemarch*."

"It *does?*" I could see the surprise in her eyes. "But don't you work at the downtown post office?"

"I do, yes. I manage the Dead Letter Office."

"Dead letters and *Middlemarch* would seem to have very little in common."

I smiled at her dry observation. It was very characteristic of her teaching style. "One would think so. But in this case, the letters are curiously bound up with the book."

"Really? How so?"

I hadn't intended to delve so deeply into the background or

particulars of the letters, but I saw no harm in acquainting Dr. Ogletree with the basic facts.

"The undeliverable letters, there are eight so far, have been arriving at regular intervals. They are all addressed to Mary Ann Evans, care of The Gardens at Old Salem. Each letter is signed 'Dorothea.' One or two other clues about the sender have emerged, but even those are tied in some way, it seems, to *Middlemarch*. It's very singular."

"Most unusual. Are you sure someone isn't having a joke at your expense?"

"Very sure. In all my years resolving the toughest undeliverable mail, I've never come across a case quite as confounding as this one. Of course, the simplest thing would be to return them all to the sender, but the absence of that information is what lands the letters squarely in my hands to begin with."

"This is all so fascinating." She sounded sincere, but I grew concerned that I'd been monopolizing her attention for too long. I didn't want to hold Dr. Ogletree hostage, and force her to continue to stand any longer in the direct sun.

"I must apologize for blathering on about this. I'm sure there are other guests you'd like to socialize with here."

She leaned closer to me. "In fact, there aren't. I only agreed to stop in because Inez insisted that I might reconnect with a former student—who we now know to be you." Her eyes twinkled. "I think she was up to some mischief, don't you? She'd know full well I'd be captivated by your present dilemma."

I thought with great irony that Dr. Ogletree would be undone if she knew the true depth of my *present dilemma.*

"Would you like to find a place to sit down, so we can be more comfortable?"

"That I certainly would agree to," she said.

We walked toward an area where Fay Marian had set up a dozen or so folding chairs, beneath some maple trees that had begun to leaf out.

We passed Fay Marian, who was busy tending two three-legged charcoal grills. Harrie was at her elbow, eager to lend her expertise if the hot coals failed to cooperate.

Mr. Hauser and his dog, Mortimer, sat on the back steps at a respectable distance from the fray. Harrie's father, Johnnie, sat beside them. I imagined that Mr. Hauser feared all the laughter and disruption being made by his boisterous neighbors would be unsettling to his schnauzer, but I could tell that Mortimer's only concern was keeping an eye on Harrie's whereabouts.

Inez was deep in conversation with Evelyn Haas and another woman I did not recognize. Inez caught my eye as we passed and winked at me.

Guilty as charged, I thought.

Once Dr. Ogletree and I were seated, she returned to her queries about my dilemma.

I'd been tempted to tell her that I'd taken to thinking of it as *The Case of the Mysterious Letters*. But I refrained because I didn't want to admit to her that I had enough familiarity with Erle Stanley Gardner novels to make the comparison.

Her opinion still mattered to me.

"So," she continued, "your letter writer obviously attaches some great significance to *Middlemarch*. That in itself should assist you in identifying her."

"Why do you say that?"

"Esther. I've taught the classics here for more than thirty-five years. And in all that time, I can count on one hand the number of girls who deigned to read *Middlemarch* with other than a yawn—or even more overt expressions of boredom and pointed pronounced lack of interest. Our esteemed department chair now considers the novel too dense and lacking in relevance for today's students. It no longer has a place in the curriculum."

"It's odd you mention that. Because the commission of my work sometimes requires that I read the letters to look for clues that might assist us with delivering or returning them. I've had to do this in this case, and I find myself beginning to wonder if the author had, at some time, been a student here at Salem College."

"Because the letters were mailed here to the garden, you mean?"

"Not just because of that," I explained. "The letters also contain fairly direct references to a community of 'single sisters,' and to working in an herb garden."

"Well, that certainly does sound like Salem College. I suppose these also could be references to Moravian College in Pennsylvania, because it, too, has a medicinal garden—but then, why send the letters here? Do you know where the letters originated?"

"Oh, yes. They were all mailed from the same post office in Paradise, Virginia—a small town near Roanoke."

"Hmmm." Dr. Ogletree seemed lost in thought. I noticed the rhythmic tapping of her index finger against the aluminum arm of her chair. I recalled that this had always been one of her quirks when she'd been lost in thought. "Well." She looked at me with determination. "I think it would be fairly simple to search alumnae records for any students who hailed from Paradise, Virginia—and who may have majored in English. There should even be notations in the records about any extracurricular activities—for example, membership in the garden club."

I had never considered that. But Dr. Ogletree made it sound

like the most obvious—and simplest—task in the world to undertake.

"Could I do that?" I asked with wonder.

"Well, no." She smiled sadly. "*You* probably could not. However," she nodded toward Inez, "*she* certainly could. Or," she lowered her voice, "if she is unwilling, I could, as well."

It was an ingenious idea—one that might even stand a chance at yielding results.

Fay Marian called out to her assembled guests that the hamburgers were ready, and we should all make our way to the food tables. Dr. Ogletree and I got up and walked across the narrow scrap of lawn to join the queue forming alongside a row of folding tables covered with red-and-white-checked cloths.

"Now," Dr. Ogletree declared, "while we wait, you may regale me with a fantastic explanation for why you never returned to complete your degree . . . "

After the cookout ended and the guests had all departed, I stayed behind to help Fay Marian and Inez clean up. Harrie and Johnnie were on hand, too, collecting folding chairs and tables and moving everything back into Fay Marian's shed. So much clearing and debris removal had taken place, the once neglected space was barely recognizable anymore. Fay Marian's next step was to have the soil tilled. After that, we'd be ready to start planting.

It didn't take long for Inez to ask me about how my talk with Lydia Ogletree had gone.

"That was very sly of you, you know." We were in Fay Marian's kitchen, washing up serving bowls. "How did you figure out that she'd been my favorite professor?"

"It was a lucky guess. I knew that Lydia had traditionally taught both sections of English Lit, and since you'd confessed that you actually *enjoyed* reading *Middlemarch*, it seemed to make sense that she'd probably been your guide."

"Well, you were correct. It was very good to see her. And she even waited a respectable amount of time before demanding an explanation for why I never reenrolled."

"Oh, dear . . . how did that go?"

"About the way I thought it would. No excuse short of death—meaning my *own*—dismemberment, or alien abduction would ever have been acceptable to her. But we did manage to find common ground when it came to discussing strategies to identify our mysterious letter writer. She actually had a rather brilliant idea." I hesitated. "It involves you."

"Me?" Inez dried her hands on a hand towel that bore a festive, floral print. I found it curious that such a fussy item would be found in Fay Marian's kitchen—it didn't mesh with the rest of her style. "Don't keep me in suspense," she demanded. "However does her idea involve me?"

"How does what idea involve you?" Fay Marian entered carrying a tray loaded with an assortment of mismatched serving spoons and relish forks. "That's it, folks—the last of the cleanup."

"EJ was just explaining that Professor Ogletree had a brainstorm about solving the letter mystery—and that her idea involved me."

"*Requires* you, is a more accurate description," I added. "Although she was quick to say that if you were unable or unwilling to do it, she could."

Inez leaned against the kitchen counter. "Okay, now I'm extremely curious. What is it? Does it involve espionage?"

Fay Marian chuckled. "You'd *love* that."

"Well," I explained, "I shared with her that I had been able to determine that our letter writer might have been a student at Salem College at one time, and that she probably volunteered in the garden, too."

"No kidding?" Fay Marian seemed surprised. "When did you put that together?"

"Only a few days ago, after I'd read the rest of the letters."

Inez raised an eyebrow. "You read *all* of them?"

I nodded.

"Why Miss Cloud," Fay Marian teased, "wasn't that a flagrant breach of protocol?"

"It may have been a tiny breach, but it wasn't flagrant. We'd reached the point where we'd all but realized our only remaining option would be to destroy the letters—so reading them didn't seem to signify much."

"Hey. I'm gonna go out on a limb here and suggest something wildly extravagant."

Inez and I both waited for Fay Marian to share her idea.

"I say we forget about washing the rest of these dishes right now and have a cocktail. That way, we can relax, unwind, and debrief. Thoughts?"

Inez looked at me. "I'm in."

"Okay," I agreed. "I suppose so."

"Excellent." Fay Marian clapped her hands together. "Who's mixing? You or me?"

"I'll do it." Inez gently nudged Fay Marian out of the way so she could access the cabinet where the drink paraphernalia was stored. "I have a healthier respect for correct proportions than you do."

"Says the woman who doubted I could entice the enchanting

Miss Cloud to part with her hairpins for an afternoon fête."

"It was a moment of weakness." I resisted the impulse to smooth my hair into its proper place.

"Well, I hope you'll have many more. All joking aside, EJ," Fay Marian fixed me with an earnest gaze, "you're a stunning woman, and there's nothing wrong with letting the world know it."

I didn't know what to say, and my expression must have indicated as much.

"Mark my words: the more you do it, the less conspicuous you'll feel."

"I hate to agree with her, EJ." Inez paused her drink preparations. "But for once, Fay Marian is right."

"Well, damn. This is a red-letter day. How about we celebrate my elevation to the realm of *sometimes* being right by listening to a little music, too? Any requests?"

"Yes," Inez said over her shoulder. "*Not* that awful 'Happy Organ' record."

Fay Marian's face fell. "Oh, come on, Inez. It's a contemporary classic."

"It's classic roller-skating music."

"Hey, it beats those dirges you're always listening to."

"I do *not* listen to dirges—unless it's *you*, singing along with Dinah Shore during those Chevrolet commercials."

Fay Marian looked to me for support. "See what I put up with?"

I held up both hands in mock surrender. "Switzerland."

Fay Marian looked confused. "What's that supposed to mean?"

"She's *neutral*," Inez explained. "Now," she handed us each one of her signature Boulevardiers, "let's go sit down and get comfortable."

Fay Marian all but hummed after her first sip of the martini. "I do love these Bouviers."

"*Boulevardiers*," Inez corrected.

"Don't ruin my fantasy." Fay Marian winked at me. "I like thinking I have something in common with Jackie Kennedy."

"Well, if that's all you desire," Inez offered, "I could lend you a pillbox hat."

Once we were settled in the living room and Fay Marian had selected the music—she'd reached a compromise choice with Bobby Darin—Inez asked me to share Lydia Ogletree's idea, and explain how Lydia thought she could be involved.

"It's quite ingenious, actually. Dr. Ogletree thought we ... well ... *you* could search the college alumnae records and look for the names of any students from Paradise, Virginia, or environs. And pay particular attention to any girls who majored in English and may have been involved in the garden club."

"That *is* ingenious."

"I agree." Fay Marian faced Inez. "But how on earth would you know which years to search? This Dorothea person could be thirty years old—or eighty. We have no way of knowing."

"No," I interjected. "But we do know some things. The *hortus medicus* garden in Old Salem wasn't restored and cultivated again until 1930, a few years before I started college."

"I don't get it," Fay Marian said. "I thought you said you *always* worked in the garden—just like your mother and grandmother had before you?"

"That's right," I explained. "But the herb garden we kept was on my grandparents' land, out near Bethabara. After the garden in Old Salem was restored, my mother and I both began volunteering here."

"Well," Inez said, "that does narrow the search field somewhat."

"It's still decades, Inez." Fay Marian sounded dubious.

"Oh, I don't think our Dorothea is likely to be a recent graduate."

"Nor do I," I added. "Dr. Ogletree said *Middlemarch* was no longer part of the curriculum because students didn't find it relevant."

Fay Marian chuckled. "That's putting it mildly."

"She's correct, of course," Inez agreed. "And it certainly wasn't being taught when I joined the faculty here five years ago. I can ask when it fell from grace."

"How onerous a task do you think this will be?" I was wary of intruding too much on Inez's free time.

"Not much of one, actually. Those records are all indexed by class year, and by geographic region after that."

"How come?"

"It helps the college with fundraising and organizing regional events. In any case, most of our girls come from North Carolina and Virginia—with the exception of Pennsylvania and Illinois, where there are other established Moravian communities."

Fay Marian still wasn't convinced. "Based on what you've told me about how much these girls prefer the male companionship they find on the Wake Forest campus, I doubt that religion played much of a role in their decision to study here. And I use the term 'study' very loosely."

"Another reason why our Dorothea is not likely to be a modern girl." Inez looked at me. "Don't you agree, EJ?"

"I do, actually. There's also an old-school method to her . . . phraseology. Her writing style is decidedly not modern."

"You mean she uses verbs?" Inez swatted at Fay Marian. "Hey! You're the one who told me they can barely write complete sentences."

"Behave yourself, Fay Marian. We *are* talking about EJ's alma mater."

"Don't worry," I assured her. "I'm not at all offended. Economy with language and a disregard for proper rules of correspondence is endemic these days."

"I blame our complete disregard for teaching the Classics," Inez declared.

"I'm inclined to blame television," I added.

"*I* blame Eydie Gormé." Fay Marian ignored the withering look she got from Inez. "Face it: everything gets loose when Eydie sings the blues." She batted her eyes at Inez. "Did I tell you this Bouvier tastes great?"

The rest of our conversation that evening bounced back and forth between Inez's ideas about how to conduct the search of alumnae records, and Fay Marian's obvious enjoyment of her "Bouviers."

I spent most of Sunday doing my normal tasks. After church, I took some time to sort through a couple of gardening books that had belonged to my mother and noted some ideas about the best landscape designs for Fay Marian's backyard space, taking into account the presence of tree cover and amount of available sunlight.

Afterward, I sat down on my front porch to read the paper. Of special interest to me was the report that the goodwill committee Winston-Salem Mayor Kurfees had appointed to explore remedies to the lunch counter sit-in standoff was reported to be nearing the end of its deliberations.

I recalled how Lottie had expressed a lack of confidence in the process when it had been announced.

"Twenty *men*?" she'd asked with scorn.

I told her that I'd found the idea encouraging. "Yes, but ten of them are white and ten are Negroes."

"So what? It won't amount to a hill of beans for us."

I told her that I was choosing to remain more hopeful. "If the Negro community has a voice in the discussions, the outcome might be better for everyone."

"You did say it was twenty *men*, right?"

"Yes."

"So let me ask you, when was the last time a group of *men*—no matter what color they are—has ever done anything to make life better for us?"

It finally became clear to me what she was getting at. "You mean women?"

"Yes, ma'am, I do. And mark my words: no matter what rights and privileges them men may or may not decide to extend to my people, *we're* still gonna be the ones who cook the food and clean up after 'em. That ain't likely to change anytime soon, believe me."

"You sound like a feminist, Lottie." My voice was teasing, but underneath, I knew what she was saying was the truth. Women seemed fated to always remain second-class citizens—and in her case, that was doubly true.

"I ain't no damn feminist," she retorted. "Lord knows I've read enough about how all them sanctimonious white women from them fancy northeastern colleges don't pay no never mind to what affects women who look like me."

I wanted to disagree with her, but I couldn't summon up any ready examples of arguments that proved her thesis wrong.

Still . . . it would be interesting to see what the goodwill committee recommended.

I continued to read the rest of the paper and concentrated on enjoying the remainder of my time outside on the porch.

It was there that Harrie found me an hour later. She roared around the corner from Race Street on her red scooter, hopped off it in front of my house, and scampered up the steps to join me.

"Hi ya, Eej. It's been a *day*. I could use a Postum. How about you?"

"Why hello, Harrie." I lowered my paper. "Postum, you say? I think I can manage that."

Harrie collapsed onto a chair. "Thanks.

I was intrigued. It wasn't that it was unlike Harrie to be so dramatic—but something in her demeanor was different. She seemed almost . . . *rattled*. I hoped nothing had happened to Mortimer.

"You take it easy," I told her. "I'll go fetch our drinks."

She accepted that suggestion without comment—another anomaly.

When I returned to the porch with our hot beverages, I half expected Harrie to have struck off in some other direction, as she was wont to do. But there she still sat, with that same serious expression on her young face.

"Is everything all right, Harrie?" I set her mug down on the table between our chairs. "You seem agitated."

"You didn't hear the ruckus at our house?" she asked. "It was crazy."

In truth, I hadn't heard anything. But then, I'd been working inside after church, and had had the radio playing. I liked to listen to the rebroadcast of the weekly Metropolitan Opera performance that our local station played on Sundays.

"No," I told her. "I didn't hear anything. What happened?"

Harrie launched into an enigmatic account of what all had

occurred that morning in Fay Marian's backyard.

"Fay Marian had some fellers with a dump truck come over to haul off some of them bigger car parts. They was doin' real good, too. They had this one last hunk to get loaded up, but it was the biggest one and real tough to get lifted up high enough so they could get it in the back of the truck. One of the men got behind it with this big board and tried to scooch it up closer so's they could move it—but the board busted clean in two and the car fell back on the man's leg."

"*Oh, no. That sounds awful, Harrie. Was he hurt?*"

Harrie was nodding vigorously. "He was bleedin' real bad on account of how old and rusty that metal was. Fay Marian tried to wash the cut off right quick, and wrap it up with some towels, but it kept soakin' right on through. There was blood all over the place, too. Miss Inez got kinda faint when she saw that, and ran inside to call for an ambulance."

That was strange. I hadn't heard any sirens.

"Did they come and take him to the hospital?"

"Nope." Harrie's expression was somber. "Miss Inez come back out and told us they asked first if the feller was colored. When she said yes, they told her they couldn't take him, and said she'd have to call across town for the colored ambulance."

My heart sank and I closed my eyes in mortification. *How were these things still happening?*

"Fay Marian got so mad she was cussin' up a storm—rantin' around the yard and throwin' things. Finally, Daddy heard the ruckus and come out. He helped her and the other feller get the hurt man in our car, and Daddy drove him to the colored hospital his self. Fay Marian rode right along with 'em. They only got back a little bit ago. Daddy said as how the hurt man got twenty-eight stitches in his leg—and they had to give him some kinda shot so he don't get lockjaw from that ol' car." Harrie sipped her drink. "That'd be strange, wouldn't it Eej? If a feller got lockjaw from one of them French cars? I thought maybe he'd get that French pox you told me about, so I asked my Daddy about that."

I was aghast. "Tell me you didn't."

"Yeah, and he asked who told me about that French pox, and I said you."

"Harrie . . ."

"Daddy just shrugged and said as how lockjaw was easier to treat these days." She seemed thoughtful. "I reckon that's the same as what Carla told me about the clap."

For the first time in my life, I thought about having a cigarette.

I hardly knew what to say about all Harrie had just experienced. It had been horrific—and was another shocking example of the brutality of segregation.

I reached over and touched her knee. I noticed that some of her recent scrapes had started to scab over. "I can imagine how much that all upset you."

Harrie sighed. "I didn't get as upset as Miss Inez. Fay Marian had to borrow one of Morty's nerve tablets from Mr. Hauser." She looked at me knowingly. "He says they help Morty sleep at night. But between you'n me, I think *he's* the one who needs 'em."

I didn't doubt Harrie's surmise at all. "How is Miss Inez now?"

"Fay Marian said she's sleepin' it off."

"And how are *you?*"

Harrie shrugged.

"That was a lot to go through. Do you want to talk about it with me?"

Harrie took her time thinking it over.

"Okay," she said. "But can I get another one of these if I do?" She held up her mug.

"Of course. You can have as many as you want."

"Good." She sighed and shook her tousled head. "You know, Eej, some things in life just take more'n one Postum."

I knew exactly what she meant.

It felt right for me to walk over to Fay Marian's after dinner and check on Inez. Harrie's account of what had happened that day sounded harrowing. I knew that Fay Marian and Inez were avid anti-segregationists, and I could only imagine how angered and frustrated they'd both been by the heinous refusal of the volunteer emergency squad to dispatch an ambulance to pick up a Negro man—no matter how serious or potentially life threatening they knew his injury was.

It had been next to impossible for me to explain the flawed system behind that bigoted response to Harrie. In the face of her repeated "whys" and "how comes," I'd finally given up and told her the simple truth: it had happened because we lived in a place where many of God's people were still regarded as unequal, and so were not treated fairly.

"But if they're God's people, then how can they be unequal?" she demanded to know.

"That's the same question many people are asking, Harrie."

"You mean like Jerome?"

"Yes." I said. "*Just* like Jerome. And many others, too—including me."

"I don't get it. Carla told me one time that God was color blind. But I thought she meant He couldn't tell the difference between red and green, just like them charts at the eye doctor's office." She absently swung her legs while she stared at the boards on my porch floor. "But I guess maybe this is what she was talkin' about."

It was the first time I'd held out hope for the state of Carla Hotbed's soul.

Fay Marian was outside smoking a cigarette when I approached the house. I could see that she'd just been sweeping off her front porch. She seemed happy to see me. And not, I realized, just because I was wearing my hair down again.

"Well, if you aren't a sight for sore eyes." She leaned her broom against the door frame. "Harrie told me she filled you in our little tableau today."

"She did. I'm so sorry you had to experience that, Fay Marian."

"Yeah," she said with more than a trace of disgust. "It makes me want to sell up and blow this pop stand. I don't know how much more of 'quaint, small town life' we can endure. This place," she spread her arms to encompass the neighborhood, "is damn near pathological with its shallow pretensions extolling life in a simpler time."

"You mean Old Salem?" I wasn't very surprised to hear the forceful energy behind Fay Marian's condemnation of life in our rather closed community. Lately, I'd begun to feel the same way.

"Not just here," she explained, "the whole goddamn South." She ground out her cigarette and pocketed the butt. "I've just about reached my limit with the pace of so-called *progress* in our fair city. They say Rome wasn't built in a day? Well by my calculation, we've had nearly three hundred years to get this mess figured out, yet we just keep spending all our time digging a deeper damn hole to climb out of."

"I know. Lately, I've begun to feel so ... *culpable* ... for walking these cobblestone streets all my life with blinders on. Things like what happened here today? They're the responsibility of *all* of us who haven't spoken out or worked to change things. Coming home every night to my storybook life no longer makes me immune to the ways our world has to change."

"Don't I know it?" She tossed her head toward the house. "Don't we *both* know it?"

"How is Inez? That's actually why I came by. Harrie told me she'd been very upset by everything that happened today."

"God bless you, EJ Cloud." Fay Marian let out a deep breath and smiled at me. "You always seem to know the right thing to do."

I could think of a hundred examples that would disabuse her of that opinion.

"Not really . . ."

Fay Marian ignored my protest. "Come on inside. I know she'd love to see you."

"Oh, no . . . I sincerely don't want to intrude."

"Don't be silly." Fay Marian opened the front door and stood aside so I could enter ahead of her. "You're practically family here. Don't you know that? Even Mr. Hauser likes you."

Mr. Hauser? I'd barely spoken two words to her antisocial tenant.

"I somehow think that's unlikely," I assured her.

"Trust me." Fay Marian lowered her voice. "The old codger's got a thing for hot redheads."

For the first time, I was tempted to try out one of Inez's characteristic socks on the arm. But I resisted temptation. Fay Marian was *her* public works project, not mine.

I had my hands full with Harrie . . .

When we got inside, Inez seemed genuinely thrilled to see

me. She'd been sitting in a chair by the window, reading. She got up when I entered the room and rushed over to embrace me.

"How glad I am you're here." She released me and stood back, still holding onto my arms. "It means the world to me that you came by to check on me." Her eyes looked red and puffy. I was sure she'd been crying. She stepped back and waved me toward a chair. "Sit down, please. And talk to me about *anything* else. I'll lose my mind if I keep thinking about it. Not even this," she held up her book, "could distract me."

Inez had been reading *Middlemarch*.

"I'm surprised you selected that one if you were looking for a distraction."

Fay Marian laughed. "I said the same thing. I even offered her my copy of *The Price of Salt*. I was *sure* that one would distract her—and in some pretty happy ways, too."

I was unfamiliar with the title.

"What is that book about?" I inquired.

Fay Marian and Inez exchanged glances.

"It's rather *eclectic*," Inez explained. "A romance by a British author named Claire Morgan."

"You should read it, EJ," Fay Marian offered. I saw Inez's eyes grow wide. "I think you'd find it illuminating."

"Fay Marian . . ."

"Maybe I'll request it at the library. I have a book to return next week."

Fay Marian laughed. "You won't find it there. You can borrow my copy."

"How about a cocktail?" Inez had practically shouted her suggestion. We both looked at her in surprise. She spread her hands. "I'm feeling festive since EJ is here."

"Do you think you should?" Fay Marian expressed concern.

"Especially after taking that sedative?"

"That was *hours* ago, and I feel just fine now."

"Okay." Fay Marian got up and headed for her kitchen. "You know I'm always game. How about you, EJ?"

I sincerely wanted to decline. But, in truth, Inez's beloved Boulevardiers were beginning to eclipse Postum as my favorite beverage.

I didn't know how I'd ever break the news to Harrie.

I told Fay Marian I'd be happy to join them.

We passed the next hour talking in generalities about gardening, the warm weather, and Inez's intention to begin her perusal of the alumnae records tomorrow, after her last class concluded at 2 p.m. I shared with them that Harrie and I were planning another trip to Roanoke, including a stop in Paradise to explore the town garden.

"When are you going?" Inez asked.

"On Tuesday. That schedule seemed to work well for Harrie's aunt, since it's her day off. We'll have the opportunity to ask the other clerks in her department if any of them can describe the customer, Brooke Casaubon. If so, that can at least reveal something about the woman you'll be searching the records for—like her age, for instance."

"What are you expecting to find in this town garden?" Fay Marian asked.

"I don't know. Possibly any indication it might provide that shows a connection between it and our garden here in Old Salem is real, and not imagined."

"I predict you'll find it. I think you're *very* close to solving this puzzle, EJ."

"I wish I had your confidence, Inez."

"It's not confidence," she insisted. "It's common sense. Too many things are falling into place. We'll find our Dorothea. And when we do, the only problem you'll have is what to do about it."

Fay Marian had no trouble solving that problem. "I'd say borrow some of her perfume. That stuff smelled *great* on you the other night."

Inez and I exchanged weary glances.

"I don't know about you," Inez held up her martini glass, "but I could use a refill."

"Not me, thank you." I got to my feet. "I haven't been sleeping well lately, and I want to get to bed early tonight. So, I'll be on my way. Thank you both, as usual, for the hospitality." I smiled at Inez. "I'm glad you're feeling a bit better."

Inez smiled back at me. "Thank you, my friend."

Fay Marian walked me to the door. But before I could leave, she stopped me. "Hold on a second. I want to get something." She trotted off to her bedroom and returned a moment later with a book. "Here you go," she handed it to me. "I think this will make a good bedtime story."

I heard Inez begin to chastise her before I'd even made it to the porch.

Levisticum officinale
(Lovage)

"He has made everything beautiful in its time.
He has also set eternity in the human heart ..."
—Ecclesiastes 3:11

I felt like a seasoned traveler on our second trip across town to Union Station. This time, I was the one who led the way to the ticket counter and requested two returns for Roanoke. We were making the trip earlier this time. We wanted to arriver sooner in Paradise, so we'd have more time to explore the garden and allow me to do a spot of research in the town's small public library.

Harrie and I took our seats in the waiting room, and I was sure I recognized some of the same weary-looking business travelers who'd been in there the last time. I tried to imagine what it would be like to have a job that required spending so many hours commuting on a train, but I didn't get very far. A ten-minute bus ride was about as much as I could comprehend. There had been times in my life that I'd regretted never leaving home—especially after my mother died. I wondered about the ways my life might have been different if I'd been brave enough to branch out and apply to the postal service for transfers to other cities. Rumors had been circulating that the postal service might eventually close all of our regional DLOs and centralize operations someplace like Atlanta.

I'd asked Lottie once what she would do if that happened.

"Probably join them rats up in the attic," she'd said. "I'm too old now to be thinkin' about startin' over in a new place. If Uncle Sam don't have nothin' else for me here? Well. I guess I'll just see about drivin' one of them Safe Buses like my husband. Lord knows, they're gonna have to hire women sooner or later to keep up with demand. And I'd be a damn sight better driver than Marvin Bean, any day of the week."

For my part, I had a hard time imagining moving to a city as large as Atlanta. And truthfully, I didn't think I wanted to relocate to a place that was even more rigidly entrenched in its regressive *and* repressive practices.

When Harrie had met me this morning for the bus ride to the train station, I'd been happy to see that she seemed to have rebounded from her moribund mood on Sunday afternoon. She'd chattered away on the ride across town, striking up a lively conversation with the driver and querying him about how many people he reckoned missed the slot when they tossed their coins into the fare bin.

I assumed she was hoping that our trips to Union Station might result in a new revenue stream for her.

Once we'd taken our seats on the train, Harrie talked about how excited she was to see Darnelle and Paula again.

"Aunt Rochelle told me they handle most of the special orders."

"That would be useful, Harrie. I appreciate you coming with me on this trip. I know it's not as much fun as when you get to stay overnight with your aunt."

"That's okay, Eej. Aunt Rochelle says I'm welcome to come up anytime."

I smiled at her.

"Except on nights that Hal feller is in town," she added. "I reckon they have a lot of perfume business to take care of."

I told her that I expected they did.

"Are you excited about seein' them herbs in that garden by the post office?"

"*Those* herbs. And, yes, I am. I'm very excited. And interested to see how similar it is to our garden in Old Salem."

"Mr. Truitt said the best time to visit is in September, when they have their big town party. He said that's what the garden is there for—growin' stuff they all cook up for some special dish they eat at that celebration. He called it a Homecoming Garden. Have you ever heard of that, Eej?"

"I have actually. I think many small towns have those kinds of annual celebrations. Sometimes, they're called Founder's Days, to commemorate the date the town was actually started."

"Why do they cook the same food every year? That sounds kinda boring."

"Probably because it's part of tradition, Harrie. In the same way some towns will cook big pots of chowder from old, original recipes, or how sugar cakes are an important part of celebrating Easter in Old Salem."

Harrie had perked up at my mention of sugar cakes.

"What are them . . . *those*, Eej?"

I was surprised. "Haven't you ever had sugar cake, Harrie?"

"No," she said with glumness.

"Sugar cake is a sweet bread that's topped with cinnamon and butter—similar to coffee cake, but much lighter in texture and generally much sweeter. The early Moravian settlers brought the recipe with them from Germany and Slovakia, and originally baked it as a sweet treat for breakfast on Easter morning. Moravian churches still serve this cake, and a special version of sweet buns, at Lovefeast celebrations during the Christmas holidays."

"They eat cake in *church?*" Harrie asked in amazement. "We never got cake at Speedwell Baptist Church." Harrie sat lost in thought. I assumed she was rethinking the apparent wasteland of her cake-less religious upbringing. "I gotta tell Carla about this. She always said the reason church people were so mean was 'cause they're full of piss and vinegar."

"I don't believe Moravians are like that, Harrie."

"Carla needs to know about this cake, Eej."

"Maybe one day you can tell her about it."

"I think I might need to check this Lovefeast thing out."

"I'd be happy to take you with me, Harrie. We can ask your daddy to join us, too, if he wants to go."

"That'd be good." Harrie was still thinking it over. "I don't expect I'll need the eye patch, though. Do you?"

"No. I don't think so. Everyone is treated equally and there's always plenty of sweets for sharing."

"Okay." Harrie seemed to accept that logic without question.

We rode along in silence. When the train slowed for its whistle-stop in Mayodan, Harrie stretched and sighed, before looking up at me with a serious expression.

"I been thinkin', Eej. We might should invite that lunch counter man at Woolworth's to go with us to that cake service, too. Seems like he ain't heard about sharin' sweets before, neither."

I wanted to hug her.

"I think that's a great idea, Harrie."

Our train pulled into the Roanoke Station on South Jefferson Street right on time. When we exited the building, we saw no sign of Aunt Rochelle's yellow Thunderbird—not in the loading zone and not in the parking lot. Since the train had run late the last time, I thought maybe Rochelle had allowed herself more leeway in arriving to pick us up.

A smartly uniformed porter approached us.

"S'cuse me, ma'am." He touched the shiny brim of his cap. "Is you Miz Cloud, by chance?"

"Yes, I am."

"Ma'am, Miz Rochelle from Heironimus called and said for us to tell y'all that she's been held up for just a little bit. She's real sorry, but said for y'all just to wait inside and she'd have somebody from the store come and fetch you real soon."

"Oh. Well thank you so much for telling us."

"Yes, ma'am." The porter nodded his head and turned to walk back toward the station.

"Hey, Mister?" Harrie stopped him. "Ain't the store just right up this road here?"

"Why, yes, ma'am, it is. Not more'n a few blocks."

Harrie tugged on the hem of my jacket. "Why don't we just walk, Eej?"

"Well . . ."

"I bet we get there before anybody can come get us." Harrie was already tugging on my hand. "C'mon, Eej. Let's go."

I looked back at the porter. "If anyone comes to get us . . ."

He nodded. "Yes, ma'am. We'll tell 'em y'all already done walked on to the store."

I thanked him again.

"You be careful crossin' them streets now, young lady," he called out to Harrie.

"I will," she hollered back. "Thanks, Mr. Porter."

The porter had been right. We reached the entrance to the store in less than fifteen minutes. When we stepped inside, Harrie diverted immediately to review the imposing display of Osterizer blenders. I saw her face fall.

"They ain't on sale no more, Eej."

"I'm sure they will be again, Harrie."

She didn't seem convinced. "Daddy started me a Christmas Club at the bank. He puts in a dollar every week. I was gonna use that money to buy us one of these."

"Stores always have big sales at Christmastime, Harrie. I bet they'll do that with these blenders, too."

Harrie sighed. "Carla said you gotta fish or get off the pot."

"I think she meant . . . *never mind.*" In that circumstance, *not* correcting Harrie was to everyone's ultimate benefit. "I predict they'll be on sale again." I squeezed her shoulder. "Now let's go find Darnelle and Paula before anybody gets sent to the train station to fetch us."

Harrie reluctantly left the blender display, and we made our way to the cosmetics department. It was still early, and Darnelle and Paula appeared to be occupied getting their display counters set up for the day. The store had only just opened.

Paula saw us first. "Here they are!" she called out to Darnelle.

"Hey you two," Darnelle said when she saw us approaching. "I was heading out to the station to pick you up right after I got these things set out. Was your train early?"

"It was right on time," Harrie declared.

"Which means it was early," I added.

Darnelle smiled. "Rochelle got . . . *held up* . . . this morning."

"It's Tuesday. I reckon Hal was in town."

Darnelle looked at Harrie with wide eyes. "She *told* you that?"

"Harrie has a *very* good memory," I clarified. "We decided to walk in from the station. It wasn't far, and it's such a pleasant morning."

"Would either of you like anything to drink?" Paula asked.

Harrie's face lit up.

"Go on," Paula encouraged her. "You know where the Yoo-hoos are."

Harrie was off like a shot.

"Will Rochelle be coming by today?" I asked. "I know Harrie will want to see her."

"Oh, she'll be here," Darnelle said with confidence. "There's no way she'd miss seeing that kid. She adores her."

"It's mutual." I smiled at her.

"So, EJ," Paula said. "I notice you've got your hair back up. Would you like another comb out while we chat? No charge, of course."

"Well . . ." I demurred.

"Oh, go on and let her, EJ." Darnelle was restocking a countertop lipstick tester. "We don't get our hands on hair like yours very often. It's a treat when we get to work on women who come in with such great raw material."

"She's not kidding," Paula added. "Believe me, most of our makeover clients are more like Hermione Gingold than Rita Hayworth."

I gave up on my determination to stay out of the "comfortable chair" on this visit. After all . . . they were doing me a favor by allowing me to ask them questions about their customers. I owed it to them to be more accommodating—especially when they seemed to enjoy working with my . . . *raw material.*

"All right," I said, timidly. "I suppose it wouldn't hurt."

"Great!" Paula snatched up a cape and snapped it out with a crack. "Have a seat."

When Harrie reappeared with her bottle of Yoo-hoo, she didn't seem at all surprised to find me in the chair. Again.

"Nice goin', Eej. We'll get right to the front of the line again on the trip home."

I heard Darnelle chuckle as she continued to sort her lipsticks.

"I told EJ her hair is great raw material to work with, Harrie." Paula was wielding her hairbrush with a flourish. "I'm thinking we need to try a French twist today. It's less rigid than that straight pullback and pin number—and you can do it yourself on days you don't want your hair loose."

Harrie nudged me. "French, Eej."

While Paula set about styling my hair, I began my inquiries about anything either of them might recall about the special-order customer named Brook Casaubon.

"She was one of only two women who purchased *Vol de Nuit* and live in Paradise," I reminded them.

"Is she the one who always wears the cloth coat and the black brogans?" Darnelle asked.

"No. That's Doris Hanes." Paula looked at me. "Sad story. Terrible underbite." She tapped her lower lip. "Youngest daughter of the Hanes clan. Poor thing will try *anything* to get a man." She faced Darnelle. "I think Brooke Casaubon is the one with the saggy boobs and the lisp."

"I *know* that's not her. That's Stella Martindale. She was just in here yesterday."

209

"Wait a minute," Darnelle asked. "Let me check when she last picked up an order."

She walked to a wooden file box and flipped through some cards.

"Here it is." She held a card aloft. "She was just in here last week. I didn't wait on her so it must've been you or Rochelle."

"What day was it?" Paula asked.

Darnelle consulted the card. "Tuesday."

"That's Rochelle's day off, so it had to be me." She looked at me apologetically. "I'm sorry, EJ. I just don't remember. The day got extremely busy after you two left."

"Well, at least try to narrow it down for her, Paula. You must remember *something*. Was she fat or thin? Tall or short? Old or young?"

"I'm trying . . ."

Darnelle consulted the card again. "It says here she ordered some more Erno Laszlo hand cream, too."

"Oh," Paula brightened up. "I *do* remember her." She looked down at me. "That stuff costs more than my weekly paycheck. Let's see . . . she's kind of average height. Medium brownish or blackish hair. Maybe shoulder-length? I'm not sure about that. She could've had it pulled back. Not fat . . . I don't think. She was wearing a lightweight coat, so it was hard to tell. But her face looked normal. Plain-ish features generally—but could be pretty if she tried. Mostly kind of churchy looking, you know? She had short nails. That's about all I recall."

"Well, geez, Paula. That describes two-thirds of the women who shop here."

"Give me a break, Darnelle. It was busy that day."

"You don't recall anything else?" I asked. "How about her age? Was she young? Old?"

"She wasn't young, I don't think. Not too old either, though. Maybe . . . late thirties? Or mid-forties? Could've been fiftyish, *maybe*—but not much older than that . . . I don't think. She paid cash. I remember that."

"Really?" Darnelle asked sarcastically. "Did you get the serial numbers on the bills?"

Paula glowered at her. I was sure that if Harrie hadn't been present, she'd have made a colorful retort.

"You've both been very helpful," I said.

The wall phone rang and Darnelle scurried over to answer it. After a second, she held the receiver out toward Harrie.

"It's for you, punkin. It's your Aunt Rochelle."

Harrie rushed over to take the phone from her.

"Hi, Aunt Ro-Ro." Harrie glanced over at me. Paula was putting the finishing touches on my updo. "Yeah. Eej is in the chair again. No. Just her hair this time. It's some French thing." Harrie looked at Paula for help.

"Twist," Paula supplied. "It's a French twist."

"It's a French twist. Yeah, it looks real good. Paula said she has great raw material." Harrie giggled and looked at me. "Aunt Rochelle says Hal said the same thing about you last week." She returned her attention to Rochelle. "That's okay. We have to head on for Paradise soon, anyway. I gotta show Eej the garden there. Yeah? That's nifty! I'll tell Daddy. He'll be really excited you're coming down to see us. I love you, too. Bye, Aunt Ro-Ro."

Harrie handed the phone back to Darnelle.

"She's still held up," she explained. "So, she won't get here today."

"I'm sorry about that, Harrie." I was, too. I knew how much Harrie had been looking forward to seeing her aunt. "But I know she felt bad about missing you today."

Harrie nodded sadly. "That's what she said. But she's comin' down to Winston to see us next week. She said there's some kinda cosmetics show goin' on there at one of the big downtown stores."

"That's right," Paula added. "It's a buyer's meeting at Thalhimers."

"So, maybe we can show her around, Eej?"

"I'd like that, Harrie."

"Okay, madam." Paula removed my cape dramatically. "You're all set." She grinned. "No pun intended."

"Wow." Harrie seemed awed. "That French thing looks real good on you, Eej."

"You think so?" I asked.

"Yeah. It's dishy."

Great. Just what I was going for.

"Thank you, Paula. You're . . . quite good at your craft."

"It was my pleasure, believe me. You and Harrie come back anytime—whether Rochelle is here or not."

"Thanks for the Yoo-hoo!" Harrie took hold of my hand. "C'mon, Eej. We got a train to catch."

Harrie led me out of the store, only pausing briefly to admire her blenders. Before I knew it, we were back at the South Jefferson Street station.

And, just as Harrie had predicted, admiring business travelers *did* wave us to the head of the line for boarding.

We arrived in Paradise shortly before 11 a.m. We departed the station and Harrie led me directly to the garden that flanked the post office building. Fortunately, there was no sign of the cranky postmistress, Mrs. Troy. No matter how much Lottie had tried to push me into barging in on her and demanding her cooperation, I was just as happy to avoid seeing her on this trip.

"Over here, Eej." Harrie led the way along a narrow path to a spot near the center of the garden. She stopped beside a space that was about twelve feet by twelve feet, neatly laid out with tidy rows of herbs.

I was shocked by her discovery. Harrie had been right: the bed did contain Angelica plants and Rue. Numerous other herbs were present, too: Lemon Balm, Tansy, Lovage, Rosemary, and the Alba Rose—the White Rose of York.

It was a miniature version of the *hortus medicus*.

The whole thing was incredible. Yet here they were—the same herbs that had been grown by the Moravians at various sites around Old Salem since 1761. And they all seemed meticulously tended. It was evident that the beds had recently been weeded and mulched with hardwood bark. The newer seedlings had obviously been cultivated in a climate-controlled environment and were newly planted.

I knelt down and felt the soil. It was damp.

Maintaining a garden like this was not easy. It took constant care and attention. The tender plants needed to be watered every day. And care needed to be taken to protect the young seedlings if nighttime temperatures dipped close to the freezing mark—which still happened frequently this time of year, especially in an area this much farther north.

But who was growing these herbs? Who was caring for them so lovingly?

I looked around the rest of the large garden space. It was planted with an impressive variety of vegetables and flowering plants. Most of those plants looked healthy and well-tended, too—but no other section of the garden exhibited the same level of pristine care. And I didn't think it was any accident that the self-contained herb garden was exactly in the center of the shared community space. It was well shielded on all sides by rows of other, more typical plants like broccoli, Brussels sprouts, cabbage, cauliflower, lettuces, and spring onions.

Some makeshift cold frames were visible along one edge of the garden, closest to the white frame house. And some enterprising gardeners had apparently felt confident enough about the warmer temperatures to plant tomatoes, peppers, and eggplant. Although I did see a pile of flattened grain sacks that probably were used to protect young plants on cooler nights.

"You were right," I said to Harrie. "This *is* like our garden at home."

"What kinda special food do you think they make with all these vegetables, Eej?"

"I'm not sure. Maybe something like Brunswick stew? That's usually an autumn dish. Didn't you say the Homecoming dinner is in September?"

"That's what Mr. Truitt told me. Hey . . ." she looked up at me. "Why don't we go ask him about who grows these herbs? That's what you want to know, isn't it?"

"Well . . ."

"C'mon, Eej." Harrie dug her eye patch out of her pocket. "I know where their house is. He won't mind us stoppin' in. He said they don't do nothin' but come over here once a day to get their mail."

I supposed we were too early for Mrs. Troy to have the day's mail sorted and put up yet. As I recalled, it arrived on the later train from Roanoke. So there wouldn't be much chance the Truitts would happen by while we were admiring the garden.

And maybe they could give me a list of the people who grew plants in the community space. That might help Inez narrow her search of the alumnae records at the college.

Lord knows, Paula's physical description of Brooke Casaubon wouldn't get us anyplace . . . She could've been a composite of every woman who'd ever shopped their department.

"Okay. Maybe that is a good idea, Harrie."

"*Great.* Let's go." Harrie turned on her heel. "Follow me, Eej. I know the way."

I had a hard time keeping up with her. Harrie marched us around the corner beyond the house beside the garden, and along a side street that was dotted with more houses and a diner that seemed to be doing a brisk business. She turned on Mill Street and made a beeline for a dilapidated brick bungalow that stood next to the dirt road entrance to the Paradise Lumber Company. Two people were seated in painted rockers on the front porch. Harrie waved at them enthusiastically.

"Hey, Mr. and Miz Truitt! We came back."

Mr. Truitt raised his hand in a salute but didn't say anything.

"Can we come up and chat a spell?" Harrie asked. "It's official post office business."

Mr. Truitt nodded before spitting into a small, blue-tinted Mason jar.

We approached the brick steps that led to their porch. Several of the brick risers had been broken off. And someone had installed a hand railing that was made from cast iron plumbing pipe.

I hoped the Truitts had a less treacherous egress from their house.

"Mr. and Mrs. Truitt, hello again. I'm EJ Cloud, a postal inspector from Winston-Salem. We met briefly last week?"

Mr. Truitt nodded. "A-yup. I remember. You was over at the post office."

"Yes, sir. That's right. And that's why we're back in Paradise today, to do a spot of research about your town garden. It might help us complete the delivery of some items I've been trying to process. Would you and Mrs. Truitt know any of your neighbors who grow vegetables and herbs there? If you do, it would be very helpful."

He exchanged glances with his wife. "Waaallll. We know most ever'body that works 'ere. There's a whole crop of 'em." He smiled at his own joke. "Lessee. There's ol' Dot Crabtree an' her daughter, Dorothy Sue. An there's them Loomis gals, too. What's their names, Ma?"

"Dana and Dorsey," Mrs. Truitt answered. "They're twins and do ever'thin together. Don't they, Pa?"

"Sure do. They used'a sing in the choir at the Baptist Tabernacle until Dorsey got that throat cancer from smokin' them Lucky Strikes. Who else grows things there, Ma?"

"Dottie Purvis. She makes the best coleslaw in this county with that there red cabbage she puts in ever year. And Martha Langdon used'ta always work there, too, until her arthritis got so bad."

I'd been writing all the names down as they rattled them off. I had no idea how old most of these women were, but it should be easy enough to find out by looking them up in the City Directory.

"Is that pretty much everyone you can think of?" I asked.

"Who plants them 'maters?" Harrie asked. "I bet they're real good."

"Best 'maters you ever 'et," Mr. Truitt agreed. "Ain't they grow'd by that fussy feller that lives over the hardware store, Ma?

Dorothy Boitnott's son? What's his name?"

I perked up at once. There had been a Boitnott on the list of special-order customers Rochelle had given to me.

"*Kevin.*" Mrs. Truitt had a look of concern on her face. "That boy ain't right if you ask me."

"Is he related to Darlene Boitnott, by chance?" I asked.

Mrs. Truitt gave a slow nod. "His sister. But she don't live 'round here no more. Works over Roanoke-way. Only comes home for visits these days."

I made a note about Kevin, the "fussy feller," anyway.

"Anyone else you know of?" I asked.

Mr. and Mrs. Truitt exchanged glances. Then he looked at me. "Nope. I reckon that's it."

Harrie jumped into the fray. "Do either of y'all know who planted them herbs in that middle part?"

"Herbs?" Mr. Truitt looked confused. "What kind'ly herbs?"

"You know," Harrie began to explain. "In that big middle part where all them paths join up. There's all kind of little plants. Some of 'em with flowers. They're special kind a plants . . . not 'maters or peppers or anything. Herb plants. Back there by them roses."

The roses detail must've worked. Mrs. Truitt spoke up.

"Y'all need to ask Miz Troy about that. It's her garden so she can tell y'all who put what in."

Great. Just what I wanted to avoid . . .

But I had to hand it to Harrie. She'd done a masterful job getting more information out of the Truitts than I could've done in a month of Sundays.

I thanked Mr. and Mrs. Truitt profusely and wished them a good day. Harrie and I descended their broken steps carefully, intending to head back toward the garden.

"Say," it appeared Harrie had thought of one more question to ask before we took our leave, "what dish do you all cook up for that Homecomin' dinner, anyway?"

"Brunswick stew," Mr. Truitt offered. "Best you ever had, too. Y'all should come back fer it in September."

Harrie gave me a smug look before replying. "That's what we figgered. We'll plan on bein' here for it—won't we, Eej? See y'all then."

She gave her new friends a hearty wave and we continued along our way.

When we approached the Paradise diner, I asked Harrie if she'd like to get some lunch.

"That'd be great, Eej. I am a mite peckish, I have'ta say. Do you think we can get somethin' to take back to the garden so we can eat at that picnic table?"

"I think we should be able to do that."

We went inside and approached the counter. I tried to ignore the stir we created and how many people—men mostly—were staring at me.

In fifteen minutes, we had foil-wrapped sandwiches, potato chips, and paper cups of iced tea. We carried our lunch satchel with us back to the garden space. Harrie spread out our feast atop the picnic table before biting happily into her grilled ham and cheese sandwich and moaning with pleasure.

"I love a good ham-n-cheese. Don't you, Eej?"

"They are pretty hard to beat."

"Especially when they're all melty like this one."

"I think that's the Velveeta cheese."

Harrie took another bite. "It's sure a lot better'n that government cheese."

I did not disagree with her. In truth, I'd eaten my fill of

government cheese, too.

"Weren't Mr. and Miz Truitt nice?"

"Yes," I agreed. "They were very helpful."

"Wonder what the story is with that Kevin feller?"

I was surprised that Harrie picked up on that nuance. "I'm not sure, Harrie."

She lifted her eye patch so she wouldn't have to look at me sideways. "Do you think we need to go check him out?"

I pretended to give the idea fair consideration.

"No. I don't think so. We have a long enough list of . . ." I struggled to find the right word.

"Suspects?" Harrie supplied.

"Well. Not exactly. But, yes, we have a long list already."

"Are you gonna eat all them chips, Eej?"

"*Those* chips." I slid my foil packet toward her. "You may share them with me, Harrie."

"Thanks. I love this kind. They got a good scald on the edges. So, what are you gonna do with all them names? Are we gonna go visit all them . . . *those* . . . people?"

What was *I going to do with them?*

I considered the list on my notepad. If I included Kevin—and his sister, Darlene—that added up to seven names. Of course, I'd also have to include the garden's owner, the irascible Mrs. Troy. But I had a difficult time imagining *her* having the patience to tend plants. I sighed. On the surface, this would seem to be a random collection of people who had little in common with Dorothea—apart from a preponderance of names beginning with *D*. I looked up at Harrie, who was busy munching on scalded chips.

"I'm actually not sure."

Harrie was regarding me with a curious expression.

"Hey, Eej?" She lifted her eye patch again. "That sun hittin' your hair almost makes it look like your head's on fire."

"It does?" Instinctively, I raised a hand to my head and checked the French twist. It still felt like it was holding.

"Yeah. I wonder if Paula hit you with one of them . . . *those* . . . shiny sprays?"

Shiny sprays? I certainly hoped not. It had taken me the better part of thirty minutes to remove all traces of Rochelle's magic the last time.

"Fancy seeing you two here . . . *again*."

I closed my eyes and cursed our misfortune before looking over to meet the disapproving gaze of Postmistress Troy. Neither of us had heard her approach.

"Hey, Postmistress!" Harrie was still holding up her eye patch. "Me'n Eej are havin' lunch."

"So I see." She looked at me. Her expression wasn't as marked with disapproval as I'd expected. It was more . . . I wasn't sure what it was. "What brings you back to Paradise? Or do I even to need to ask?"

"We come to see the garden," Harrie explained with energy. "Then we visited with Mr. and Miz Truitt and they gave Eej a list of all the folks that plant stuff in this here garden." She lowered her voice. "Do you know what's up with that Kevin feller who lives over the hardware store?"

Troy seemed amused. "Kevin Boitnott?"

"That's the feller," Harrie declared.

"There's nothing 'up' with him as far as I know. He grows the tomatoes here." She looked at me. "But I assume you already know that."

"The Truitts were very kind to give us so much time."

"And information, apparently." I saw Troy's eyes take in the list of names on my notepad.

"They did share the names of some of your volunteer gardeners."

"*My* gardeners, Miss Cloud?"

"We were led to understand that the garden space belongs to you. Was that inaccurate?"

Troy took her time before answering my direct question. "No. That's not inaccurate."

"Take a load off, Postmistress." Harrie slapped the bench beside her. "You want some chips? They're the good kind."

"I see that." Troy looked down at the foil package spread open between Harrie and me. "I like the ones with the browned edges, too."

"See, Eej?" Harrie looked at me proudly. "I told you they was the best kind."

"*Were* the best kind."

I looked at Troy with surprise. She had taken the words right out of my mouth.

Harrie's face fell. "*Great.* Now there's two a y'all."

"If you wouldn't mind, Mrs. Troy," I held up my notepad, "it would be helpful if you could take a moment to look over this list of names. Perhaps, since you know them all, it might jog your memory about the possibility that any of them could have mailed the letters we discussed on our last visit?"

She looked back and forth between us while she considered my request. "I suppose I could. I'm on my lunch break."

Harrie slapped the bench again. "Have a seat, Postmistress."

To my amazement, Troy followed orders and carefully sat down beside Harrie, who magnanimously slid the packet of chips toward her.

When Troy reached out to take the notepad from me, I

noticed that she had pretty hands. Long fingers and nails trimmed short. I remembered that the Truitts had told Harrie her house had a concert grand piano in it—and we now knew the house beside the garden belonged to her.

"So, what am I looking for, exactly?" she asked me.

"For starters, do you know all of these people?"

She scanned the list and looked up to meet my eyes. "Yes. But Darlene Boitnott doesn't work in the garden. Her brother, Kevin, does, as we've already established."

"Do you think any of these people could be the one who mailed those letters?" I asked hopefully.

"I can't be sure." She stared at me. I thought her gray eyes held a tinge of suspicion. "Not without seeing the handwriting on the letters again. I don't suppose you happen to have them with you, tucked inside that old mailbag, do you?"

"I, um . . ." I rested my hand on the big leather bag. "I do, actually." I tugged the bag closer and reached inside it to withdraw the packet of letters.

"That was her *daddy's* bag," Harrie volunteered. "He was a mailman, too. Eej carries it everyplace. Don't you Eej?"

"Yes." I was flustered. "He was a mail carrier for many years. I have a . . . sentimental attachment to it."

"She even puts her gardening stuff in it when we go to town to pull weeds. It has lots of pockets in it for stuff, don't it, Eej?"

"I see." Troy reached out and selected one of Harrie's chips. "Is pulling weeds another one of your hobbies, Miss Cloud?"

"Well . . . not pulling weeds, exactly." I knew I was blushing. *How had I allowed the conversation to shift to me?* "I volunteer in the herb garden at Old Salem. That's actually why . . . *how* . . . the letters came to me in the first place."

"Do tell?" Troy bit into the chip. "That seems providential. I mean, since you also manage the DLO."

"Yes. The master gardener thought so, too." I handed the stack of letters to her.

Troy took her time looking them all over.

"Nope. Don't think this handwriting matches any of your prime suspects." She handed them back to me. "A pity."

To my ear, she didn't sound the *least* bit regretful.

"What about that Kevin feller's?" Harrie asked. "Does his handwritin' match them . . . *those* . . . letters?"

"His least of all." Troy smiled at Harrie. I was surprised by how the simple act changed her appearance. She looked less formidable and much more attractive.

What was wrong with me? I was starting to sound just like my mother.

"I do note that all of the letters appear to have been opened," Troy observed. "That's a change."

"Well . . . yes." I didn't offer any further explanation.

But Troy seemed unwilling to let it drop. "What about that forty-five-day requirement?"

"Excuse me?"

"Didn't you say that postal procedure required you to wait forty-five days before opening dead letters?"

"Yes. That's correct." I was getting a sinking feeling.

"Based on the dates of the postmarks, you haven't had custodial control of them all that long." Her eyes seemed to look right through me. "So why were they all examined?"

"Mrs. Troy," I struggled with how to explain the subversion of procedure to her with minimal self-incrimination, "my position invests me with certain authorities that allow me to override processes that would seem moot in the normal commission of our duties."

"So, you read them all?"

I blinked. Her directness was extremely off-putting. "The letters were all examined for any possible guidance they might offer."

"And did you discover anything useful?"

I was losing patience with her inquisition. "My presence here today would seem to indicate that I did not."

"I repeat," she continued to stare at me, "a pity." She got to her feet. "Thank you for sharing your chips, Harrie. Now, if you'll both excuse me, I need to head home and make my own lunch."

"Of course. Thank you, Mrs. Troy, for your help."

"Believe me," she smiled, "it was the *least* I could do."

I thought her tone suggested that she'd intended for her remark to sound as ironic as it seemed. I didn't understand that—but in truth, nothing about this annoyingly mercurial woman made sense to me.

"See ya, Postmistress!" Harrie called after her.

We both watched her walk toward the big frame house. Along the way, she stopped to pull an errant sprig of wild onion that had cropped up near some border plants and tossed it into a nearby wheelbarrow.

"She's a nice lady, ain't she, Eej?"

I was surprised by Harrie's estimation of the confounding woman. I looked at her quizzically.

She was already busy finishing up the chips.

"But I still think we might should check out that Kevin feller," she said between mouthfuls.

Harrie and I made one last stop in Paradise before heading back to the station to wait on our train home.

The Paradise Public Library was a one-room building with a musty-smelling basement that housed most of its reference materials. The dour librarian told me that was where I would find the City Directories.

"But," she explained, "we hadn't got a new one since '55. They cost too much money now."

I told her I thought I'd still be able to get the information I needed.

"I expect." She returned her attention to the books she was checking in. "Not much has changed 'round here since then."

Harrie asked her if she had any comic books.

"We don't get much call for 'em here," the librarian explained. "But there are some nice picture books up front that Boitnott boy donated. You might like them."

Harrie perked up. "Kevin Boitnott? That feller that lives over the hardware store?"

The librarian looked surprised. "Why, yes."

Harrie looked at me knowingly. "I'll check them books out, Eej."

"Good idea." I left her to head downstairs to consult the City Directories.

I was primarily interested in ascertaining the ages of the women, because it would help me refine the search window for Inez and her review of the college alumnae records.

I jotted down the entries I found for each woman, adding five years to their ages to correct for the information cited in the 1955 directory:

> Crabtree, Dorothy (Lester Crabtree). Age 64.
> 214 Water Street.
>
> Crabtree, Dorothy Sue. Age 43. 214 Water Street.

Loomis, Dana. Age 72. 118 Poplar Street.

Loomis, Dorsey. Age 72. 118 Poplar Street.

Purvis, Dorothy (Raymond Purvis). 67.
326 Salem Avenue.

Boitnott, Kevin. Age 44. 95-B Station Road.

Boitnott, Darlene. Age 46. 228 High Street.

Langdon, Martha (Rev. Alton Langdon). Age 69.
44 Church Street.

I'd returned the book to its place and started for the stairs when I got a whim. I went back to the shelf and took the book down again.

There was one more entry I wanted to search.

As I suspected, I found no listing for anyone named Brooke Casaubon. That didn't surprise me. But what *did* surprise me was why I hadn't recalled until that moment that Mrs. Troy had placed a checkmark beside that name last week, when I'd asked her to identify the names of any of the special-order customers who lived in Paradise. *How had Inez and I both overlooked that?*

Troy had to have known that no such person with that name lived in her town . . . even if she'd had no reason to grasp its literary significance. *So why would she have checked it?*

On impulse, I looked up one more name and added the information to my list.

Troy, Beatrice L. (Aubrey J. Troy, dec'd). Age 47.
101 3rd Street.

The train trip back to Winston-Salem unfolded like the previous one had. Harrie chattered away for the first thirty-five minutes—mostly about her enduring suspicions about "that Kevin feller"—before I noticed her eyelids beginning to droop. She was sound asleep with her head tucked snugly against my shoulder before we reached the state line.

I thought over the events of the day.

There hadn't been much of real consequence that had transpired. Paula's everywoman description of Brooke Casaubon hadn't clarified much of anything. And the list of community gardeners who may or may not have been responsible for planting the mini *hortus medicus* garden in the Paradise town garden hadn't exactly been illuminating, either.

The list of women—and Kevin—ranged in age from 43 to 72. If we excluded Kevin from the list, which seemed advisable, we could narrow the alumnae records search field to this list of seven names.

Unless we included B.L. Troy . . .

But that seemed pointless. What a singular person she was. It had almost felt like she'd been toying with me—making fun of my interest in solving the mystery of the letters. She'd certainly had no desire to be helpful. Maybe Lottie had been right about her, and she was one of the worst examples of our new generation of cavalier and disengaged postal workers?

But that wasn't right. Troy was 47 years old—just two years older than me. I had no idea how long she'd had her position in Paradise—but even in rural communities, you had to do diligence within the postal service before acceding to any senior management position. And that was especially true for women.

So clearly, Troy had worked for the postal service long enough to become postmistress of the branch in Paradise.

I wondered vaguely what her story was—and why she was so determined to be disagreeable—and outright misleading? I even mused briefly about the possibility that *she* had written the letters—but dismissed that idea as quickly as it cropped up. The irascible Troy would seem to be the last person inclined to pour her heart out to a stranger.

Not that it mattered. I'd have no reason ever to visit Paradise again. Not unless Inez was able to find a needle in the small haystack of names I was about to hand her. And that possibility seemed increasingly unlikely.

I stared out the window at the passing landscape. I could clearly make out the distinctive smoky-blue contours of Pilot Mountain off to the east. That meant the train hadn't stopped in Mayodan. We'd be back in Winston-Salem well before dinnertime.

Harrie slept on. I envied her ability to relax so easily. It certainly wasn't a trait I'd ever managed to acquire.

I pulled the novel I'd been reading out of my bag. It was the one Fay Marian had lent to me on Sunday. I'd barely set foot outside their door when I'd heard Inez upbraid Fay Marian for lending the book to me.

"What on earth could you be thinking?" she'd demanded to know.

Fay Marian's response had been too muted for me to make out.

Even though I knew from the cover notes that the content was considered to be downright scandalous, I'd quickly become captivated by the story of the mysterious Carol, and her burgeoning—and fraught—relationship with a young female salesclerk. It seemed hardly realistic to me. But my recent experiences with Rochelle and her various . . . *intrigues* . . . made me think that perhaps the story wasn't so farfetched. Either way, I was hooked and wanted to see where a story with so many ominous overtones went.

"They must—and do—pay a price for thinking, feeling and loving *differently*," the cover declared.

Although I understood that the story the book told was considered taboo—I, nevertheless, felt it would be a justifiable diversion from the *other* mystery complicating my life.

Or so I hoped . . .

Rosmarinus officinalis
(Rosemary)

"For the land that you are entering to take possession of
is not like the land of Egypt, from which you have come, where
you sowed your seed and irrigated it, like a garden of herbs."
—Deuteronomy 11:10

Inez and Fay Marian were sitting on their big front porch when I came by to drop Harrie off back at home. They seemed so genuinely excited to see us that I wondered if they'd been waiting on us to arrive.

"Come on inside, you two," Fay Marian insisted. "Have you had supper? We were just going to make something, weren't we Inez?"

"Yes," Inez agreed cheerfully. "We'd love it if you would join us."

Of course, Harrie accepted their invitation right away.

"What are we havin'?" she wanted to know. "Have you ever made Brunswick stew?" she asked Inez.

Inez held the door open for her. "No, I haven't. But I've heard about it. Maybe we should try it when the weather gets cooler."

I eyed Fay Marian with skepticism. "Why do I think you were lying in wait for us?"

"Maybe because I couldn't wait to see what hairdo you came back with today?" She took my arm and guided me toward the door. "It looks fantastic, by the way."

"Do you honestly think so? Harrie said it made me look like my head was on fire."

Fay Marian laughed. "Oh, yeah. *It works*. It's very Inger Stevens. Only," she held the door for me to enter ahead of her, "it's far *steamier*."

"*Fay Marian* . . ." Inez had obviously overheard Fay Marian's comment.

"That woman has better ears than that RCA dog, Nipper," Fay Marian whispered. "I can't get away with nothin'."

"*Anything*," Inez corrected.

We entered the apartment. Harrie was already preoccupied with checking out what TV shows were on. I could hear Inez busy with something in the kitchen. For the first time, I hoped it might be cocktails. That realization surprised me. I could hear echoes of one of my mother's favorite refrains: "Honestly, Esther. You're behaving like a common trollop."

It was a good thing she wasn't around to know about the book I'd been reading . . .

"Come into the kitchen you two," Inez called out. "I'm making Boulevardiers."

We joined her and claimed seats at the kitchen table.

"Let me just run a cola in for Harrie." Inez took a small bottle from Fay Marian's refrigerator and made use of the opener fastened to a kitchen cabinet. "Be right back."

"I feel guilty crashing in on you again like this," I said. "The last thing I want is to become a pest."

"Don't be silly. We love spending time with you. We wouldn't ask, otherwise. Inez worries that *we're* imposing too much on *you*."

"No. Not at all. It's been good for me to get out . . . some. Or more accurately, *at all*." I grimaced. "I suppose I have been a determined homebody for too long. It's been refreshing for me to become acquainted with so many new people—with you two, especially."

"And with Harrie, no doubt."

I smiled. "And with Harrie, no doubt."

Inez rejoined us and proceeded to pour our cocktails.

"Harrie is watching a movie."

"Let me guess," Fay Marian asked. "A Western?"

"Right first time. She's watching 'The Four Star Western' on UHF. I think I recognized Barbara Stanwyck and Melvyn Douglas."

"*Annie Oakley*?" Fay Marian started to get up from her chair.

"Hold up, cowboy." Inez placed a hand firmly on her shoulder. "Sharpshooters don't get Bouviers."

That seemed to snap Fay Marian out of her reverie.

"Sorry, EJ," she apologized. "I love Barbara Stanwyck. She always looks so ... formidable."

When we were all seated with our cocktails, Inez asked me if I'd learned anything useful on the trip to Paradise.

"Sadly, nothing earth shattering," I told her. "But I think I was able to narrow the field on our alumnae search. Thanks to Harrie's inquisitiveness, we discovered that someone is keeping a miniature *hortus medicus* in the center of the town garden in Paradise. Again because of Harrie, we gleaned a list of names of the people—almost entirely women—who help to maintain the garden." I withdrew the list and the notations I'd made with the corrected information I'd gleaned from the City Directory and showed it to Inez.

"These stand to be the only women with any possible connection to both Paradise and gardening."

Inez scanned the list. I saw her eyes widen. "*Kevin?*"

"He's an anomaly, I'll admit. But you can see that most of the women are likely too old to be our Dorothea."

"What makes you so sure about that?" Fay Marian asked.

"I neglected to tell you that Paula, the cosmetics clerk who was determined to do my hair this visit, clarified that our 'Brooke Casaubon' customer was an average- to nice-looking woman in her mid-thirties to mid-forties. As you can see, all of the women on this list are far older than that."

"Not all of them." Inez pointed to a name on the list. "Darlene Boitnott is here—even though you noted that she no longer lives in Paradise."

"True," I agreed. "But her brother does."

"Kevin?" Inez asked.

I nodded. "Precisely."

"And," Inez recalled, "she was on the original customer list, too. Was she not?"

"Yeah, but so was Brook Casaubon," Fay Marian pointed out.

"But we've already determined that the nonexistent Brooke *must* be our Dorothea," Inez insisted. "Isn't that right, EJ?"

I nodded. "But somehow, we both missed one glaring detail."

Inez seemed surprised. "What was that?"

"If Brooke Casaubon doesn't exist, why would the postmistress have placed a check mark beside her name when I asked her to identify the women she knew who lived in Paradise?"

Silence fell around the table.

"Oh, good *god*." Inez hastily consulted the paper again. "Okay. So, who is this last person on the list named Beatrice L. Troy?"

I met her eyes. "One guess."

Inez's mouth fell open.

Fay Marian sat back and guffawed. "*The Postmistress Always Rings Twice.*"

"We don't *know* that," I hurried to add. "All we know for certain is that Mrs. Troy seemed determined to toss me some kind of red herring."

'You mean you think she could be protecting someone else?" Inez asked.

"That's what I suspect, yes."

"My money's on that Kevin feller." It was Harrie. "Can I have another RC Cola, Miss Inez?"

When I got home from dinner that night, I had a hard time settling down.

Inez had told me she was planning to spend Wednesday afternoon in the alumnae office, combing through records. She said she didn't have classes after 11 a.m., so she'd have plenty of time to conduct the search. Since we'd effectively narrowed the field to a fairly short list of names, she was optimistic it wouldn't take long to go through the files to seek out the names of any girls from Paradise or the Roanoke area—especially girls who had majored in English and participated in the garden club. She'd promised to let me know what she discovered, if anything, right away.

I was antsy and distracted. I tried to busy myself with

mundane chores around the house, but it was pointless. My mind kept going back over details from the day—especially my unsettling interaction with Mrs. Troy.

Why was that woman such an enigma?

No matter how I tried to parse it, I couldn't come up with an acceptable reason for her to want to sabotage my research. But neither could I shake the feeling that we were on the cusp of solving the entire mystery.

I was tempted to sit down and reread all the letters again, in the hope I might discover something else I'd managed to miss. But I knew that would be a mistake. I was already restless and wakeful. The last thing I needed was to become even more overstimulated.

I thought about trying to lose myself in something on television. But the offerings for a Tuesday evening were limited. My only options were *Wyatt Earp, Dobie Gillis,* or *Alfred Hitchcock.*

It was far too early to go to bed, so I made myself a mug of Postum and took it out front to enjoy the quiet and solitude on my dead-end street. The moon had fully risen when I heard the first unmistakable call of a whip-poor-will. I didn't know if I'd ever heard one of the distinctive calls of the nocturnal birds this early in the spring before. Growing up, my grandmother had always been adamant about telling me I could never go barefoot until I'd heard the first whip-poor-will.

I heard the bird a second time. The sound seemed to be moving nearer to where I sat, no doubt indicating that the bird intended to forage for insects that liked to hide beneath the eaves on the roof.

To me, the sound the bird made was always so sad and doleful. Maybe that was because it seemed so timeless and tied to my earliest childhood memories—and also because we only ever heard the calls at night, when the moon was bright. I knew the old superstitions. Some insisted that the sound of a whip-poor-will singing near a house meant that death was imminent. I never forgot that one, because I thought I'd heard one of the birds repeating its insistent call in the woods near St. Philip's Church the night my mother died. But since I hadn't been sure I'd actually heard it, I didn't know whether to believe in the myth or not.

Other superstitions abounded, too. Another one I'd grown up hearing oft repeated suggested that if a single woman made a wish when she heard her first whip-poor-will in the springtime, she would be married within the year. Of course, I had no way to test the veracity of *that* theory, either.

So instead, I sat in the white moonlight with my warm mug between my hands and listened while the enterprising bird advanced closer to the house from his hiding place in the woods.

It was after I'd heard his fourth or fifth call that I closed my eyes and made a wish.

Because I'd slept so fitfully the night before, I was up and ready to head for work much earlier than usual. It was very early, and Winkler's Bakery hadn't opened yet. So, I stopped in at the Krispy Kreme doughnut shop on South Main Street to see if they had any hot doughnuts left after they'd made all their store deliveries. I was in luck. Rudolph Armstrong sold me the last two dozen of the tasty, glazed treats he'd made overnight.

I knew how much Lottie loved them, so I was careful not to give them all away to other riders on the bus that morning. There were far fewer passengers than normal since it was barely 6 a.m., but I made sure that every one of them had a hot doughnut. I didn't miss the way the driver watched me in his mirror as I made my way along the aisle to the colored section and handed out the last doughnuts in one of the boxes to the three riders seated back there.

I already had the coffee perked when Lottie showed up a few minutes before eight. She stopped dead in her tracks when she saw me—and I quickly realized it wasn't because I was holding a plate of Krispy Kreme doughnuts. She stared at me like she was seeing an apparition. It went on for so long that I grew uncomfortable.

"For heaven's sake, Lottie. Don't just stand there—say something."

"I never thought I'd see the day."

"What?" I looked down at the plate in my hands. "That I'd get up early enough to get these doughnuts you love?"

I saw something flash behind her brown eyes. I knew it presaged the end of her reverie.

"Of course not." She snapped her hand toward me dismissively.

"What is it, then?"

She fluttered her fingers around her head. "It's *that*."

Oh, good grief. She meant my hair.

I hadn't even thought about it. After I'd brushed it out that morning, I'd decided just to wear it loose. I'd done it so many times lately that it was starting to feel more comfortable to me. And, frankly, even if I had been tempted to try Paula's French twist again, I knew the Inger Stevens look was a little too formal for the basement of the post office.

"I didn't mean to shock you." I set the plate of doughnuts down beside our ancient percolator. "I just thought this was an easier style."

Lottie took off her lightweight coat and stored her purse in her locker.

"Easier? Since when have you ever done anything that was easier?"

"Do you start every day in this kind of mood?"

"What kind of mood?"

"*This* kind of mood. Like you're God's avenging angel."

She actually laughed. "Give me one of them doughnuts."

I poured our coffees and added milk and sugar to Lottie's before handing the mug to her. She took it from me gratefully.

"Thank you. I need this." She sipped it before picking up one of the glazed doughnuts and holding it to her nose. "And *this*, too." She bit into it and made happy sounds. After she'd swallowed, she narrowed her eyes and took a closer look at my hair. "I'd just about given up on miracles. But damn if this ain't one—starin' me right in the face."

"Come on, Lottie. It's not that big of a deal."

"*No?* Have you looked in a mirror? If not, I suggest you do. And if you see what I see, you'll never pin that mane of hair up into one of them tight-assed buns again."

"Could we please move on?"

"You keep lookin' like that and *you'll* be the one movin' on . . . and right quick, too."

I wondered if she'd heard the whip-poor-wills last night, too?

"I have no desire to move on—unless we're talking about getting to work. I'm sure you have a backlog from working alone down here yesterday."

"It wasn't that bad. I got through most of 'em. There's only a few that are problem children."

I nodded. "Maybe we'll get lucky and today will be slow."

Lottie clucked her tongue. "I doubt it. People just seem to be gettin' stupider. How damn hard is it to look up an address and write your own information on the outside of an envelope? Answer: it ain't hard."

"Well, with luck, zone codes will catch on."

"Zone codes?"

"Yes." I looked at her over the rim of my mug. "They'll certainly expedite accurate mail delivery."

"Of course, *you'd* think that—you and whoever wrote all them racy letters. And it figures, too—because you're also the only person on the damn planet who can remember Ricky Ricardo's phone number."

I reflexively opened my mouth to repeat it, but managed to refrain.

Lottie cupped a hand beside her ear. "Go on. You know you want to."

"*Fine.* It was MUrray-Hill 5-9975."

"The defense rests, Your Honor."

"More like the *prosecution*," I muttered.

Lottie pulled out her desk chair and sat down to enjoy the rest of her doughnut. "So, when are you gonna fill me in on your trip to Shangri-La yesterday?"

"Don't you mean Paradise?" I sat down, too. We liked to start our days with these short debriefing sessions.

"Uh huh. Did you get to see your little girlfriend again?"

Girlfriend? I had no idea who she was talking about. My face must've shown it.

"That Helen of Troy—or whatever in hell her name is." She waved a hand dismissively. "That lazy-ass postmistress with the attitude problem."

"Oh. You mean Mrs. Troy. Yes, I saw her—by accident,

actually. We were eating our lunch outside at a picnic table and she happened by."

"Happened by?"

I nodded.

"Was she out cruisin' on her broomstick or somethin'?"

"*No*. She was on her way home for lunch. Her house happens to be next door to the post office."

"Well, ain't that convenient. You get any more information outta her?"

"Nothing useful. I had a new list of names for her to review—townspeople who work in the Homecoming Garden there. They have an herb garden that's like a mini replica of the garden in Old Salem. It seemed like a connection that might have significance."

"Lemme guess: she didn't know nothin' about any of it."

I sighed. "Pretty much."

"Well, that reminds me." Lottie pulled open one of her desk drawers. "I got a present for you yesterday." She withdrew a letter with unmistakable features and held it out to me.

My heart sank. Reluctantly, I reached out to take it from her. It felt lighter than the others.

"Why are these still coming?"

Lottie shrugged. "Maybe they don't get good TV reception up there in them boonies."

I stared at the letter and the tidy handwriting on the front. "I think I'm too old for this."

"Child, if you ask me, you're just gettin' started."

I had no idea what she meant, and I was not in any kind of mood to ask for an explanation. I got up and carried the letter over to my locker so I could put it into my bag.

"I'll read this at home tonight."

"You do that, Miss Cloud."

I turned to look at her. "What's that supposed to mean?"

"Nothin'." She held up her hands. "Just don't get burned by that *Spring Fire*."

I'd had about enough of her teasing. "Let's just get to work, okay?"

We spent the next twenty minutes reviewing the problem children she'd identified from yesterday. Shortly after that, the buzzer sounded, and we heard the mechanical grinding of the dumbwaiter lowering our new bin of undeliverables. It was always a guessing game to try and predict how many there would be.

When the service elevator creaked to a halt, I walked over to retrieve the bin. It was overflowing.

Reluctantly, I pulled it out and wrangled it over to our sorting table.

"Well, damn it all to hell," Lottie said with disgust. "Are you thinkin' what I'm thinkin'?"

I met her eyes. "Does it involve another doughnut?"

Lottie smiled before she pushed past me to head for our makeshift break room.

"Child, I don't need no damn zone code to find those . . ."

When I arrived home that evening, I discovered a folded piece of paper stuck inside my screen door.

> *EJ,*
> *Please stop by my apartment when you get home?*
> *I've completed the records search and have*

information about Dorothea.
    Inez

I quickly ate a sandwich—because I was determined not to let them coerce me into eating dinner with them again—and changed into more casual clothes before walking over to Fay Marian's house on Main Street.

Inez had said I should go to *her* apartment, so I ascended the stairs and walked to her door. I thought I saw a shadow moving beneath the door to Mr. Hauser's apartment and wondered if Morty was expectantly lying in wait for Harrie and the advent of Ken-L Treats.

Fay Marian opened the door almost immediately after I knocked. She seemed excited and happy to see me.

"Come in, come in," she urged. "Inez has been going crazy waiting on you."

When I got inside, I heard Inez in her kitchen. "I'm just getting dinner on. I hope you'll join us, EJ."

I was relieved that I could decline their invitation. I was beginning to feel like a freeloader.

"No thank you, Inez. I've already eaten." I saw Fay Marian's face fall. "Would you like me to stop back later on, after you've finished your meal?"

Inez came out of the kitchen to greet me. "Absolutely not. Would you at least keep us company and join us for a cocktail?"

"It's useless to resist." Fay Marian steered me toward a chair in the living room. "We won't take no for an answer."

I capitulated. The truth was that I enjoyed spending time with them and genuinely looked forward to our cocktail dates—which seemed to be evolving into a regular event.

"Thank you." I sat down. "That would be lovely."

"Tell the truth, EJ," Fay Marian teased. "You love those Bouviers as much as I do."

"That reminds me," Inez said. "I read today that Jackie Kennedy is pregnant."

"No kidding?" Fay Marian seemed impressed. "That'll put a run in Pat Nixon's nylons."

"I doubt she planned it for that reason," Inez said drily.

Fay Marian grinned at her. "I doubt she *planned* it at all. He looks like a randy bastard to me."

"You need to stop reading *Photoplay Magazine*."

Fay Marian stuck her tongue out at Inez before winking at me. "I like the pretty pictures."

That reminded me of Harrie, doing investigative research on the photo books "fussy" Kevin had donated to the Paradise Public Library.

"I think Jackie Kennedy is a genteel addition to American politics," I observed. "It's too bad she'll now have a reduced role in the run-up to the election."

"What makes you say that?" Fay Marian asked.

"I'd imagine she'll need to keep a lower profile during her confinement."

"Her *confinement?*" Fay Marian laughed at my quaint expression. "She lives in Georgetown, not *Middlemarch*."

"Don't mock EJ, Fay Marian." Inez looked at me in solidarity. "I feel the same way about pregnancy."

"It's true," Fay Marian admitted. "Inez once compared having a baby to doing forced labor in a gulag."

"No pun intended." Inez was busy at her cocktail cart, making our martinis.

"Well, I suppose I can sympathize. I'm not blessed with maternal instincts, either."

"All evidence to the contrary." Inez distributed our cocktails and sat down on the sofa beside Fay Marian.

"What do you mean?" I was confused by her objection.

"You. Harrie. If that's not a match made in heaven, I don't know what is."

Fay Marian agreed. "Face it, *Eej*—you're the reigning mother figure in that kid's life. And she's damn lucky, too."

I appreciated their assessment of my relationship with Harrie, but I hardly thought the ten-year-old regarded me as any kind of mother substitute.

"I am exceptionally fond of Harrie, as you know. But I don't think she sees me that way at all. Our relationship is more . . ." I searched for the right words to describe it. "*Equal.* Harrie and I are attached to one another as friends, I think. I have to force myself sometimes to think of her as a child."

"She is pretty precocious," Fay Marian agreed.

"It's more than that. Harrie is advanced for her age, certainly. But what makes her unique is not so much what she knows—it's what she *understands.*"

"Hard knocks will do that to a kid." Fay Marian sounded like she knew what she was talking about.

Inez looked at her with affection. "You've done all right."

"I had help." Fay Marian reached out and gently touched Inez on the knee. "Good help."

If I'd felt the need for any kind of gazetteer to help me appreciate the unique geography of the landscape their relationship inhabited, I felt like I was acquiring one in real time.

Well . . . maybe from these intimate interactions and what I was learning from the Claire Morgan novel Fay Marian had insisted I read.

Sooner or later, I knew my day of reckoning would come. Fay

Marian would demand to know what I thought about the story of forbidden love. So far, I didn't have the slightest idea what to tell her. But bearing almost daily witness to the obvious love that existed between these two women—my friends—I found it difficult to think ill of them, or of the worldly character Carol and her wide-eyed store clerk, Therese.

I decided to navigate to safer territory.

"So, Inez," I began. "I was happy to find your note in my door this evening."

"Oh, yes." Inez picked up a notepad from the end table beside her chair. "An assistant in the alumnae office was happy to help me with my search. We were able to comb through the records in next to no time at all."

"I cannot adequately express my gratitude to you for taking the time to do this, Inez."

"Don't thank me yet," she said with a smile. "You don't know what I found."

"All right. I'm all ears."

Fay Marian looked me up and down. "*No*, you aren't," she said with obvious admiration.

Of course, Inez swatted her. It was back to business as usual.

"There were only eleven girls from the Roanoke area who graduated from Salem during the relevant era. Only *two* of them were from Paradise proper. One of the two girls married and moved to California more than twenty years ago."

"What about the second girl?"

"She was the daughter of a Methodist minister and graduated in 1935. Her name was Bea Ellen Langdon. Unfortunately for us, however, she did not major in English."

That news was certainly disheartening. But there had been a woman on the list from yesterday I recalled . . . a Martha

Langdon. Mr. Truitt said she'd stopped working in the garden because of her arthritis. But she still lived in Paradise. So that might lead to something.

"What was this Bea Ellen's major?"

Inez consulted her notes. "Music. I gather that was pretty typical during those years?"

It was true. About a third of the girls I'd gotten to know well in my class were music majors. Most of them had gone on to have careers in the church.

"Well." I sighed. "That sounds like another dead end. I suppose I should expect them by now."

"Oh, one other thing was noteworthy. I discovered that none of the girls from the Roanoke area had participated in the garden club. I thought that was the death knell for our research. But the office assistant explained to me that there had been *no* garden club until 1937. Before that time, girls who worked there just volunteered, and no record was kept of those activities."

"I should've remembered that." I was embarrassed. "I was a volunteer in the garden for part of that time myself."

"But you don't recall any other girls who did likewise?"

"Not many. But then, I mostly went on the weekends with my mother. On those days, we were usually the only volunteers. Most of the other girls were off on any of the innumerable social junkets the school sponsored."

"Ah, yes," Inez remarked. "The infamous mail-order bride circuit."

I smiled at her. "I take it you're familiar with the practice?"

"Oh, yes. I think it's barbaric that it still goes on. Why can't they realize this is 1960, not 1690?"

"Inez calls these school-sponsored fishing expeditions 'groping for trout.'"

"*Fay Marian . . .*" Inez apologized to me. "It's Shakespeare. *Measure for Measure.*"

I admitted that I'd never heard that one before.

"One other thing," Inez told me. "The office assistant told me that, as far as she knew, there hadn't been any other students from Paradise enrolled since 1935."

"That makes sense. I gather the population there is primarily geriatric—or at least, trending that way."

I finished my cocktail and prepared to take my leave.

"Are you sure you have to go?" Inez got to her feet as well. "We have plenty of food."

"I'm quite sure. But thank you, just the same. And thank you, again, for doing all this research."

"I'm sorry it wasn't more conclusive."

"That's all right. I think we've reached the end of the line with any shot at solving this mystery."

"Maybe not." It was Fay Marian. "I have an idea."

"It's not that one about using aluminum foil to extend the range of UHF antennas, is it?"

"*No.*" Fay Marian scowled at Inez. "It's about the list . . . well, *all* of the lists, actually. Why don't you run them by Professor Ogletree and see if any of the names resonate for her? I mean, let's face it: if anybody knows who was keen on *Middlemarch* during those years, it'd be her. Right?"

Inez and I looked at one another.

It was a brilliant idea, and we both knew it.

"Fay Marian, you're a genius." Inez kissed her on the cheek.

"I have to concur. It's an inspired idea." I looked at Inez. "Could I borrow the list you pulled together today?"

"Of course." Inez tore the pages out of her notepad and handed them to me. "Are you going by her house tonight?" She sounded as anxious as I was feeling.

"I don't know about that. It's seems awfully impertinent just to show up this late in the evening."

"It's not late at all." Inez consulted her wristwatch. "It's barely six-forty-five."

"You brought your bag," Fay Marian observed. "Do you have the other lists of names in it?"

I nodded.

"How about I ring her? I have her number." Before I could protest, Inez had crossed the room, picked up the handset of her telephone, and dialed the number for Lydia Ogletree.

"Lydia?" she said. "This is Inez. I'm calling because Esther Cloud is here, and she could use your help looking over the names of some students you may recall. Yes. *Exactly.* They may very well have relevance to solving her dead letter case. You are? That's wonderful. I'll tell her to come straight over. Thank you, Lydia. You bet . . . I'll tell Fay Marian you said hello. Bye."

Inez replaced the receiver and faced me with a smile. "She's expecting you."

I was overwhelmed.

"But, I don't know where her house is . . ." I began.

"That's easy." Fay Marian pointed north. "She lives right up Main Street—on the left in the yellow house, just after you pass Winkler's Bakery."

"Her house is number 520, to be exact," Inez added. "It's a little more than three blocks from here."

"Do you want me to walk you there?" Fay Marian offered. "I'd be happy to."

"No." I held up a hand. "That's kind of you, but I think I can find it."

Inez walked me to the door. "And EJ?"

"Don't worry." I smiled at her. "I promise I'll report back."

"Good. There's another Bouvier in it when you do."

That was beginning to have the ring of an offer I couldn't refuse.

Dr. Ogletree received me very enthusiastically.

"I honestly don't know why we haven't done this before now." She took my arm and led me into her small living room. The house was quaintly but tastefully furnished with many antiques and colorful paintings that looked original. Books were stacked on nearly every available surface. A wood fire was burning in the small, stone fireplace, even though the night wasn't cold. I surmised it must be as much for ambience as warmth. It did lend the space a cheerful and inviting air.

"Esther, you need to meet Sofia Becker, my housemate."

A tall woman with long silver hair stood to shake hands with me. She was wearing round, wire-framed glasses that could not conceal her stunning blue eyes.

"Esther," she said in heavily accented English. "It is always a pleasure to meet a former student of Lydia's."

"Sofia is the librarian at Salem College, Esther. But she came well after your time."

"I'm honored to meet you." I returned her warm handshake. "When did you begin working at the college?"

"In 1942," Sofia explained. "My mother and I were refugees. My father was killed by the Nazis in Berlin. We were fortunate to have relatives in Winston-Salem who would give us lodging."

"Sofia studied library science at Woman's College in Greensboro, and that's how she got the position here at Salem."

Dr. Ogletree beamed at her companion. "We are very fortunate to have her."

"Do not believe a word she says, Esther. I fear dear Lydia is in her dotage."

I was charmed by their relationship. I had to confess to a fleeting thought that perhaps they were like Inez and Fay Marian . . . but I quickly put that aside. It seemed vaguely blasphemous to entertain any personal speculation about the private life of my most esteemed professor.

"Come in and sit down, Esther. Inez said you've acquired more pieces of your puzzle—and some of them are things you'd like for me to consider?"

"Yes, if it's not too much of an imposition."

"It's not an imposition in the slightest. I explained to Sofia that you're a sort of postal detective and are working on solving a fascinating case involving the authorship of some dead letters that may have been written by a former student."

"That's an accurate description," I agreed. "And a much more succinct and coherent explanation than I could have offered."

"If you were a student of Lydia's, you should be accustomed to her ability to skim the schmaltz."

"That's *cut the fat*, Sofia." She looked at me like we shared a secret. "Immigrants."

"Well, apropos of the aphorism," I withdrew the various lists from my bag, "let me get to the point, so I don't take up any more of your evening."

"Your visit is not an imposition in the slightest," Dr. Ogletree assured me. "But I confess to being very curious about what you brought to share with me."

"I have two lists," I explained as I passed the papers to her. "The first is a list of the names of people who live and volunteer in the community garden in Paradise, where," I took pains to note, "they maintain their own mini version of our *hortus medicus*. I looked the names up in the town's City Directory, and was able to access the current addresses and determine the ages of the women. Inez used this same list when she searched records in the alumnae office yesterday, looking for any overlap."

"And did she find any?"

"Sadly, no—and none who majored in English. But she did go ahead and make a second list of all the girls who'd attended Salem from Paradise and the Roanoke area during this time period. I was able to determine that timeline from the in-person description I got from the store clerk who sold our mysterious 'Brooke Casaubon' the distinctive *Vol de Nuit* perfume the letters are all scented with."

Dr. Ogletree nodded and began to review the lists.

"It actually was Fay Marian who suggested you might recognize some of the girls from your classes. Particularly any you recall who'd been fans of *Middlemarch*. I recall you told me there weren't many."

"That certainly will refine these lists even more." Dr. Ogletree continued to review the names. After a moment, she looked up at me. "I don't recall any coeds named *Kevin*."

"Well. No. I'm sure you don't. I opted to include that name only because it had particular resonance for my . . . *associate*. He is, however, the brother of one of the women who special ordered the perfume—Darlene Boitnott."

"I see that. But I don't recall a student by that name."

Dr. Ogletree flipped to the second list of names—the one Inez had gleaned from the alumnae records. She took her time reviewing it.

"As we can see," Sofia observed, "Lydia doesn't exercise the same level of dispatch in every task."

"Shhhhh," Dr. Ogletree hushed her housemate. "I'm concentrating."

"Oh? Is that what I smell burning?" Sofia winked at me. "I thought it was creosote on the inside of the chimney."

Dr. Ogletree lowered the papers to her lap. "The more you interrupt me, the longer this will take. Rome wasn't built in a day."

"While we wait for the construction of Rome to be completed, would you like to join me in a schnapps, Esther?"

"Thank you, Sofia. But I must gratefully decline. I've already had a Bouvier . . . I mean, *Boulevardier* with Inez and Fay Marian."

Sofia chuckled. "That girl does love her mixed metaphors."

I looked at her quizzically.

"She calls it a French drink, but Campari is an *Italian* liqueur." She shook her silver head. "*Armes Mädchen.* But while Lydia is concentrating, perhaps you can explain why solving *this* particular mystery has become so personal for you?"

"Personal?" I was flustered by her question. "It's . . . actually part of my job."

"Oh," Sofia waved that explanation off. "I understand *that* part. But you have become very invested in the outcome. Is that not accurate?"

"I'm . . . I suppose I am. I haven't ever thought about it in quite that way."

"Interesting. I suspect it will become clearer to you in time."

Sofia left the room and went into their kitchen—I assumed to get her glass of schnapps.

"Well," Dr. Ogletree lowered the papers and faced me, "I can report that I clearly recall three of the girls on this list." She held up the notes from Inez. "You may wish to note these."

She waited while I withdrew my own notepad and pen.

"One of the Roanoke girls on this list, Celia Archer, was an avid reader and took several classes with me. She was particularly fond of the novels of Eliot and the Brontë sisters. She wrote one of the best papers on *Middlemarch* I'd ever had submitted—until the three others came along."

"Three others *besides* Celia Archer?" I looked at her for clarification. "Did I misunderstand you? I thought you said there were *only* three girls from the list you recalled."

"The fourth girl is you, Esther." She smiled.

"Oh." I blushed. "Sorry."

"To continue . . . the second girl from the alumnae list, Rosemary Byrd, was a true scholar. Her family lineage was impeccable—she came from one of Virginia's first families. As I recall, her father was a direct descendent of William Byrd, the tremendously successful planter who founded Richmond. She created quite a stir when she enrolled at Salem. I think the trustees had high hopes for netting a hefty endowment from the Byrd family. Rosemary was a quiet girl—very pretty and studious. She was arguably one of the brightest students I believe I ever taught—and the only one who'd already read *Middlemarch* before I assigned it in class. But sadly, she met a very tragic end."

"What happened to her, Lydia?" Sofia had returned with two glasses of schnapps, and she passed one to her housemate.

"I believe she had some deep-seated mental health issues. She'd had to withdraw and return home to Virginia before the end of her senior year. She never came back for commencement, even though she'd completed enough credits—with distinction, I might add—to graduate. We received word months later that she'd taken her own life. Drowning, I believe. It was a devastating loss—and a true waste of so much potential."

"That's horrible." I hardly knew what to say. A young woman like that . . . with every possible advantage and so much talent, *gone*—and by her own hand? It was unconscionable.

"It *was* horrible," Dr. Ogletree agreed. "And word of it roiled the campus community, too. As I said, she'd been a quiet girl, but had been much beloved by the faculty."

"*Ein sinnloser Tod.*" Sofia muttered before looking at me. "A senseless death."

"The only other girl I recall is actually from the town of Paradise. Bea Ellen Langdon, Class of 1935. She, too, was a great scholar of the British classics—and a joy to teach. She had a lively personality, as I recall, and was very quick-witted. I tried to persuade her to major in English, but she was quite an accomplished musician and was determined to major in music. I gather it was a family expectation, as well."

"Organist?" Sofia asked.

"No. Piano. I attended her senior recital, and it was a virtuosic performance."

"Why do you say her family expected her to major in music?"

"Her father was a Methodist minister. I gather the Langdons were—and are—a very church-centered family. And, as you know, many girls came to Salem to study sacred music."

I was intrigued by her observation. "But why do you say they *are* a church-centered family?"

"Because," she held up the first list—the one I'd compiled of the volunteer gardeners in Paradise, "her *mother* is on this list. Martha Langdon. I recall meeting her several times while Bea Ellen was a student. They came every year for the May Day celebration. Her mother was a Salem alumna, too. Mrs. Langdon had been raised Moravian. I believe she met her husband, Alton, while she was a student here. He was in the divinity school at Wake Forest."

"Do you know what happened to Bea Ellen after she graduated?"

"I think she worked briefly as a music director for several of the larger churches in Roanoke—until her marriage, which took place a year or so after graduation. I gather her husband was a man of means, and she gave up her music career. I lost touch with the family shortly after that. I haven't seen her on campus for many years now. Of course, that doesn't mean she hasn't visited—I just haven't happened to see her."

I closed my notebook.

"That's all very helpful. Thank you both for taking the time to see me this evening."

"Of course. I'm sorry I didn't find your smoking gun, Esther."

I smiled at her simile. *Perhaps I wasn't the only one who loved a good mystery novel.*

"At this point, I don't believe there are any smoking guns to discover."

"Well," she said, "the only other thing you might consider is asking Elizabeth McCarthy if she recalls Bea Ellen volunteering in the gardens."

I remembered Elizabeth McCarthy very well. She'd been the master gardener when I'd been a student—and she'd been single-handedly responsible for the restoration of the *hortus medicus* in 1930.

"Why would you think Bea Ellen might have volunteered in the garden?" I asked.

"Oh, it's a random thought. But I do recall that Bea Ellen always had a fondness for flowers. She often brought bouquets to me. Very beautiful they were, too—especially the white Roses."

I recall she once said they were her favorite because they smelled like heaven."

I felt as though the floor had given way beneath my feet.

There had been White Alba Roses growing in the Homecoming Garden in Paradise.

And Martha Langdon, who still lived there, could tell me how to locate her daughter . . .

I did as promised, and telephoned Inez when I reached home to update her on what Lydia Ogletree had shared. She, too, believed that we might have discovered our Dorothea. The question was, how to contact her?

I was certain that her mother, Martha Langdon, held the key.

The best way to approach Mrs. Langdon, of course, would be in person. But frankly, the thought of yet another train trip to Paradise held little appeal for me. And I felt guilty about the undue burden my repeated absences from the DLO placed on Lottie.

If only there were some *other* way to get the information I needed.

I recalled Lottie's oft-repeated assertion that the cranky postmistress in Paradise worked for Uncle Sam, just like we did—and that I simply needed to pull rank on her and *compel* her to cooperate. If I *could* get Troy to assist me in locating the whereabouts of Martha Langdon's daughter, it would simplify things greatly—and save me another train fare. I wasn't sure about much, but I did suspect that Troy would be as invested in my not having to make a return visit as I was.

I recalled that she'd written down her contact information for me during my first interview with her. I doubted that she'd have given me her home telephone number, but at least I'd be able to reach her as soon as her tiny post office opened at 8 a.m. sharp.

I was entirely confident that someone as persnickety as Troy would open her office on time.

It took me a while to locate the folded piece of paper in my bag—mostly because I quickly became distracted by the newest Dorothea letter Lottie had given me earlier at the office.

I could try to pretend otherwise, but I knew I was going to read it. I wouldn't be able to sleep if I didn't. Left unopened, the letter would be like another whip-poor-will, circling my house, challenging my serenity, and portending the advent of something unforeseen. It took an effort, but I managed to set the letter aside while I continued to look for the note that contained Troy's contact information. Finally, I found it, tucked behind our punched return tickets from the two train trips to Roanoke and Paradise. I deposited both items on the table beside the letter and returned my bag back to its hook in the foyer.

For once, a mug of Postum didn't sound appealing. I actually wished I had another one of Inez's "Bouviers" . . . the *Italian* cocktail, as Sofia had pointed out.

Sofia's direct question about why the resolution of the mystery mattered so much to me personally was still unsettling. I'd wanted to disagree with her surmise—but knew that it would be untruthful to do so. I *was* invested in the outcome. I just didn't know why—or what I wished for.

I thought about Fay Marian and Inez, and how much getting to know them had changed my life. It was past time for me to entertain my new friends at *my* home—including dinner *and* cocktails. Of course, I'd never bought liquor in my life, but I was pretty certain Lottie could fill me in on whatever I needed to know. I decided that I would invite them to join me on Saturday, if they were free. The only other thing I had planned for the weekend was having Nelson come by to clear those branches from my roof. That would give me plenty of time to shop and plan my menu.

And perhaps by then, the mystery would be solved, and we could spend our time talking about other things.

Like Fay Marian's book . . .

I still wasn't ready for *that* conversation—although I was certain I'd have finished reading the story long before Saturday. I fervently hoped the ending wouldn't be tragic, as the dark direction of the story seemed to suggest. I didn't need any more sadness in my life. *None of us did.*

Harrie's book sat on the table where I'd placed the letter and the paper with Mrs. Troy's contact information. *The Cricket in Times Square.* I'd promised to begin reading it to her when she finished her Ramona book. Harrie had taken pains to tell me that she'd read the last chapter of *Ramona and Beezus* on Monday night, and she'd been impatient to know when we could begin the new book.

I smiled. *Perhaps I'd make a date with Harrie for the weekend, too?*

Although I didn't need to orchestrate opportunities to spend time with her—Harrie had essentially commandeered my schedule since the day I'd first met her, standing with her skinned arms akimbo, in the center of Fay Marian's so-called French burial ground. What a sea change the ten-year-old had wrought in my life. Through Harrie's eyes, I'd learned to see the world as it really was.

An ironic feat, considering the fearless youngster seemed to prefer the view with one eye occluded. Maybe that was her secret?

You had to work harder to see things with one eye.

Now I was beginning to sound like Carla Hotbed . . .

With resignation, I picked up the note from Mrs. Troy. Maybe I'd be in luck, and she'd have written down her home telephone number, too? *Fat chance.* Troy wasn't about to do anything that would make my job easier. I unfolded the paper and read what she'd written down that day in her office.

As predicted, no home telephone number had been provided—just her name and the private number for the telephone in her office. She'd also written down the hours of operation for the post office. So, I resolved to call her bright and early tomorrow morning, as soon as the tiny branch opened.

When I returned the note to the table with the letter and Harrie's book, I noted what a curious kind of triptych the three items created. They were wholly unrelated, yet strangely interconnected. It was odd how seemingly disparate things in life could still overlap like circles in a Venn diagram. No matter how dissimilar you believed things to be, they still contained points of logical relation to each other.

That was when I saw it.

Oh, my dear sweet God . . . the handwriting.

The cursive script on Troy's note bore a striking similarity to the handwriting on Dorothea's letter.

It was impossible. And yet? I picked them both up and held them side by side.

I felt the blood rush to my head.

No one would deny that there was a near perfect match between the two.

But how could Mrs. Troy possibly be the student Dr. Ogletree spoke of with such fondness? What words had she used to describe her? *Vibrant personality and quick-witted.*

Neither of those things sounded like the dour woman I'd met on two occasions.

Yet, upon reflection, I had to admit there *had* been traces of wit . . . but it had always been cloaked in irony and sarcasm.

I felt like I was at sea.

I recalled the City Directory listing for Mrs. Troy: *Troy, Beatrice L. (Aubrey J. Troy, dec'd). 47.*

B.L. could easily be an abbreviation for *Beatrice Langdon*—daughter of Martha Langdon, the pastor's wife who lived on Church Street. And if Troy were forty-seven years old, that would mean she'd probably have graduated from college in 1935—the same year as Bea Ellen Langdon, the Salem College student who loved flowers and British novels—and the same student who had played the piano beautifully, just as I was becoming certain B.L Troy did, since I knew she had a concert grand piano in her home.

And someone was growing white Alba roses in the town garden . . . the garden B.L. Troy owned.

In that moment, I felt as if I'd just run a full marathon: exhausted, dehydrated, depleted—but also exhilarated and slightly euphoric.

No wonder Troy had quizzed me about why I'd read the rest of the letters. It made sense. She must've felt some version of the same things I was feeling right now. After all, she'd mailed the letters here, to the *hortus medicus*, for some reason. She must've longed for someone who was intimate with the garden that had once meant so much to her to find connection with her anguish and loss.

But if my suspicions were right, what would I do with the information?

I could hardly return the letters to her now, without any

real certitude that she had authored them. And in some way, I understood that Troy's discovery that someone had read them—*that I had read them*—might just have fulfilled her very purpose in writing them in the first place. She had finally told her story. And the lone person, who now knew her truth, did not turn away from it—but had, instead, become relentlessly committed to reuniting the storyteller with her elusive, lost love.

I stared at the newest letter Lottie had given me that day. Its postmark indicated that it had been mailed just two days after Harrie and I had made our first visit to Paradise. If, as I now suspected, Troy was the author, she knew the letter would come straight to me.

I picked it up with trepidation. What would she have to say now ... *to me?*

There was only one way to answer that question.

I opened the letter, withdrew its pages, and began to read.

Dear Mary Ann,

I find myself in a whirlwind of confusion.
You have chosen to confound me at every step,
and your latest interference is no exception. Why
have you sought to unmask me and lay me bare to
the censure of the world? Why have you granted
me license to pour out my heart and the deepest
longings of my soul, only to have my words
rebound like taunts from Echo, the great trickster?
You have chosen to goad and torment me by
instilling within me vain imaginings incited by
another fair emissary—one possessing the hypnotic
voice of a siren and hair made of fire.

What is your purpose, Mary Ann? What if any good can you seek to effect by awakening within my heart this faint and timid beat of hope—while my head retains the harsh clarity that you intend for nothing but a malicious repeat of former, vexatious outcomes? I know that I shall once again be rendered lost, alone, bereft of hope, and made foolish by the exercise of my weakness and inability to resist the temptation you have seen fit to set before me.

Why, Mary Ann? Has not my previous suffering been enough for you? Why must you now flatter me with vain hopes and fleeting sleights of hand? I have not the strength to remain steadfast in my resolve if your continued assaults on my newly awakened senses continue. I beg you to take pity on the shallow veneer of strength I cling to and leave me to cultivate my garden as before— with my only companion being the cold comfort of base solitude.

Dorothea

It was impossible for me to string any set of coherent thoughts together after reading the letter.

If I'd suspected that the words it contained might be addressed to me, I now had proof. "Dorothea" was asking *me*—pleading with *me*—to give up my quest and to leave her alone—if not in peace, then at least in solitude. Knowing that, it would be unconscionable for me to continue to pursue her by citing a flimsy point of procedure as my justification—no matter how much my own heart might be pushing me to continue our connection.

Although it was a mortifying admission to make, I had to own that I had permitted myself to become a participant in her suffering—*a willing voyeur*. And Dorothea's last, latest lament was aimed solely at begging me to stop. Last, because I knew with certainty that no other letters would follow.

After carefully folding the pages scented with *Vol de Nuit* and returning them to the envelope, I resolved to make my own *night flight*: when the full moon hid its face, I would destroy the letters.

I made an uneasy peace with my decision. But throughout the long night that followed, my dreams were haunted by echoes of a siren with hypnotic eyes, and hair made of fire.

Rosa x Alba
(White Rose of York)

"Now I know in part; but then I shall know even as I am known."
—I Corinthians 13:12

Inez and Fay Marian accepted my dinner invitation without hesitation. It was strange to think that neither of them had ever visited my home. With shock, I realized that I had known them less than a month. It was impossible for me to reconcile the swift intimacy and affection that had grown up between us in such a short period of time. But I chose not to question it and resolved instead to be grateful for the richness their friendship had added to my once solitary life.

Lottie'd been more than a little bit curious about the content of the newest letter. I managed to give her the barest gist of what it contained, without compromising the writer or myself, and I told her of my decision to destroy the letters.

"I don't think we'll be receiving any more of them," I declared.

For once, Lottie accepted my statement at face value. At least,

I *thought* she did. Her only comment was to remark that, in her opinion, it was about time for me to "cut bait."

I didn't ask her to elaborate because I was too afraid that she'd see through my veneer of pretense.

Later that morning, when I asked her for help navigating the purchase of the liquors I'd need to make the Boulevardiers, she stared at me open-mouthed for at least ten seconds—although it felt like much longer. When finally she spoke, it was to ask for assurance that I hadn't come down with some kind of brain fever.

"Child, have you overdosed on some of them herbs you got growin' over there in that hocus pocus garden?"

"I think you mean *hortus medicus*—and no, I have *not* overdosed on any herbs. Nor do I have a brain fever."

"Well, what in hellfire *has* come over you? First you start comin' to work lookin' like Maureen O'Hara, and now you're wantin' a road map to the damn liquor store."

"*Nothing* has come over me," I lied. In fact, something had come over me, and its effects were more far-reaching than the simple ingredients of a French-Italian cocktail. "I'm having some friends over for dinner tomorrow night, and I'd like to serve cocktails. To do that, I have to know how to find the ingredients."

"*You're* havin' people over for dinner?"

I nodded.

"Tomorrow night?"

"Yes. Tomorrow night."

"If that don't beat all." She shook her head in what lately was becoming her characteristic response to just about anything I did. "What kind a cocktails do you wanna make?"

I was reluctant to tell her the name of the fussy drink.

"It's French . . . and Italian."

Lottie narrowed her eyes. "What in tarnation is it? Some kind of damn U.N. treaty in a glass?"

Glass! I realized I'd totally forgotten about the glasses. I couldn't serve Boulevardiers in water tumblers. *Even though I knew that Fay Marian probably wouldn't complain about the proportions . . .*

"I'll need to get some martini glasses, too," I added. "Where would be the best place to acquire those?"

"I need to sit down for this . . ."

"Come on, Lottie. It's not *that* dramatic."

"Hold your horses." She dropped into her desk chair. "Give me a minute to think this over."

"Does that mean you don't know where I need to go to get the ingredients?"

"No, it does not. It means I need to find a church that still does damn *exorcisms*."

In the end, Lottie set aside her concerns for my mental health—and eternal salvation—and consented to provide me with the information I needed. She suggested that a store like Thalhimers would be the best place to find martini glasses that wouldn't break after one use. And she told me the general areas in the liquor store to find the rye whiskey and the Campari. The sweet vermouth, she explained, would be found in the grocery store with the sweet wines. She pointed out that to make a proper martini, I'd also need something like a beaker that was large enough to mix the ingredients together with ice, and a strainer.

Oh. And I'd need a measuring cup, too, so I could measure the components accurately. That was the only thing I already possessed.

This was all like a foreign language to me. But I dutifully wrote down all of her instructions. And I no longer wondered why Inez made use of a special cart to transport all of her cocktail paraphernalia.

Thankfully, I was on more familiar terrain with the menu. I was making a bona fide stalwart of the town we lived in: chicken pie. I had my grandmother's recipe—the same one that single-handedly had raised enough money at a benefit to add a new roof to her church in Bethabara. With it, I'd serve redskin potatoes and green beans. And I'd also make my grandmother's applesauce cake for dessert.

I picked up the "Bouvier"-making materials during my lunch hour on Friday. I'll never forget the expression on Lottie's face when I stashed the whiskey and other ingredients inside my locker.

"People who don't believe the Lord still does miracles need to be seein' this."

The rest of my shopping, I did on Saturday morning. I'd had to make two trips into town on the bus, because I'd been determined to give into a wild impulse and acquire one other item that wasn't on the menu. But even with that, I took care to be finished with my errands and back at home with plenty of time to spare before Nelson arrived to remove those pesky branches from the back of my roof. Ever since I'd seen them from the windows of the Harts's apartment, I'd been in a tizzy to get them cleared away. Nelson had been working on the grounds at St. Philip's the previous weekend, and when he stopped by to say hello, I'd asked him if I could borrow a ladder from the church that was tall enough to reach my roof. He made it clear in short order that he was having none of that.

"Miss Esther, you got no call gettin' up on any roof. Ruthie would have my hide if I let you get into somethin' like that. I promised your daddy I'd always look after you if he wadn't around. Now what would he think if I stood by knowin' you could fall and do yourself a harm? Now you just tell me whatever it is that you need doin', and I'll take care of it."

I'd been reluctant to even ask him about the ladder because I knew he'd react precisely as he had. But I also knew it would be pointless to argue with him. And I'd long since learned that trying to pay him for his help was a non-starter. Instead, I made quiet donations to the maintenance fund of his beloved St. Philip's Church. Predictably, Nelson declared his intention to come by my house on Saturday around lunchtime to take care of the branches.

Shortly after noon, Nelson arrived carrying the tall extension ladder from St. Philip's. We walked around to the back of my house, and he proceeded to secure it before climbing up to remove the fallen branches and some other debris that had accumulated up there after all the early spring storms.

While he worked, I busied myself tidying up some of the flower beds along the back fence. I hadn't been aware that I'd been humming, but Nelson must've overheard me. When he finished clearing the roof and had descended the ladder, he teased me about it.

"It's been a long time since I heard that ol' velvet voice of yours—not since before your daddy died, and you two would sing together." He slowly shook his head. "Not many things in life sounded prettier'n that."

I was embarrassed by his praise. "I guess I haven't felt very inclined to sing since he left us."

"Now you know he wouldn't want that."

"I suppose not." I wiped my hands on an old towel. "I do miss it, actually. I still love music so much."

"Then you have an obligation to be sharin' them gifts, Miss Esther. Listenin' to you up on that roof, I could just feel your daddy smilin' up in heaven."

That image warmed my heart. "Thank you for saying that, Nelson."

"Well. I never had no trouble speakin' the truth."

After Nelson had collected and carried off the smaller debris, he painstakingly broke down the larger segments of tree limbs and stashed them inside a kindling box next to the hutch that housed my firewood.

"Those'll dry out real nice by fall and make it easy for you to get a good fire goin' when the weather turns cold."

I had to admit the picture he summoned up had great appeal to me—especially, as I told him, if I'd be warming myself up while snacking on some of Ruthie's Sweet Potato Jacks.

He flashed me that million-dollar smile of his—the one that made me believe every good thing in life was possible if only we did right, worked hard, and never lost faith in the grace of God.

"Now you know that Ruthie only makes them treats at Thanksgiving—and that's a long ways off yet."

"Not so far off," I argued. "It'll be here before we know it."

"Why're you in such a hurry to race ahead to wintertime, when we got the whole promise of summer just barely comin' on? I know it ain't just to get some of them sweets."

"Well . . . maybe I just need to have something to look forward to."

I'd intended the remark to be flippant, but Nelson seemed to hear everything unsaid that hid behind my explanation.

"Miss Esther? One thing I know for sure is how fast the time we're allowed gets gone. And knowin' that, I believe that wasting a single bit of it might be the greatest sin of all. So instead of worryin' about gettin' some kinda sweet treat more'n half a year from now, why not open them pretty green eyes your daddy give you, and look at all the sweet gifts God has already put right in front of you?"

I suddenly felt like crying, and I didn't know why.

But one thing I didn't have to wonder about: one of the greatest gifts God had ever put in front of *me* was standing right there on my front porch.

"Do you think Ruthie would mind if I came over to visit some time, and watch her bake?" I asked him.

"Why, Miss Esther," he said, "I believe she'd be as pleased as punch."

About thirty minutes before Fay Marian and Inez were due to show up, I was surprised when I heard a knock, meaning another visitor had arrived at my front door. When I went to answer it, I was surprised to see Johnnie Hart standing there, twisting his hat with obvious uncertainty.

My first thought was one of panic . . . had something happened to Harrie?

"Hello, Johnnie." I held the screen door open. "Is Harrie all right?"

"She's fine, ma'am."

I was immediately relieved. "Won't you come inside?"

"No, ma'am," he said. "I won't take much of your time. I was just wantin' to stop by quick and thank you."

I joined him outside on the porch. "Thank me? Thank me for what?"

"Well, ma'am, it ain't no secret that you been spendin' a bunch of time with my girl. And I'm real grateful to you for that. She ain't never had much contact with grown-ups—'specially not ones who can set her a good example. I feel real bad about that. Ever since her mama run off . . . well. I've had to try to be both mama and daddy to her—and I don't think I get it right most of the time. Womenfolk are a mystery to me, to tell you the truth."

I was touched by his obvious devotion to Harrie.

"Johnnie, I have to disagree with you. I think you're an excellent parent to Harrie. You provide for her in all the ways she needs. She's very self-confident—and most of that comes from knowing she has a daddy she can count on."

"Well . . . I don't know about all that. She's always been kinda headstrong, you know? Like her mama. But I try to do right by her. Rochelle tells me not to worry 'bout that. She says Harrie's got a good heart 'n better sense than her mama had. But I know good people like you'n Fay Marian and Miss Inez—well . . . you all make my job a whole lot easier."

I stepped forward and hugged him. He seemed as surprised by the gesture as I was. But belatedly, he gave me a gentle hug back.

"Johnnie, you need to know that the *best* thing Harrie's got going for her is that she got you as a daddy."

He seemed embarrassed. I watched as he pulled a bandana from his back pocket and wiped at his neck. It was obvious that my words meant something to him.

"I think you know Rochelle is comin' down next week. Harrie and me would like it a lot if you could come 'n have supper with us."

"I'd love that, Johnnie. You let me know what I can contribute, okay?"

271

"Yes, ma'am. I sure will." He backed toward the steps. "Miz Cloud? I know'd Rochelle done things to your hair while you was up there on them store visits. I hope she didn't offend you none. She can be kinda pushy." He gave me a small smile. "Kinda like Harrie."

"Believe me, Johnnie. I wasn't at all offended."

He looked relieved. "That's good." He turned to leave. Halfway down the steps, he turned around to look at me. "I don't mean no disrespect or nothin', but your hair does look real good that way, ma'am."

"Thank you, Johnnie." I smiled at him. "You know what? I think so, too."

Inez and Fay Marian arrived right on time. They exclaimed over my house and loved the improvements I explained I'd made to it after my mother's death. Inez especially liked that I had a formal dining room. The one regret she had about her apartment, she said, was the eat-in kitchen.

I was bold enough to suggest that the other aspects of her living arrangement more than made up for the lack of a dining room. Inez looked at me with wide eyes, and Fay Marian laughed out loud.

"Don't think I won't start reminding her of that every time she complains about it," Fay Marian joked.

"I don't know what you're making, EJ," Inez observed. "But it smells divine."

I told them I'd baked us a traditional Moravian chicken pie.

"No way!" Fay Marian was ecstatic. "I *love* those! Does it have a double crust?"

I smiled at her. She was about as excited as Harrie got whenever she was near a Yoo-hoo.

"Of course it does," I explained. "It wouldn't be authentic otherwise. And just so you know, my grandmother always insisted that it be served with extra gravy—so that's how I make mine, too."

"Dear God . . . I think I've died and gone to heaven." Fay Marian looked like she meant it.

"Well, you might need to hold your applause," I cautioned. I proudly displayed the cocktail fixings I'd acquired. "*This*, on the other hand, was a brand-new experience for me."

"Glory be to God." Fay Marian clapped her hands together.

I was quick to ask if one of them would please consent to make the drinks.

Fay Marian volunteered right away.

"Dang, EJ," she exclaimed when she picked up the bottle of rye. "You bought the *good* stuff."

To be fair, I'd had no idea a line of demarcation separated cheap booze from *the good stuff*. I said as much, and pointed out that when I'd finally screwed up my courage and asked Lottie for help, she hadn't explained that nuance to me.

Inez seemed to get a kick out of my story. "I can only imagine the reaction she had when you appealed to her for help buying whiskey."

"Trust me," I said. "I don't think you can. First I stunned her with the new hairstyle—then I added insult to injury by asking her for information about shopping in a liquor store." I sighed. "She thought I'd been possessed by demons."

Fay Marian laughed. "If you have been, they're at least the fun kind."

"There's a difference?" Inez asked with a raised eyebrow.

"Hell, yeah. A *big* difference." Fay Marian winked at Inez. "You, above all people should know that."

Inez chose not to disagree with her.

"I suppose I do," she said quietly.

After Fay Marian had poured our drinks, we carried them out to my front porch to enjoy the early evening. It was a lovely night, and the days were beginning to lengthen. I thought about Nelson's admonition to enjoy the good things that were right in front of me. These warmer evenings were part of that. So was having the companionship of good people like Inez and Fay Marian. Looking out across my front yard toward the simple majesty of the old St. Philip's African Moravian Church, I was reminded of the impermanence of life—but also the staying power of faith and love. Those things abided long after we'd departed these lives. We were only tenants of God's creation. Stewards, actually. Our job was simple: care for the things He'd provided, and do our part to make them better for the next generation.

"You seem lost in thought," Inez said gently. "What are you thinking about so intently?"

I chose to answer the question I thought she'd intended to ask. "It's about Dorothea and the letters. I've decided to let them go."

"Meaning?" Fay Marian asked.

"I'm going to destroy them, and not pursue her mystery any more. Some things, by design, are intended to remain private—and I've come to believe that Dorothea's heartrending laments about a great love, gained and lost, are among them."

Inez didn't question my decision. I think she understood it. But she did ask me about one thing.

"Why do you still call her 'Dorothea,' when you now know

274

her real name?"

It took me a few moments to reply to her predictably direct question. I dearly hoped she would accept my response at face value and not press me for more elaboration than I thought I could provide. It wasn't that I wanted to avoid disclosing anything to her. It was more that I honestly had no real idea how to explain my reactions to anything related to Dorothea or the letters. It had all been changing so rapidly that even I was finding it impossible to track the evolution of my understanding.

And my *feelings* ... well ... they inhabited an unknown realm.

"It's difficult to explain," I finally said. "Once I learned her true identity, the persistence ... the passion ... I'd invested in finding her felt ... *inauthentic*—inappropriate, even. I felt that by pursuing her, I'd intruded on something that had always been intended to remain private. Her letters to Mary Ann, in fact, *did* constitute a kind of death. And when I reached that realization, I finally understood the true, finite, and limited scope of my involvement—and that understanding dictated that the only legitimate action available to me was to destroy her letters."

I wanted to add, *and set her free*. But I didn't.

Inez listened to my explanation intently. She made no reply, but eventually gave me a slow nod and a smile that was confined mostly to her eyes.

Fay Marian, for once, remained quiet, too.

It was gratifying to me that my new friends, even if they didn't understand my motivations, cared enough about me to respect them without argument.

We had easy conversation while we finished our Bouviers, and then moved back inside to have our meal. Both women exclaimed over the chicken pie—even though I kept insisting that it was my grandmother who deserved the credit for any perfection they perceived in the crust.

It was while we were eating our slices of applesauce cake that Fay Marian finally decided to ask me if I'd finished reading the Claire Morgan book—and proceeded to quiz me about its unique storyline.

"So, EJ? What'd you think?"

I decided to make her work for it.

"What did I think . . . about what?"

"Well." She stole a glance at Inez. "About the relationship between Carol and Therese."

"Oh." I kept my voice as matter of fact as possible. "I found it charming that two such dissimilar women were able to develop such a close friendship."

Fay Marian was clearly at a loss for how to respond to my summary.

For her part, Inez held out for as long as she could before breaking out into peals of laughter.

"What's wrong with you?" Fay Marian demanded.

"I'm just amazed at your gullibility," Inez replied, still chuckling.

Fay Marian looked back and forth between the two of us. "What am I missing here?"

"From my perspective, I'd say just about everything."

Fay Marian glowered at her. "Come on, Inez. You know what I'm referring to."

"Yes. I do. And obviously, so does EJ."

"What do you mean?" Fay Marian looked at me. Then she noticed that I was having a hard time keeping a straight face, too. "You two must've been separated at birth," she declared. "I think I need another Bouvier."

"Help yourself," I said magnanimously.

Fay Marian got up to head for the kitchen. "Any other takers?"

"Sure." I said. "If we're going to have an in-depth discussion about depictions of homosexual relationships in popular fiction, we might as well grease the skids."

Inez tittered gleefully.

Fay Marian stood rooted in place like a statue and blinked at me. "Who *are* you?"

"Lately I've been asking myself that same question. Let me go and retrieve your copy of the book and maybe we can discuss it?"

So, we did—for the better part of an hour. The night before, I'd even taken the time to make a few notes on passages I'd found to be particularly revelatory—and relevant for me. I shared those with the two women who had come to mean so much to me.

> "It would be Carol, in a thousand cities, a
> thousand houses, in foreign lands where they
> would go together, in heaven and in hell . . ."

And:

> "She had heard about girls falling in love, and
> she knew what kind of people they were and
> what they looked like. Neither she nor Carol
> looked like that. Yet the way she felt about
> Carol passed all the tests for love and fitted all
> the descriptions."

Our conversation gained energy and traction as we explored the risks the author, who Fay Marian said was rumored to be the well-known American novelist, Patricia Highsmith, had taken by allowing her principals to have a happy ending.

Although Inez hastened to add that having to give up custody of her child was hardly an unqualified happy ending for Carol. That led us to a conversation about hypotheticals. What would we each be willing to give up to have a great love?

Fay Marian was bold enough to immediately answer, "Anything."

Inez chided her. "Even your beloved Bouviers?"

"Of course. Because without you, they'd be like drinking bitter herbs."

I was brought up short by her response. I thought immediately about Dorothea . . . *about Beatrice* . . . and what she'd been forced to give up—even though I didn't know the circumstances that had led to her great loss. And that led me to think about myself, and the enormity of what I was poised to give up, without ever having had it.

"What about you, Inez?" Fay Marian asked. "What would you surrender for happiness?"

"You mean besides an apartment with a formal dining room?"

Fay Marian grinned at her.

That left me—the only one who'd not yet answered the question.

I knew my friends would be careful not to push me into a response they knew I wasn't ready to make. After all, how *could* I make any response? I wasn't a woman of little experience: I was a woman of *no* experience. I didn't know the first thing about the choices Carol had been forced to make to have a life with the woman she loved. I was barely beginning to comprehend that a world existed where such choices were even possible.

But I *was* learning something about loss . . . and regret. About the death of hope, and the probability that both Beatrice and I would live out our days alone—tending our patches of bitter herbs in gardens that would forever be divided by fate, geography, and the capricious whims of history.

None of these things I shared that night. But I did take a measure of comfort from the examples set by my dear companions, who I knew had barely begun to teach me the things I'd need to know to find my way forward. For that night, at least, it was enough.

Harrie appeared at my door not long after lunchtime on Sunday. I'd been sitting on my front porch with the newspaper and had just begun to read the local news when I heard her calling out to me from the corner of Race Street.

"Eej! Eej!" She was out of breath. "Have you heard the news, Eej?"

She dropped her scooter in the yard and dashed up the steps to join me.

I folded my paper and reached out a hand to calm her down.

"Slow down, Harrie. Take your time."

She dropped into a chair beside me and took several deep breaths.

"Now," I asked, after her level of excitement had settled down. "What's your news?"

"That mean man at Woolworth's is *gone*," she declared. "And we can have pie with Jerome, now."

I was surprised by her report. "What do you mean, he's gone? What happened?"

"Daddy told me this morning that the city changed the rules about them lunch counters. We can all eat together now, Eej. So can we go have pie with Jerome?"

Was she talking about the mayor's goodwill committee? I picked up the paper and opened it to the local news section. Sure enough . . . the headline was right above the fold.

Lunch Counter Mixing Is Approved In Winston

WINSTON-SALEM Variety store merchants in this tobacco city have voted to integrate lunch counters "in the near future."

The action came at an afternoon meeting of Mayor Marshall Kurfees' "Good Will Committee."

The committee issued this statement:

"At a meeting of the mayor's committee with merchants it was unanimously recommended that the lunch counters be desegregated. The merchants agreed with this recommendation, and with the committee are working on a plan to put this into effect in the near future."

It would be an understatement to say I was every bit as excited as Harrie was. If I'd thought I could've handled it without breaking a leg, I'd have jumped on her red scooter and taken off on a few celebratory laps around the block myself.

"This is wonderful news, Harrie!"

"Ain't it?" She noticed my subdued grimace. "*Isn't* it?" she corrected.

"Yes, it certainly is."

"Can we ask Jerome to meet us for pie, now, Eej?"

I thought about her simple request. "I don't see why not. I bet he would enjoy that as much as we would."

"Fay Marian said she heard that mean manager feller there

quit when he heard the news."

I told her I wasn't surprised one bit.

"Carla always said good riddance to bad garbage. I reckon he's what she was talkin' about."

I didn't want to compromise our celebratory mood by dissecting the witticisms of Carla Hotbed. I thought the better part of valor was to change the subject.

"Why don't we do something special to celebrate?"

"Sure." Harrie perked right up. "What'cha got in mind, Eej? They're showin' a bunch of *Lone Rangers* on UHF all afternoon."

"I was thinking about something more . . . interactive. Like how about we start reading your *Cricket in Times Square* book together?"

"Really?" Harrie sat up straighter in her chair. "That'd be great, Eej."

"But I've been sitting out here a while and I'm kind of thirsty. How about we go into the kitchen and rustle up something to drink?"

"Okay." Harrie hopped off her chair and held the screen door open for me. "Postum, Eej?"

"Hmmmm. Maybe not today. Let's see if we can find something more exciting."

Harrie followed me to the kitchen. I heard her gasp when she crossed the threshold.

"*Eej* . . ." She was staring open-mouthed at the new appliance on my counter.

"Do you like it?" I asked.

She looked at me with eyes as wide as saucers. "*It's an Osterizer.*"

"Yes, it is. I thought we needed one—just in case they don't go on sale at Christmas."

Harrie approached it tentatively and ran her fingers across its shiny, mint green base.

"It looks way bigger in here than it did at Aunt Rochelle's store." Her tone was reverential.

"I thought so, too. I'm not sure where I'll keep it when we're not using it. But I'll figure something out."

"Can we try it out?"

"Of course. Why don't you go to the fridge and get out some ice."

"Okay, Eej." Harrie turned away from the blender reluctantly and walked over to the fridge so she could retrieve the ice trays from the freezer compartment. "Eej!" she called out. "There's *Yoo-hoos* in here!"

"I know, Harrie. I thought we needed them to make milkshakes."

Harrie turned away from the chocolate spectacle and rushed across the room to throw her arms around me. I was surprised by her sudden, affectionate onslaught—and very touched.

"Thanks, Eej," She muttered into me. "This is the best present *ever.*"

As I hugged her back, I thought about telling her that *she'd* been the best present ever to me—but I knew I'd have lots of opportunities for that in the future. Right then, we had another agenda.

We had Yoo-hoo shakes to make—and a new book to read.

Monday at work passed quietly.

Our work in the DLO moved along at its normal, determined pace. Lottie and I processed bin after bin of dead letters. The mounds of mail came and went with the same balance of both simple and complex challenges.

But nothing new arrived from Dorothea.

I wasn't the only one who noticed. I could tell by how she'd steal looks at me each time we finished sorting a new stack of letters that Lottie was aware of my disappointment. But to her credit, she never verbalized her concern—or teased me with speculation about what had happened to my "pen pal."

I suppose the sadness I tried so hard to conceal didn't elude her. Lottie'd known me for too long, and was intuitive enough to understand that I'd reached a personal turning point stemming from my involvement with the mystery of the garden letters.

Instead, we talked about the lunch counter decision and what it meant, and didn't mean, about the changes beginning in our city. Lottie surprised me when I asked her if she thought Jerome would agree to meet Harrie and me for pie at Woolworth's. Not only did she say he was foolish enough to accept, but she also said she might just join him.

"It's about time you and I split a dessert in public, instead of down here in this damn basement."

I told her I couldn't think of anything I'd rather do.

"Don't get too excited, Esther Jane," she told me. "Bad pie is still bad pie, no matter where you get to sit down and eat it."

I told her to hush, and just for once—to try and enjoy the moment.

To my amazement, she didn't disagree.

"You know how to climb them five hundred steps, don't you?" she asked.

"One step at a time?" I was brave enough to answer.

"One step at a time," Lottie repeated with a smile.

When I left the post office for home that night, I felt more tired than I had in weeks. I knew that was because I'd had so many sleepless nights. It was time for me to move on and to reconnect with the things in my life that I could control—and to channel my energy and focus into my new friendships: Harrie. Fay Marian. Inez. Even Dr. Ogletree and Sofia. And I needed to do what Nelson had reminded me to do: keep my eyes focused on all the sweet gifts God had already set before me. I was sure I could learn to do that. Lottie had already told me how.

One step at a time.

As I walked home from the bus stop and passed so many familiar sights, 1 was struck by how much my world had expanded—and in ways I never could have imagined. I still lived inside the same quaint snow globe. All of its treasured features remained familiar to me. But when I looked at it now, I saw more than a frozen monument to a gentler past. I saw its hidden truths, too. The humble buildings constructed of bricks made by the hands of slaves. The cobblestone streets traveled by Union Cavalry officers who brought the news of emancipation to a faith community that had looked the other way. The hidden bridge over Salem Creek—a natural barrier defined by the Brethren to keep the Negro community they'd named "Liberia" separate. The silent but enduring witness of St. Philip's African Moravian Church. The abiding grace and dignity of unmarked graves in the Negro God's Acre. All of these things were now one with the life I lived here, and had become part of the history I now shared.

And, of course, the promise of the garden, and its steadfast reminders of the resilience of God's creation, would endure, too.

I began to understand that the story of my life in Old Salem was being rewritten as a story comprised of many voices. Young and old, friend and stranger, white and Black, seeker of truth and peddler of deceit, guardian of the past and harbinger of change—all of them raising their voices together in a grand chorus. Our sacred obligation as members of this community was not to deify an idealized past—but to realize the best and noblest ambitions of our founders by working together as one and discovering the best ways forward. Only then could we fulfill the original promise of this place—and of all places.

My head was full of these thoughts when I reached my house. As I approached my porch from the street, I was thrilled to see that the Lenten roses my father had planted so many years ago were in full bloom. Every year, against all odds and despite the capriciousness of the elements, the dusky purple flowers would spring forth just in time for Easter. They, like the ancient herbs we cultivated in the *hortus medicus*, were among life's everyday miracles. They kept right on happening, year after year. No matter how many bombs we built, treaties we broke, or natural resources we squandered, the earth remembered—and always honored its commitments.

I was nearly inside before I realized there was mail inside my little box beside the door. That was curious, because the carrier normally delivered my mail directly to me in the DLO before he went out on his rounds. I figured it was probably just an aberration—the result of some locum filling in during a vacation or other kind of leave. When I reached inside the box to pull the items out, I immediately recognized a letter written on pale stationery, addressed with a familiar handwriting.

It was from Dorothea.

But how was that possible? Why had the letter not been brought to us in the DLO as the others had been?

When I finally dared to withdraw the letter and examine it, I felt as if the porch boards had given way beneath my feet. The letter was exactly like all the others in every respect but one. This letter had not been addressed to Mary Ann Evans.

This letter was addressed to Esther Jane Cloud.

I hardly know how long I sat holding the letter without opening it. To be truthful, thoughts about its potential contents filled me with both anxious anticipation and terror in nearly equal measure. It was only when I realized that the night air was beginning to fall that I finally relented and convinced myself to read it. My hands were shaking, and it was difficult to hold the lengthy letter steady enough to make out the words she'd written. Only then did I notice with shock that this letter had *not* been scented with *Vol de Nuit*.

Eventually, I steadied my breathing and allowed my heart rate to slow enough to permit me to read the many pages it contained.

Dear Esther,

I am sure by now you have discovered my secret. I suppose I should amend that and say "secrets," because they are legion. You alone have now unhappily been made privy to the things I have kept locked inside my heart for the past twenty-five years.

Twenty-five years! Even writing that causes the words to reverberate inside my mind with the resounding ring of hammer blows. How has so much time elapsed since the day my life was changed forever—since the hour that all hope died within me, and I became consigned to lead a lonely life devoid of meaning or pleasure?

Ah, but you already are acquainted with many of these things, Esther. You have become like a priest, locked inside the dark chamber of my confessional. I revealed my deepest yearnings and disappointments to you, yet never showed my face.

But still, you managed to find me. And in every exchange we shared, I realized that you had come to know me, as well.

At first, I thought I must apologize for unburdening myself on an innocent stranger in this distant, but undeniably intimate, way. What must you have thought when first you opened a letter and saw laid bare before you an unabridged account of the forbidden passion I shared with my beloved in a garden of hope and healing? It is perhaps a supreme irony, Esther, that you would be the one chosen (or should I say fated?) to read these laments of mine. For you, too, have toiled as handmaiden in a garden that imparts all knowledge of good and evil.

I can now reveal what I suspect you already know. The garden you keep is the same one I, too, tended and cultivated while a student at Salem College. It was in that garden I fell in love with Rosemary, a soft and gentle girl from an old family in Virginia. It was in an English literature class taught by Lydia Ogletree that I first met her. We became study partners while researching our term papers on *Middlemarch*. Rosemary had already read the book many times, but it was new to me. We had endless discussions late into the night about Dorothea, and the tragedy of her marriage to the elderly landowner, Casaubon. We both viewed this outcome as a callous betrayal by the author, who chose not to allow Dorothea to flourish and pursue the independent life of philanthropy and scholarship she yearned for—and should have been heir to.

It was through our study of this seminal work of literature that we became aware of our special connection—which only grew and deepened in intensity through our volunteer work in the fledgling herb garden. With Rosemary, I learned to understand the possibility of perfect connection and the fullness of romantic love. But our special bond and growing passion for one another was soon discovered and cruelly reported to the administration. Rosemary was immediately withdrawn from school by her parents, who reviled her for her immorality and proceeded to crush her tender spirit.

We both understood that we had been forever divided from one another.

*I learned only days after graduation that
my sweet Rosemary had taken her own life. It
was after that revelation my broken heart and
woefully defeated spirit descended to a dark
and impenetrable place. My parents, at a loss
to understand my sudden retreat from them,
from all society, and even from the music that
had always sustained and nourished me, became
frantic. They quickly resolved that what I needed
was the steady, reliable and safe companionship
provided by marriage to an older man, known in
our small community to be gentle, scholarly, and
unassuming. This, they believed, would reclaim
me from my darkness and provide welcome
release from the pain of a miserable and plodding
existence working as an itinerant minister of
music. I was then abiding in a place too dark, and
cared too little about my life or prospects, to try
and dissuade them. So, within a few months, I
was married to Aubrey Troy, a quiet gentleman
with modest expectations for a wife, and very
generous means. He was nearly thirty years older
than me when we married, and was, as I soon
learned, in a state of very indifferent health.*

*Aubrey allowed me to live a mostly
independent life. He made few demands on
my time and none on my person. We never
consummated our union, and both seemed to
be at peace with the parameters of our chaste*

cohabitation. He died quietly in his sleep one night, after battling influenza for the better part of a month.

It was shortly after that I learned of the opening in the local post office—and even though I was temperamentally ill-suited to the work, I liked the anonymity of it and the few demands it made on the rest of my quiet life. My only consolation was, as you now know, working in the large garden that commands the space between my home and workplace. Crossing that humble, verdant space as I navigate from one part of my life to the other has become a kind of sacred pilgrimage for me. For I understand that it is only through tending the herbs that form my slender connection to the great love I once knew and lost, that I feel any sense of meaning or belonging.

The particular fragrance that permeated my letters to Mary Ann Evans, aka George Eliot, is—as you know—Vol de Nuit by Guerlain. It was the perfume worn by Rosemary—and it suited her very well. Soft but heady. An earthy, aromatic scent tinged with hints of jasmine and bergamot. Her mother had purchased the perfume for her in Paris, and Rosemary wore it like a second skin.

It was only last year, when I was at the Heironimus Department Store in Roanoke buying

*hand cream, that I happened to be standing
beside another customer who was testing a store
sample of the perfume. I recognized the scent in
an instant, and the full force of memory and loss
came crashing down on me once again. After that
experience, I was besieged by a fever with the heat
of a thousand suns—and I desperately sought an
outlet for my misery.*

*As a side note, you may wish to know that
Kevin Boitnott happened upon me one morning as
I passed the garden en route to work. In my hand,
I carried the first letter I'd written after receiving
my specially ordered bottle of the Vol de Nuit.
Kevin noticed the fragrance and was captivated
by the scent, and promptly importuned me to
know what it was. As I was eager not to prolong
our interview, I told him the name of the perfume,
and hurried on my way to post the letter. It was
many months later when I learned from Kevin
that his sister, Darlene, had procured a bottle of
the perfume for him. Kevin's particular situation
as a non-traditional male precluded him, or so he
believed, from ordering the woman's fragrance
himself. This you may share with your charismatic
young associate. I do hope this explanation allays
her suspicions about poor Kevin.*

*My decision to write and mail the Dorothea
letters derived entirely from my desperation to
find an outlet for an emotion that threatened to*

consume me. I began to consign my overflowing expressions of grief and loss to paper. It seemed only natural to me that these should be committed to the garden where the love Rosemary and I shared had flourished in tandem with the first blooms of the spring herbs. It did not matter to me that the letters would never be read, and would eventually be discarded or destroyed—such had already been the fate of the great love I bemoaned. I understood that I was sending these accounts of the deepest feelings of my heart into a void. But it mattered more to me to have the words find their final resting place in the same earth that had given birth to them.

It was after you and I, quite literally, ran into one another that day—and you were wearing the same fragrance that fed my deepest longings—that I realized my compulsive exercise of anguish had reached its end.

This, dear Esther, is the rest of the riddle you worked so valiantly to divine. For all the myriad ways I misled and intentionally worked to unsettle you, I sincerely apologize. I also ask your forgiveness for earlier confessing to my weakness in the face of what I knew was a growing attraction to you. It has only been since meeting you that I have begun to emerge from my stubborn cocoon of insensibility. There is no honor and certainly no expectation in my heart that

you might hear these admissions of attachment
from me with anything other than pity or, worse,
disgust. But I shall hasten to thank you just the
same for awakening within me the ability to
recognize beauty, and once again, to allow my
heart to experience the gentle stirrings of desire.

Know that I expect nothing from you, Esther.
Know also that I will not seek you out or attempt
to initiate contact with you again. If I am never
permitted the honor of a response from you, I will
go forward as I have been—but I will do so with
gratitude in my heart for the hope and joy that
knowing you, even in part, has added back to my
life.

Yours most sincerely,

Beatrice

How long I sat while the darkness gathered about me, I do not know. But when the moonlight began to shine brightly through the windows overlooking St. Philip's Church, and I heard the whip-poor-will's plaintive call, I was roused from my stupor. I was aware that I'd been overwhelmed by emotions, the depth of which I'd never experienced before—but I couldn't define them. *How much was fear, and how much was pleasure?*

I had no idea. Both responses battled for dominance.

Neither did I have any sense of how to resolve my dilemma—for I was, above all else, certain that I was swirling in the midst of something portentous.

The whip-poor-will called again.

My agitation increased. What was I expected to do?

What did I want to do?

I crossed to the small secretary that stood between the front windows of my house.

It was only when I sat and withdrew several sheets of stationery from a drawer that I began to recognize familiar things in the room.

The space I knew so well at last regained its clarity.

In the same way, things that had never before been clear to me also gained focus.

I picked up my pen and began to write.

    My Dear Beatrice . . .

About the Author

Ann McMan is the author of twelve novels and two collections of short stories. She is a two-time Lambda Literary Award winner, a nine-time winner of Golden Crown Literary Society Awards, a Foreword INDIES medalist, a four-time Independent Publisher (IPPY) medalist, and a recipient of the Alice B. Medal for her body of work. She resides in Winston-Salem, NC, with her wife, Salem West, two precocious dogs, and an exhaustive supply of vacuum cleaner bags.

Oh. She's also the custodian of this . . .

Inez Bell's Perfect Boulevardier (Bouvier)

Ingredients	Steps
1.25 oz Old Overholt Rye	(1) Combine Old Overholt Rye, Campari, and sweet vermouth with ice in a cocktail beaker and stir until well-chilled.
1 oz Campari	
1 oz sweet vermouth	
orange peel	(2) Strain into a martini glass
	(3) Garnish with orange peel.
	(4) Drink and repeat.

Acknowledgments

Daring to write this book was a terrifying departure for me. It's not inherently humorous—and I've never before attempted to write an historical narrative about anything. *Dead Letters from Paradise* is a small story about a woman who leads a quiet life. Yet the tale she shares about what happened in her small, Southern city on February 9, 1960, recounts an event that changed history for a nation. Telling Esther's story was made possible by the generous gifts of time and patience extended to me by many kind people—and I am sincerely indebted to them all.

Harriet McCarthy, the master gardener of the *hortus medicus* garden in historic Bethabara, gave me a guided tour of the garden and provided me with valuable insights on its history and uses.

Jennifer Lynch, the official historian of the United States Postal Service, took a great interest in this project, and provided invaluable assistance that increased my understanding of the peculiar history of Dead Letter Offices—and their curious methods of detection. (She also made a few plot suggestions that did not go disregarded.)

Ms. Alma Penn graciously spent hours talking with me over many seriously good cocktails at Sweet Potatoes Restaurant, sharing her memories of life as a young Black woman and her intimate experiences of racism and race relations in Winston-Salem in the 1960s. Ms. Penn also provided me with access to countless clippings, articles, and books which helped to direct and refine my research. I can never repay her for her keen interest, generosity, and kindness.

Stephanie Tyson and Vivián Joiner embraced the mission of this project immediately, and put me in touch with many people who provided valuable first-person accounts of several of the events and experiences recounted in this book. I am, as always, indebted to these two wonderful women who have made Winston-Salem a better and more welcoming place to live.

Winston-Salem Transit Authority (WSTA) Marketing Director Tina Carson Wilkins provided meaningful assistance researching the history of the Black-owned Safe Bus Company.

Donna Rothrock, librarian and archivist at Salem College, graciously provided access to digital copies of academic catalogs from 1935 to 1955.

It would be impossible to overstate the value of the digital resources of The University of North Carolina at Greensboro, which provided access to exhaustive, contemporaneous coverage of the 1960 lunch counter sit-in movements in Greensboro and Winston-Salem, NC.

Montine Bryan Scales was enormously helpful by freely sharing her colorful memories of life as a coed at Salem College.

I remain indebted to my dear friend, Sandy Lowe, who sent me a random text message one afternoon that read, "Hey, McMan. I have a great story idea for you." (So if you hated this book—blame her!)

My trusted friends, Carole Cloud, Cheryl Pletcher, Abbie Padgett, Christine Amen, and Louise Nixon each read first drafts of the novel and gave me thoughtful and valuable feedback.

A special nod of thanks goes to my ususpecting math tutor, Skippy, for her valiant efforts to help me correct space/time inconsistencies. Trust me when I say her shrewd observations covered a multitude of sins.

I am eternally grateful to my superlative editor, Elizabeth Sims, whose skill and insights made this a better (and less cringeworthy) book—and me a better writer. At least, that's the hope. If the effort wasn't successful, I probably should've plied her with more Moravian sugar cakes.

My copy editor, Nancy Squires, continues to improve and refine everything she touches. I'd be lost without her.

Elizabeth Andersen, my stalwart proofreader (and slayer of ill-used em dashes), never fails to make me sound smarter than I am.

My Bywater Books family provides consistent and unending support. I am so proud to be in your midst.

My younger sister, Rhonda, had little to do with the telling of this story—but *everything* to do with enriching the real-life story I lived while writing it.

And special, enduring, and loving thanks are due to my longsuffering spouse, Salem West, who never tires (or if she does, she never shows it) of talking the minutiae of these literary outings to death. Without you, your endless patience, and your selfless engagement in this and everything I do, this little story would never have been told. Thank you for the richness, joy, and meaning you add to my life every single day.

My love and gratitude to you all.

–Ann McMan
Winston-Salem, NC

Select Bibliography

Ashbrook Center. "Christianity and Slavery: The Moravians of North Carolina, 1753-1858." Ashland University, *Religion In America*, 2018

Csencsits, Sonia. "Growing Remedies: Apothecary Garden Is Restored with 1700s Medicinal Plants." *The Morning Call*, June 8, 1997

Dalton, Mary M. *I Am Not My Brother's Keeper: Leadership and Civil Rights in Winston-Salem, North Carolina*, documentary film, Wake Forest University, 2001

Davis, Lenwood G., Rice, William J., and McLaughlin, James H. *African-Americans in Winston-Salem/Forsyth County*. Donning Company/Publishers, 1999

Dixon, Amy. "Medicinal Garden Holds Special Place in History—and Today." *Winston-Salem Journal*, May 13, 2016

Ebony Magazine. "Dixie Bus Company at a Crossroads." *Ebony Magazine*, Dec. 1965

Eury, W.L., Appalachian Collection. "Across the Creek from Salem: The Story of Happy Hill, 1816-1952." Exhibit at the Gallery of Old Salem, Winston-Salem, 1998

Fullilove, Courtney. "Dead Letters—By a Resurrectionist: Liberty and Surveillance in the Tombs of the U.S. Post Office." Commonplace, *The Journal of Early American Life*, 2015

Grant-Hill, Cathy. "The Balcony Is Closed: The Only Remains of the Carolina Theater's Third-Floor Segregated Balcony are a Tossed-Aside Old Sign, and Local People's Memories." *Greensboro.com*, Feb. 12, 2020

Herbin-Triant, Elizabeth A. "Winston-Salem's Residential Segregation History." *Winston-Salem Journal*, May 17, 2019

Hinton, John. "'Our Company': Safe Bus, Started in 1926, Was Source of Pride in Winston-Salem Black Community." *Winston-Salem Journal*, Jun. 16, 2013

Hughes, Kathryn. "George Eliot's Women." The British Library, May 15, 2014

King, Kerry M. "The 1960 Winston-Salem Sit-In: The Day Wake Forest and Winston-Salem State Students Changed History." *Wake Forest Magazine*, Sept. 9, 2021

Landon, Edward. *History of the Moravian Church: The Story of the First International Protestant Church*. Allen & Unwin, 1956

Lovejoy, Bess. "Patti Lyle Collins, Super-Sleuth of the Dead Letter Office." *Mental Floss*, Aug. 25, 2015

Luck, Todd. "Former Drivers Recount Experiences at Historic Safe Bus Co. of Winston-Salem." *Winston-Salem Chronicle*, Feb. 18, 2016

Nittle, Nadra Kareem. "How the Greensboro Four Sit-In Sparked a Movement." *History.com*, July 28, 2020

Radzievich, Nicole. "Moravian Record Books Hold Little-Known History of Slaves." *The Morning Call*, May 16, 2015

Schlosser, Jim. "Blacks Bought Buses, Bypassing Jim Crow Laws." *Greensboro News & Record*, Mar. 31, 2002

Tursi, Frank W. *Winston-Salem: A History*. Raleigh, John F. Blair Publisher, 1994

Usher, Jess Alan. "An Uneasy Peace: The Struggle for Civil Rights and Economic Justice in Winston-Salem, North Carolina, 1960-1969." Unpublished Ph.D. Dissertation, University of North Carolina, 2015

Van Buren, Davina. "A Medicinal Masterpiece." Visit Winston-Salem, November 23, 2018

Watts, Kathy Norcross. "Hidden in History: Old Salem's Hidden Town: Old Salem's New Hidden Town Project Explores the Untold Story of Free and Enslaved African-Americans Living in Salem." *Winston-Salem Journal*, Feb. 1, 2018

Weaver, William Woys, translator. *Sauer's Herbal Cures: America's First Book of Botanic Healing 1762-1778*. New York, Routledge, 2001

Wilson, Christopher. "The Moment When Four Students Sat Down to Take a Stand." *Smithsonian Magazine*, Jan. 31, 2020

At Bywater, we love good books by and about women, just like you do. And we're committed to bringing the best of contemporary feminist and lesbian literature to an expanding community of readers. Our editorial team is dedicated to finding and developing outstanding writers who create books you won't want to put down.

For more information about Bywater Books, our authors, and our titles, please visit our website.

www.bywaterbooks.com

CPSIA information can be obtained
at www.ICGtesting.com
Printed in the USA
JSHW030810160622
26992JS00002B/2